The Polish Lad

translated from Yiddish by Moshe Spiegel

introduction by **Milton Hindus**

The Polish Lad

by Isaac Joel Linetski

The Jewish Publication Society of America
Philadelphia

The Polish Lad

Introduction

Milton Hindus

Literature has many mansions, and *The Polish Lad (Dos Poylishe Yingl)* may well belong in one of them. The genre to which it belongs, or aspires to belong, is, to vary the figure of speech, obviously not everyone's cup of tea— all evidence, in fact, points to its being obnoxious to many readers—but it has in all ages been regarded both as pleasurable and indispensable by a sufficient number of readers to guarantee its recognition and inclusion within the fold. In brief, the *kind* to which it belongs exposes to public view the scabrous side of a culture or civilization. It has, if I am not mistaken, some of the stigmata unmistakably associated with satire, and its publication in English now, if noticed at all, may displease and give offense to certain people.

Until quite recent times Jews have not been known to be in serious competition with those capable, like the Emperor Nero's *arbiter elegantiarum*, Petronius, of producing a *Satyricon*. The nearest they came to sophisticated, tragic, or brutal satire in ancient times is probably in the somber prophecies and jeremiads of the great man whose name has given us the word. But we have proof in the book before us that the Jews of Eastern Europe more than a hundred years ago were busily engaged in hammering out a medium of expression that seems to have important points in common with that used in some of the scandalous and successful literary artifacts produced by their descendants among us today.

In a pioneering article on Jewish fiction (both in Hebrew and in Yiddish) published in 1888 in *The Andover Review,* art critic Bernard Berenson noted what he took to be one of its peculiarities when he said of an author: "He speaks of Jewish life with a plainness that another people would not endure. It seems almost incredible, the amount of chastisement that a Jewish public will bear from one of its own writers." Nearly a century later this observation still strikes home, though the tendency to self-denigration has been checked somewhat by the fact that this literature is for the most part no longer linguistically intramural, and consequently it has unhesitatingly been brought by community spokesmen before the bar of public opinion and even of public relations.

The resulting purgation, though it could hardly assume the dimensions of bowdlerization in an age as licentious as our own, may not be an unmixed blessing. An atmosphere favorable to emasculation and censorship— in which the kind that is self-inflicted should be included —is hardly favorable to the literary enterprise, which thrives best when the writer feels most free within himself, most at home in his little world, and has no need of casting anxious glances over his shoulder to see what "they," the denizens of that great impersonal gentile world of his fellow citizens, think about him.

No more favorable than outright censorship to unfettered self-expression (which is the minimal condition for the appearance of what is generally recognized as authenticity, if not genius) is a writer's feeling of anxiety concerning his own loyalties, for before the community undertakes to criticize him, we may be sure that (if he is at all worth his salt) he has already criticized himself more severely in his own mind. As a rule, he could have saved himself the trouble. A bitter French satirist has commented caustically: "On est né fidèle, on en crève nous autres! [We are born loyal and we die of it]." The exceptions to this generalization are negligible, and many scrupulous and sensitive souls who suspect themselves of harboring the vice of disloyalty within themselves do not deserve to fall under their own imputation. James Joyce's Stephen Dedalus probably spoke on behalf of all his rebellious and experimental contemporaries in *A Portrait of the Artist as a Young Man* when he said defiantly to his reproachful young nationalist friend Davin: "This race and this country and this life produced me. . . . I shall express myself as I am."

Why Jews should be more self-critical than other people, or at least nervously tolerant of their own critics (as Berenson puts it), if they are indeed so, is an interesting question that is difficult to answer. Perhaps it is because the memory of the prophetic tradition has remained so strong and alive among the Jews, even after the cut-off date for the recognition of prophecy decreed by the ancient rabbis. Just as every stranger in ancient times among many peoples was thought to be a possible divinity or at least a divine messenger in disguise, so among the Jews every critic is suspected of being a prophet. (One may go so far as to say that the very type who to many is synonymous with the concept of being Jewish may be the prophet, particularly if he is an abusive one!) Perhaps it is because the Jew in the dispersion has for so long been despised, rejected, and persecuted that he has *internalized* this hatred and contempt of himself so that, in a sense, it is not self-hatred in such circumstances which is a sickness (as it is often represented to be) but the refusal to become conscious of the temptation to it that is slightly abnormal. According to such a hypothesis, the most devastatingly critical writers may only be the loosened tongues of their more repressed neighbors and countrymen, giving open unashamed expression to what others more decently tend to contain and bottle up. Perhaps it is, finally, because Jews are intellectuals and so are inclined naturally toward *healthy* skepticism and criticism (Jacob Epstein in his *Autobiography* noted wistfully: "Jewish people look upon the work of an artist as something miraculous, and love watching him, even though they may be extremely critical"), and it is only to be expected that this critical bent of mind should become reflexive and be turned upon the critic himself and upon the people to which he belongs.

At any rate, modern Yiddish literature begins on a strongly critical note. It was motivated by a desire to reform traditional Jewish life, to make the Jews come out from behind the walls of their East European ghettos and czarist Pale of Settlement into the light of modern civilization. (It may have been these walls of separation that Kafka symbolized in his story *The Great Wall of China*.) With an unmatched satirical ferocity, Jewish writers like Mendele and Linetski castigated the faults that they found in Jewish life, faults which seemed to them to spring almost entirely from the condition of isolation in which Jews found themselves in Eastern Europe. Segregation had become second nature to the Jew. In addition to the restrictions placed upon him by the laws of an alien world his interpretation of the inhibitory regulations of his own religion added immeasurably to his isolation. The cure at the start seemed to be some form of integration with the life of the world about him, insofar as that was possible. The model to be followed was the modus vivendi achieved by the Jews of Western Europe since the French Revolution and the conditional Emancipation, notably in Germany in the wake of the Mendelssohnian epoch and the Age of the Enlightenment. In Linetski's *Polish Lad* we see the German Jew being held up to the reader for his admiration as the pattern of all gentility, refinement, civilization, and true religion (which is not fanatical) to be emulated by the author's own backward, barbarous, ignorant, superstitious, medieval, corrupted, and unfortunate countrymen.

The name of Linetski has for various reasons virtually disappeared from our histories and anthologies. Yet in the earliest notable academic accounts of Yiddish literature—for example, Professor Leo Wiener's groundbreaking *History of Yiddish Literature in the Nineteenth Century* and Pines's *Histoire de la littérature judaeo-allemande*, which originated as a dissertation written at the Sorbonne before the First World War—it played a stellar role. Wiener has no doubt that *The Polish Lad* is a "great work." He tells us:

> *In 1867 the* Kol-mewasser *began publishing a serial story by Linetski under the name of "The Polish Boy." Its popularity at once became so great that to satisfy the impatient public the editor was induced to print the whole in book form as a supplement long before it had been finished in the periodical. The interest in the book lay not so much in the fact that it was written with boundless humor as in its being practically an autobiography in which the readers found so much to bring back recollections of their own sad youth. They found there a graphic description of the whole course of a Chassid's life as no one before Linetski had painted it—as only one could paint it who had been one of the sect. . . . Linetski had narrowly escaped being a Rabbi himself, had*

suffered all kinds of persecution for attempting to abandon the narrow sphere of a Chassid's activity, and knew from bitter experience all the facts related in his work. The story of his own life, unadorned by any fiction, was dramatic enough to be worth telling, but he has enriched it with so many details of everyday incident as to change the simple biography into a valuable cyclopaedia of the life and thoughts of his contemporaries in which one may get information on the folklore, games, education, superstitions, and habits of his people in the middle of [the nineteenth] century.

Isaac Joel Linetski was born September 8, 1839, in Vinnitza, Podolia. His father, Joseph, was a rabbi and fervent Hasid. Unlike the protagonist of his quasi-confessional *The Polish Lad*, Linetski was very precocious in his studies. It is said that he began his study of the Talmud at the age of six and that by the time he was ten years old, his teachers agreed that there was nothing left for them to teach him. He had the reputation of being an *ilui:* that is to say, one who is endowed with extraordinary abilities—not merely *an accomplished scholar* (which is the way Wiener puts it) but an undoubted genius! Such a description was not lightly or frivolously or often bestowed upon boys in Eastern Europe, where competition to excel in sacred studies was as keen and universal as interest in baseball is among our own young. Again, unlike the spoiled children of the rabbi whom we see in the pages of *The Polish Lad*, Linetski was apparently brought up in a despotic fashion—not so much by his own father as by his father's followers and surrogates, to whom the tasks of discipline were assigned as well as instruction in the mysteries and superstitions of the Kabbalah, which he later felt had nearly undermined his reason.

Rebelliousness manifested itself early in Linetski,

and he began secretly to frequent the homes of the few enlightened persons (the so-called maskilim who subscribed to the new faith in progress of the Haskalah) in his shtetl and to borrow secular books from them. These books, we are told, he studied in out-of-the-way places: deserted houses and empty synagogues. It was impossible for this to go long unnoticed in such an environment, and his "transgressions" came to the attention of his father, who decided to apply a time-honored remedy (in consonance with the customs of the time) designed to make the young man mature more quickly by burdening him with responsibilities. He was married off at the age of fourteen to a girl of twelve! This course of action didn't work very well, however, since the new husband soon succeeded in subverting his child bride, and thus there came to be two rebels in the family instead of one. The father then dissolved the marriage through a divorce, which he was empowered to grant, and compelled his son to marry a second time. This bride was deaf! But he was now sixteen years old and prepared to carry his fight against fanaticism into the open.

He battled against the Hasidim of his town for the next three years. A climax in the struggle was reached when his enemies waylaid him one dark night and flung him into the river. He was saved "as if by a miracle." Though Jews of all shades of opinion were suspicious of the czarist authorities at this juncture there seemed no way out for him but to appeal to the police for protection. He was left in peace after that. In 1858, when he was not quite nineteen, Linetski left his native Vinnitza for the big city of Odessa on the Black Sea, with which his varying fortunes were to be associated off and on for the rest of his life. Here he supported himself at first by giving Hebrew lessons to children, while studying German by himself in preparation for going to Breslau to continue his secular studies. On his way there, in a small town near the Austrian border, he was stopped by the local rabbi at the behest of Linetski's father, who had somehow gotten wind of his plans and came to fetch him home again. On their way home, they stopped at the court of one of the most influential Hasidic rabbis at the time in order that the young man might "do penance." Finally, they arrived back at the too-familiar Vinnitza. (The story of Linetski's abortive attempts to escape from the stifling atmosphere of his hometown almost reminds one of the poet Rimbaud's efforts—which, for a time, similarly miscarried—to get away from the influence of his enveloping mother and his native little town in Belgium.) Despite such horrendous experiences, the mature Linetski later told his friend and disciple Reuben Granowsky, around the beginning of the twentieth century, that he bore no grudge against his father and retained only the kindliest memories of him. Perhaps in writing his satires he had succeeded in sublimating and dissipating his resentments.

Linetski's drive to break with the shtetl and Hasidism was simply too strong to be contained even by the most vehement measures of compulsion. His creativity made him so stubborn that it was easier to kill him than to change him. Of course, he never actually served time in prison like the "hero" of his "romance." This invention was merely symbolic of the fact that his old home had become like a prison to him. He divorced his second wife and left again for Zhitomir, where for a time he attended the famous rabbinical seminary and where he made the acquaintance of Abraham Goldfaden, the founder of the Yiddish theater, who became his friend. After Zhitomir, Linetski lived for a few years in the beautiful city of Kiev, where he made his living as a tutor and composed the lyrics that later went into his first poetry collection in Yiddish entitled *The Angry Jester.*

In 1865, at the age of twenty-six, he became associated with a Hebrew publication and married a woman whom he loved and with whom he had four children: three sons and a daughter. His growing family compelled him to seek his fortune in a variety of places and occupations. He was at times a writer, teacher, and editor; intermittently he was a bookseller (like Abramovitch, who took the pseudonym Mendele Mocher Seforim from this vocation), an entertainer in a wine cellar that was also a cabaret, a traveling salesman, a peddler, and a petty trader at country fairs. During his wandering in those early years he again met Goldfaden, who at that time had not yet found himself and his real vocation in the theater. The two of them joined forces in a trading partnership. This speculative venture (like the ineffectual stock market manipulations of Sholom Aleichem's comic character Menachem Mendel) proved to be without foundation and soon came to nothing. Linetski had early turned to Yiddish prose and made a notable satiric debut in that juicy vernacular (as he called it) in the Odessa periodical *Kol Mevaser* (The Herald), number 8, on February 28, 1867. Later that same year (*Kol Mevaser*, number 16, published on June 9), the first installment of *The Polish Lad* appeared in print under a pseudonym that was an anagram based on the author's real name. The work, as Wiener has indicated, provoked a real sensation. It is said that on the day when a new installment of it was scheduled to appear, an impatient crowd would gather at the editorial offices to get the first copies of the paper "hot off the press."

The mordant satire of Hasidism had found its mark. Word of it reached into every nook and cranny of the East European Jewish world, and rumors of it even traveled abroad. The hitherto unnoticed young writer suddenly became the rage everywhere. Curiously, his popularity eventually seems to have penetrated into those very Hasidic circles where his name at first was anathema. Wiener expresses his astonishment at this phenomenon and attributes it to the absolute inner truthfulness of the caricature, which was irresistibly amusing to the subjects of it. He tells us that "the copy of the book in my possession was sold to me by a pious itinerant Rabbi, who had treasured it as a precious work." The Yiddish poet and storyteller Abraham Reisen remembered his own father reading aloud installments of *The Polish Lad* to his family each Friday night, a rare treat, to which neighbors, too, were hospitably invited. Many years afterward, the poet still vividly recalled the womenfolk on such evenings vainly trying to choke back their laughter at the very palpable hits scored by Linetski's biting wit. The objects of his lampoon were then still quite fresh in mind and memory—if not actually still in existence. Reisen makes a comparison between Linetski and his contemporary Mendele, both of whom he regarded as classics. Mendele's work, he says, appealed more to the intellectual maskilim, whose intellectuality was sometimes more aspiration than fact and who showed their approval with characteristically sly, reserved, thin-lipped smiles. Linetski's tale (though it was not lacking in its share of intellectual admirers) was capable of inspiring loud, happy, healthy laughter among the humblest and least educated members of the household, who were capable of appreciating the accuracy and felicity with which he was capable of depicting scenes that were deeply familiar to them.

But if this striking success brought Linetski fame, the general poverty of his public was capable of bringing him but little fortune. In 1867 he was living in an obscure backwater between the larger towns of Kherson and Simferopol in the Crimea. When news of his success reached him, he hopefully set out again for Odessa to collect his royalties, but on getting there he was informed that the editor felt he himself deserved to be paid by Linetski for making him famous! *The Polish Lad* was published in book form in 1869 in Odessa and was introduced by the waggish editor of *Kol Mevaser*. Linetski became a regular contributor to this paper, the contents of which were universally critical, scathing, and satiric about the state of contemporary Jewish life. Later he began to publish his own books and to peddle them in the countryside. In 1872 he published a calendar diversified with contributions of verse and prose (a utilitarian popular form which Mendele also employed for a time). Although he continued to be widely read, none of his subsequent publications attained the vogue of *The Polish Lad*.

From July 1875 until February 1876 he and his friend Goldfaden published in Lemberg a weekly called *Yisrolik*. When this enterprise also failed he returned to Odessa, where he ambitiously undertook to publish a series called *Linetski's Writings* but only managed to put out two installments. From 1878 to 1882 Linetski became a traveler once again, selling more solid, conventional, and durable goods than books in various little communities bordering on the Black Sea. But after the assassination of Czar Alexander II triggered anti-Semitic riots, particularly among the peasantry in the countryside, this manner of making a living became too dangerous.

These tragic events were of decisive importance for modern Jewish history. Emigration to America, which had already become a factor in the previous decades, vastly increased. A much smaller number of Russian Jewish emigrants chose to go to the agricultural colonies sprouting in Turkish Palestine. Some Jewish writers who were beginning to make names for themselves in Russian letters, like Simon Frug, returned linguistically and ideologically to their own people under the impact of the crisis. A great debate started among Jewish intellectuals, who attempted to answer that perennial, favorite, and recurrent Russian question: What is to be done? The year 1882 was important not only because it heralded the creation of a mass Jewish community in America but also because it saw the beginning of a proto-Zionist movement as well. Eighteen eighty-two was the year of the publication of Leo Pinsker's *Auto-Emancipation* (to which Herzl was later to pay tribute by saying that if he had been aware of its existence he would have been saved the trouble of writing his own book, *The Jewish State*). There were other historically interesting publications in that year. One of them was Ephraim Deinard's *Amerika oder Palestiner Eretz Yisroel?* (written in Yiddish). There was also a series of small pamphlets by Linetski in Yiddish, the first one of which bore virtually the same title as Deinard's, *America or Eretz Yisroel?* Another was called *Hither or Yon?* In his initial pamphlet, Linetski appealed to people not to flee hysterically to America (that "remote corner of the world" as Knut Hamsun was later to call it, which did not as yet have any immigration restrictions, since it needed people more than people needed it) but instead to prepare for the time, ideally in the near future, when mass emigration to Palestine would become possible. He apocalyptically warned his readers that there might eventually arise in America a more virulent strain of anti-Semitism than any of those known in Europe. He stressed the difficulties of maintaining a recognizable form of Jewish life in the United States and pointed out the real dangers of assimilation there. America, he concluded, might in time turn out to be but one more stepmother as far as the Jews were concerned. If they must leave Russia, it would make sense to return to their true mother, the Land of Israel.

He saw the hand of God in the latest tribulations of the Jews in Russia. If the czarist government began to permit mass emigration as a result of the pogroms (which apparently seemed conceivable to him at the time), the long-awaited messianic era might be closer at hand than anyone supposed. He felt heartened by the committees that sprang up everywhere among the Jews pledging their efforts to raise funds for the colonization of Palestine. Venturing on a literary figure of speech with strongly traditional religious overtones, he assured his readers that he had heard recently an oracular voice (a *bas kol*) which sounded the peremptory warning: "Jews! Go home!" More practically and immediately, he advocated the purchase of land in Eretz Yisroel both by Russian Jews and by the other Jews of the world.

In 1886 he began to publish in Romania a Yiddish magazine called *National*, but after twenty-one issues it folded. He also turned his hand to translations from the German of Lessing and the historian Graetz. To sell these translations he once more took to peddling and, though he never grew rich by any of his efforts, he later told Granowsky in Odessa that he had cleared more from these books than from any others—a tidy sum of ten thousand rubles, which was a considerable sum in those days. In his later satires, he spared neither the Hasidim (his old enemies) nor their opponents, the maskilim and assimilatory westernizers among the Jewish intelligentsia, whom he had once spared and even idealized a little. He was also among the first Yiddish writers (to be followed later by Peretz and many others) who belatedly began to appreciate the poetic side of the old Jewish life in the shtetl, the failings of which he had once mercilessly castigated. Linetski was also a talented public reader of his own work and gave many performances at literary evenings and "concerts" of a kind that were then in fashion.

Though he continued sporadically to publish as

long as he lived, he came increasingly to be regarded as "a man of one book." The informed judgment of Wiener, published while Linetski was still alive, was that "the farther he proceeds, the less readable his works become, the coarser his wit." That was a devastating judgment, considering how coarse he could be even in his earlier work. Wiener concludes that "Linetski's reputation is based only on his first novel, which will ever remain a classic." Unfortunately, he was destined to outlive his early fame, and it is true of him as it is of many others that "the name died before the man." His death occurred during the dark days of World War I on September 23, 1915. He is buried in the Jewish cemetery of Odessa beneath an epitaph in Hebrew rhyme which he had prepared for himself:

Here lies interred a man whose heart was full of nothing but love and trust toward his fellowman and yet who didn't himself know the taste of love in return his whole life long. Pure-hearted and a truth-seeker though he was from birth, men nevertheless rose up against him with hatred. He was a man old before his time who died with a youthful spirit. Here is the man Linetski, a scribe of the people [sofer ha'am], *who wrote in blood which he spilled like water as long as he lived, until his spirit, returning to its source, arose to heaven.*

Though a number of his jubilees had been celebrated by fellow writers (in 1890, the twenty-fifth anniversary of his debut in print; in 1899, the sixtieth anniversary of his birth), his later years had been embittered by a growing obscurity and estrangement from the broad Jewish public, and even his death (which he had confidently assured young Granowsky was bound to draw wide attention to him again and be commented on), occurring as it did in the midst of the greater tragedy of a general European war that was to end for Russia and her Jews in revolution and an even bloodier civil war, went almost entirely unnoticed.

In a certain sense, however, Linetski's confidence in his ultimate destiny may not have been mistaken. His masterwork (flawed though it obviously is) steadfastly refuses to succumb and still speaks to us in intermittent flashes of vividness and occasional brilliance more than a hundred years after it was first composed. And the Jewish world, fitfully, here and there, again and again, has shown that it has not quite forgotten him. Over the generations, more than thirty editions of his book have appeared in different places.

Most of the recognition of his historical significance has come from sources in Eastern Europe, as might have been expected, but publications about him are not lacking in either Israel or the United States. Some of the same misfortune which dogged him throughout his life seems to have pursued him after his death. In the wake of the Bolshevik Revolution he was taken up in some Russian Jewish literary circles (before Stalin destroyed them) as a putative predecessor of the proletarian writers. A publication in Moscow in 1939, designed to celebrate the one hundredth anniversary of his birth, was entitled: *Linetski—The Enlightened Democrat*. Its author, M. Natavitch, makes much of the evidence he has discovered (in the journalistic work of Linetski in the 1870s) of the author's intense hostility to the Jewish bourgeoisie of his time and his equally intense partisanship on behalf of the downtrodden Jewish masses. The satirist, according to this interpretation, was an active participant in the class struggles of his time and a harbinger of the revolutions that were to rock Russia in the twentieth century.

The interest of Jewish Communists in pushing Linetski's work stemmed in part from their struggle against Zionism and the Hebrew language. That Linetski himself was an early and ardent advocate and pamphleteer on behalf of the nascent nationalistic movement among the Russian Jews is not mentioned in Natavitch's article. What is emphasized instead is his defense of the literary respectability of the Yiddish language. Natavitch quotes Linetski's ironically affectionate description of it as "our common, workaday, delicious jargon"—the last word then being universally applied to the vernacular not only by its opponents among the Jews of Western Europe but by its users in Eastern Europe, whose mother tongue (indeed, whose only tongue sometimes) it was. Linetski, though he himself could write in Hebrew when the occasion demanded it, defended Yiddish against those exclusive and snobbish Hebraists of the time who denigrated it as a lingua franca developed in the Diaspora, a living symbol of Jewish backwardness, unfit for any higher usage. "Let us not be disturbed," he counseled those who, like himself, were writing mainly in Yiddish, "by those affected fops who slander our 'jargon' and shame it in the eyes of the people as something appropriate for use only in religious tracts meant for women. . . . Bull! We're now in process of transmuting our 'jargon' into a literature. It is only in this so-called jargon that the spirit and characteristics of our unhappy people can be mirrored; and it is only in those books in which their folk-character is accurately reflected that the true literature of our time will be found."

Even in this respect, however, the story is not so simple or unambiguous as Natavitch chooses to make it appear, for it is a curious fact that Linetski translated into Yiddish the history of Heinrich Graetz, one of the most influential German Jewish detractors of the Jewish "jargon." But perhaps this was only another sign of the literary self-confidence felt by Linetski in its destiny.

Natavitch missed one opportunity which he could have exploited had he known of it. Granowsky made it quite clear two years after his book was published that Linetski, though he was an early supporter of the "Lovers of Zion," in his later years fell out, like many other Yiddish writers of his time, with the new brand of political Zionism introduced by Herzl, which toward the end of the century once again began to divide the Jewish community.

There were other publications devoted to Linetski in Kiev in 1929 and 1937 and in Minsk in 1931 and 1939. Some of Linetski's correspondence with Dinesen and Mordecai Spector was published in Moscow as late as 1940. Publications by and about Linetski also appeared between the two world wars in Vilna. Granowsky's memoir, *J. J. Linetski and His Time*, was published in New York in 1941. The Yiddish critic Sh. Niger included Linetski in his *Story-Tellers and Novelists*, published in New York in 1946. More recently, there have been publications about him in Jerusalem and Tel Aviv. Unfortunately, in books in English that are about Yiddish his name has almost disappeared. He is unrepresented, for example, in Howe and Greenberg's *Treasury of Yiddish Stories*. He is fleetingly mentioned in Roback's *Story of Yiddish Literature*. There are brief treatments of him in Sol Liptzin's *History of Yiddish Literature* (1972) and in his earlier *Flowering of Yiddish Literature*, in an article by Elias Schulman in the *Encyclopaedia Judaica* (1971), and in Charles Madison's *Yiddish Literature* (1968). The most extensive and helpful discussion of him is to be found in Don Miron's *A Traveler Disguised: A Study in the Rise of Modern Yiddish Fiction in the Nineteenth Century*, published in 1973.

Though Linetski is a figure of considerable interest and importance in the early history of Yiddish literature, few unqualified claims to anything greater than that should be advanced. The flickering light of his fame even among those devoted to Yiddish must be attributed in part, no doubt, to the limitations of his own talent. Another less defensible reason for his dwindling renown is that, with the widespread tendency nowadays to idealize and even sentimentalize the Hasidic form of life which has largely disappeared, we are loath to look squarely at his little vignettes of Hasidic life at its worst. Caught in Linetski's pitiless lens, there is little of the quality that attracted Martin Buber to it. In the degenerate form that Linetski knew in the provinces, it does not seem signally different (as far as its departure from sound reason and balance is concerned) from what we know of the type of life that prevailed in the same areas during the Sabbatai Zevi craze in the seventeenth century. One suspects, for example, that I. B. Singer, in his book *Satan in Goray*, drew some of his historical scenes from the model of the contemporary shtetl as he himself experienced it before World War I, for that model apparently had undergone very little change over several centuries.

There is no disguising the fact that for this reason reading Linetski's *The Polish Lad* today is an experience that is a strange mixture of pain and pleasure. His sense of humor is certainly infectious; he had a fresh and funny eye, and we can sympathize with his early readers who roared with laughter at recognizing their neighbors if not themselves in his "cartoons." But there is pain, too, because so much of the book seems to violate our instinct to venerate the dead and a form of life that was almost wiped out in the Hitler Holocaust. The pain of reading Linetski now for many Jewish readers will hardly be alleviated by the fact that his picture of the Hasidim is so obviously slanted, biased, and polemical in intention. We are conscious at almost every moment in reading it that it could have served as an excellent illustration of what Berenson had in mind when he ventured upon one of his excessively broad and questionable condemnatory strictures and generalizations (in which he included modern Hebrew as well as Yiddish): "Jewish literature has never been anything but the weapon of a propaganda." The author of this book often fails to detach himself from his own splenetic prejudices and the theoretical point of view which he had so painfully achieved. It is these which sometimes seem to create his vision rather than merely springing from it.

It is true, of course, that the power of other satirists (even the best and most classic specimens of the genre: Aristophanes, Juvenal, Voltaire, Swift) lies not in their desire to be fair to their opponents but in a lethal impulse to annihilate them. They are filled with "savage indignation" and seem prepared to lay hold of any weapon that will serve them. Nevertheless, there are limits of caricature beyond which the satirist cannot with safety let himself go. Linetski repeatedly approaches these limits and occasionally oversteps them. The result is that he for the time forfeits that willing suspension of disbelief on the part of his reader which not only constitutes poetic faith (as Coleridge puts it) but which is necessary if the satirist is to be really effective. He cannot afford to permit doubt to creep into his reader's mind. "Credibility gaps" may be permissible in politics; they are fatal in literature, and that is why neither propaganda nor public relations ever manages to reach that level of distinction. Those who do not understand this or accept it may aspire to produce "poster art" but little more than that.

Even Wiener who treated *The Polish Lad* as an enduring classic found certain faults with it:

Were it not for the many didactic passages which the author has interwoven in the second part of his story, it might easily be counted among the most perfect productions of Jewish literature.

These unfortunately mar the unity of the whole. Except for these, the book is characterized by a truly Rabelaisian humor. Its greatest merit is that it follows so closely actual experiences as to become a photographic reproduction of scenes. There is hardly any plot in it, and it is doubtful if Linetski would have succeeded so well had he attempted a piece of fiction, for in his many later works he is signally defective in this direction. The mere photographic quality of the story, the straightforward tone that pervades it, the grotesque, unbounded humor which one meets at every turn, have made it acceptable to the Chassidim themselves, who grin at their caricature but must confess that it is absolutely true.

His handling of the problems of narrative is rudimentary and deficient. He seems absolutely incapable of negotiating the necessary turns in it gracefully. His ability to "dramatize" his material is limited; his characters sometimes take refuge in speechifying when we would hear them simply talk. The liveliness of his style, too, in Yiddish, despite the best efforts of the translator to recapture it and all the skill and ingenuity which he brings to his task, is only partially glimpsed in English. Yet despite all of these drawbacks, the book as a whole, in some odd way of its own, doesn't fail to live for us. It requires some patience and a great deal of tolerance to get at it, but in this respect it does not differ essentially from many other books, especially those that come to us from afar in space and time.

Even the last half of the book, though it deserves the charge of didacticism that Wiener levels against it, has certain redeeming features for us. It makes us keenly aware of the positive motivations underlying Linetski's brutally incisive denunciation of the Jewish milieu he was born in. His criticism, unlike that of some of our American contemporaries, seems basically responsible and not bent on indiscriminate negation and self-destruction.

Linetski, at the end, suddenly goes so much against the grain of everything he has been saying until then that his resolution has been described as sentimental. It is not quite that, though it is not wholly satisfactory either, because the author did not possess sufficient imaginative power to digest the philosophy he would teach us and to make the complete reversal in the world outlook of his hero really persuasive.

In a definition that appeals to me, a writer of satire is said to be engaged in a perverse quest for love. The epitaph prepared by Linetski for himself seems to indicate that this view approximates the one which he took of himself and his own activity. What I myself like about his last chapters—discounting the flagrant and incongruous pedantry of their tone—is the humanistic position which they reveal their author to be striving for. They reveal him as someone a cut above the mere propagandist for a particular point of view; the "proletarian" writers who later claimed him as their forerunner shared some of his weaknesses but were never capable of rising to the plane of disinterestedness and universality which is the final standpoint of his work. He is no extremist himself or a defender of extremists. He is not one of those who, by dint of railing against idiots, becomes somewhat idiotic himself. He does not aim to inculcate into his reader a "sound spirit of hate" even for the most misguided of his ideological opponents. He can see what has brought them to their present pathetic pass. In the initiators, founders, and earliest adherents of the most diverse, hostile, and clashing movements, he is aware not only of the original good intentions and good will but, quite simply and genuinely, the good itself. Hasidism in the person of the saintly Baal Shem Tov is as admirable and novel and beneficent a doctrine as is Misnagedism (its traditionally and conservatively oriented rabbinical opposition) in the person of the scholarly Vilna Gaon or as Haskalah is in the person of the philosophical Moses Mendelssohn. The trouble with mass movements that spring from individually admirable saints, scholars, and philosophers, as far as Linetski is concerned, lies in the fact that they decline from the purity of motivation in the founding fathers and become progressively more incomplete, intolerant, and mutually exclusive. Their descendants and epigones in many cases unconsciously misrepresent or misunderstand the noble doctrines in the name of which they claim to be acting, and this in turn only serves to widen the gulf between them and to exacerbate the hostilities which they feel toward each other. Linetski's unexceptionable humanistic purpose is to mediate the quarrels between the parties, to combine their varying views wherever possible into a harmonious whole, and to hold up for our admiration the unexciting and unromantic classical ideals of decorum, proportion, measure, and civilized self-restraint. He does not seem to have aspired to the stature of a giant (who is, more likely than not, rather monstrous in his one-sidedness) but simply to that of a decently full-grown man among a lot of stunted ones. His satiric fire and indignation is aroused only because he feels that his own human potential has been dwarfed by those too crippled by their own conditioning clearly and consciously to realize what they have done to him.

In Granowsky's memoir of him, as from his own work, Linetski emerges triumphantly not only as a bright-eyed and amusing companion and raconteur but as a representative man insistent upon his own human worth and dignity. In Odessa, in his later years, he dressed almost with the care of a dandy. His neckerchief, his gloves, his footwear were all sartorially elegant. He was grave in his manner, and his speech was deliberate, slow, and weighty. It was as if he were intent in every respect on putting a maximum of distance between himself and the indignity of his Hasidic shtetl origins.

His proud demeanor was all the more striking in that he was (at the age of sixty) dependent financially upon one of his sons who, out of an income of fifteen thousand rubles a year, gave his father and mother an allowance of a hundred rubles a month. On one occasion when he quarreled seriously enough with this son not to wish to accept his support any longer, he asked Granowsky to appeal to certain wealthy individuals in the Jewish community of Odessa who had publicly pledged (on the occasion of an anniversary of his work) to support him in style if he were to permit them to do so, in recognition of his literary services to their people. They proved to be only too eager to redeem their promises of patronage in this hour of his need, but after they had sent their initial subvention to him, the son composed his quarrel with his father and they resumed their former affectionate relationship. This is a sad story but not an uninspiring one. Linetski in his later years seems to have been treated by those around him as a person of at least former well-merited note and consequence. He was not simply cast off as a has-been belonging to the past. He was a "pensioner," but a pensioner who commanded respect. Long after his death, his daughter, who was very close to him and who was described as "her father's daughter," published some notes about him in the city of Minsk in 1931.

It was as if many people realized that he was singled out from among his contemporaries by his unique work, which seemed likely to exert a claim on the remembrance of his people, and perhaps of mankind, long after the generation to which the author belonged was gathered in the earth.

Satire was once defined waggishly by George S. Kaufman as "a play that closes on Saturday night." And literature, according to Anatole France, is a parcel passed on to us from previous generations, which we are content to leave unopened though we piously pass it on to other generations: "The classics which everybody admires are also the ones nobody cares enough to look at!" By daring to use such words as satire and literature about this unpretentious book, therefore, one may seem to be issuing an invitation on its behalf to both veneration and neglect. It deserves, however, neither of these extreme responses. It is clearly not a bible. Think of it what you will, call it what you like—document, history, fiction—it invites first-hand perusal, examination and reflection. Linetski's voice is hoarse—"as if from long silence and disuse"—but if we listen to it long and sympathetically and carefully enough, it may prove to have some things of interest to say to us not merely about our ancestors but about ourselves.

The Polish Lad

by way of foreword

If my father had been able to foresee even a thousandth part of the trials I was to endure he might have been rather less ardent on the night my mother conceived me. . . . Now, of course, that is all water over the dam. Naturally, I shall always lament the unhappy moment when I was snatched from my secure and comfortable place in the spacious realm of heaven for the dreary constriction of the womb. And, as if that were not enough, I have been doomed on earth to a life of unbroken misery, the good Lord alone knows for how long—or for what reason. . . .

It is true that the Torah, which an angel taught me while I was still in my mother's womb, to some degree eased my plight. But, as fate would have it, this angel turned out to be a drowsy being, especially on the Sabbath, when my parents woke from their afternoon nap; after they had finished their meal of boiled chick-peas and perry, I had to listen to their talk about my coming into the world. From their words I could hardly surmise what sort of persons they were—or for what sort of life I was destined.

Once on the eve of Tisha be-Av, the fast day com-
memorating the destruction of the First and Second
Temples, my angel was sleeping soundly—since on this
day the study of the Torah is forbidden—while my par-
ents-to-be sat on the ledge outside the house. I could not
help hearing what they said.

"Do you think, Yossel, that it will really be a boy?"
my mother asked.

"What are you babbling about, you fool?" my father
irritably returned. "The rebbe has positively said it will
be a girl—and you still have your doubts?"

"What are you angry about?" my mother said in a
placating tone. "Did you think I was serious? I was only
joking. I mentioned it in passing because yesterday the
doctor was muttering something about my carrying a
boy. Actually, not one of them would know beans with
the bag open."

"Silly thing," my father chided in a humoring tone.
"Even if it was to be a boy, the holy rabbi himself, the
tzaddik, could have turned it into a girl; just remember,
he distinctly told us he had predicted a girl even before
you became pregnant. So what more is there to say?"

"Of course, you're absolutely right," my mother
apologized. "We have witnessed such miracles before
from our tzaddik, may his life be long!"

"Such miracles, did you say?" my father retorted.
"You call this a miracle? I'll have you know, foolish
woman, that it was he who transformed the duke of Far-
tzelvika into a werewolf, and who, with a flourish of his
cane, scattered the clouds on a pitch-dark night. He did
that in order to observe the Blessing of the New Moon.
Can anything be more remarkable? So why waste words
on a trumpery miracle like this?"

"The devil take those old women, those crones!"
my mother ventured to exclaim. "They believe every-

thing that old woman, that numbskull of a doctor, says to them, as if it were gospel; they swear that all his predictions come true. But don't mind me. You know what they say—a woman's hair is long but her wits are short." She fell silent, but then very quickly went on, "I have an idea, my dear—the moment the lightning splits the sky, let us both cry out, 'Lord of the Universe, please grant us a boy!'—and the chances are our wish will be fulfilled."

But at this crucial moment of spurning the prophecy of the saintly rabbi, my father turned on her in a fury. "You always were a fool," he cried, "and a fool you'll always be!"

Overhearing such a disagreement made my blood run cold. What woe for me if, God forbid, I should be transformed into a girl! I remembered the appalling thing I witnessed through my casement in paradise whenever the Jewish girls in Poland were being dragged down to Sheol—unkempt, slovenly, and downcast every one of them, every one of them with carious teeth and with her head shaved, according to the marriage ritual of all strictly Orthodox Jews. When called to account for their actions on earth, they would stare out of their beady eyes, like startled mice after an earthquake. Even during my stay in paradise I was in mortal fear of just one thing —of coming into the world as the daughter of a Polish Hasid. But I would take heart in the thought that even if I were doomed to be born female, perhaps it was my destiny to be a genteel lady in some aristocratic Jewish home—one of those very noblewomen who were rarely ushered into paradise, but who were so well-bred, so exquisitely dainty, and so clever that a mere glimpse of them was like a feast for the soul.

Now that I had heard the woeful prediction that I was to be born a girl, you can well imagine my anxiety.

True enough, there was hardly anything attractive or admirable about the Polish Jews who were likewise relegated to Sheol. They, too, were unkempt, as full of ill will and vindictiveness as any fiend from Sheol, that abode of the dead; still, they were less contemptible than the so-called fair sex. They may have been good-for-nothing ne'er-do-wells and rascals, as well as walking skeletons— but all the same, they were *men!* Though a Polish Jew may be a miserable louse, a stammerer, and a booby, among his fellows he is still considered a man, the lord and master over the prettiest, the most erudite and accomplished woman. Be that as it may, I was scared out of my wits by the tzaddik and the doctor, and found myself between Scylla and Charybdis, between the devil and the deep blue sea. Now that I think of it, surprisingly, I never heard during my interval in paradise any such terms of address as rebbe, or preacher, or righteous Jew. Who knows—perhaps all these professional doers of good were busy in Gehenna purging and condemning the wicked souls of the Jewish damsels from Poland. . . . In short, throughout those nine painful months I suffered mortal fear of coming into this world as a girl! Please pardon, dear reader, so foolish and groundless a fear! I was, after all, hardly able to rationalize, while imprisoned in my mother's womb, that the handiwork of nature cannot be undone by so much as a jot. And even if all the saintly Hasidic sages of Poland were to join the headmasters of the yeshivas of Lithuania, supplemented by the six-and-thirty *lamed vav*, those Men of Righteousness on whom the existence of the world depends, their collective powers would not be able to change the tiniest sinew of the microscopic flea! Or, even if a pennant were fashioned from the cane of the maggid of Zazulenitz and the *tallit katan*, the undergarment with ritual fringes that had been worn by the saintly sage of Nazarenitz, and if this pennant were fastened by the Yom Kippur sash of the rabbi of Rachmestrivcka, and finally, even if the *lamed vav* sages were to wave this thrice-sanctified pennant from now till the Messiah comes, they could still not disperse the merest wisp of cloud, let alone alter a human being, the supreme creation of nature. Yet in Poland, grown-up Orthodox Jews—still with their ritual earlocks of course—had been so credulous as to believe in the power of a so-called miracle-working rebbe to transform a child in the womb from a male to a female one!

Naturally, I could not grasp such things at the time; however, I did resolve that if the Almighty were gracious enough to let me come into the world as a boy and not a girl, I would proclaim to the world that the miracle-working rabbis carried far less weight with the Lord of the Universe than the unpretentious country doctor in Strizevka. But, alas, during my passage into this world, my angel tweaked my upper lip and I was struck with forgetfulness.

It was only after my father had consulted with the rebbe, and after the rite of circumcision was over, and I first heard my name—Itzhak—that I knew I was a boy. And, hard as it may be to believe, our tzaddik proceeded to revise his wrong prediction into a fresh miracle, exclaiming as he rolled his eyes heavenward, "Oho! This child must be endowed with a special soul. For some reason, during my vision the Divine Presence showed me the word 'daughter' instead of 'son!' "

At any rate, regardless of whether I was highborn or low, no real harm had been done since I had not been born a girl.

1

The hero's life during his first three years

The moment I was ushered into this world, I became aware of a kitchen knife and a small well-worn book lying on my mother's bed. Several hours after my birth, I noted certain scribbled psalms, good-luck charms, that had been pinned to the curtains and pasted on the doors and windows of the room. At the sight of the kitchen knife, I was all but frightened out of my wits: there rushed through my mind the chapter of Genesis concerning Abraham's would-be sacrifice of his son Isaac on Mount Moriah, of which my angel had told me while I was still in my mother's womb. I supposed that carving knife was intended for a similar use on me. But since childish notions are shortlived, especially in the new-born, the knife was dismissed from my thoughts. I now became engrossed in the ancient small book, wondering what it could be about—when suddenly it popped open, as though by itself, and—wonder of wonders!—proved to be the very miniature Pentateuch out of which my angel had taught me while I was still in my mother's womb—the very same book that is so worshiped and revered in paradise! How, then, dared they leave it in so profane a place? Presently I dozed off, and when I woke I became aware once again of the amulets dispersed about the room. I also caught sight of a little box with the names of the patriarchs engraved inside it, and on top of it a *shir hamaalot* inscribed with a psalm of King David, of blessed memory. Naturally, I was very flattered by all this; indeed, I had personally known the whole crew in paradise; and more than once I had actually heard David himself chant this particular psalm, accompanied by a choir of seraphim. Needless to say, I felt quite at home.

But clearly I was not destined to enjoy such bliss undisturbed. Atop the little box, in bold type, loomed the name of "Satan," and underneath the word "witch" was repeated three times over. This discovery gave me endless distress and exasperation. It was woe to contemplate the very notion of setting up such devilish beings as guardian spirits to persons so noble and sacred—the very essence of *Homo sapiens!* And finally, what was the meaning of the last line? Try as I might, I could not understand a single word of it—and after all, while I was still in heaven, I had been well versed in the proverbial seventy languages. I should have been able to decipher a few words, even if it had been Tatar or Turkish. Though I tried to render it into one dialect after another, my efforts were all to no avail. Before long my poor brain would have been addled by the strain of trying to fathom the meaning of that line, had my grandmother not picked me up and plunged me into a basin of hot water.

Nor were my trials and perplexities ended when my mother's lying-in was over. That old crone of a grandmother had to come into my life. Three or four times a day she trussed me hand and foot in swaddling clothes as though I were a serf, blowing on my face from time to time, mumbling incantations and calling up spirits, and yawning. When I yawned in emulation, she would spit into my mouth. Then, having got rid of the old witch, and survived the rite of circumcision, I found still other woes and anxieties awaiting me. If I had a bellyache, or if I suffered from the heat, or itched from the bite of a flea or a mosquito, and cried out in distress, my mother or the servant girl would shake me with such frenzy that my bowels churned and my head spun like a top. If that expedient failed, an udder of almost suffocating size would be thrust into my mouth. Or if my mother had to attend to business as the breadwinner, there would be stuffed into my mouth a grimy, wadded rag soaked in sugar and water, which I was left to gag on for hours at a time.

At the age of two months I was put into a crib—but not before, in accordance with tradition, a cat had first been rocked in it. And there I might have been content: to be rocked is more pleasant than to be stifled in a pillow. But apparently the finding of any solace or relief in my own wretched existence was not to be my fate. There was hardly a day when I didn't fall from my crib. One day, one of the four cords holding it up would snap; the next, the hook to which the cords were attached would break loose; or else a knot would become untied. And from day to day, as the cords were untied and refastened, my crib was being hoisted a little higher so that within a few months I found myself brushing against the ceiling. Not in vain had our tzaddik proclaimed me to be a lofty soul. . . .

However, the higher my soul ascended, the greater the downfall in store. At times when I took a fancy to what I thought was an outline of Satan on the ceiling, or when I stared at the light, or when I kicked up my heels in the middle of the night, it was the invariable response of my mother or the housemaid—in order to lull me to sleep, so that they, too, could get some rest—to scare me out of my wits with tales of a demon *and* a vampire *and* a ghost *and* a goblin *and* a wicked beggar, until I shrank in terror from my own shadow. To this day, I need only to glimpse my shadow in the moonlight, or to see a white billy goat nibbling at the thatched roof of a peasant hut, or to observe the reflection of the moon in the window of a darkened house, and immediately it is as though I beheld a demon, a walking corpse, a vampire—and I feel the earth give way beneath me.

To sum it up, things are more easily said than done. But somehow or other I reached and passed my first birthday, by which time I was creeping on all fours into every nook and corner, rummaging through every sort of junk and garbage, and putting the ashes from the oven into my mouth. Eighteen times a day I would meet with an accident, and after each one, my mother would pull off my shirt and, having splashed a little water on the bump, would press down the flat of the kitchen knife, and murmur some charm. Whereupon—lo and behold!—the pain would miraculously cease. If, God forbid, the house had been lined with mirrors, I would have died several times a day simply from catching sight of myself. A scabby crust covered my entire head; my face was plastered with soot and filth; I drooled from the mouth and the upper lip my angel had tweaked was drenched with snot; my hands and feet were always dirty; and I was wrapped in yellowed, greasy rags.

And, indeed, who was there to look after me? Our housemaid, who was paid all of six rubles a year, plus my father's discarded shoes—in return for which she had to tidy up the house, care for the children, light the furnace, drive the cow to pasture, empty the pails of slop, and pluck feathers, besides wiping her own nose and continually scratching her head with both hands—could hardly be expected to. And my mother, of course, could hardly be reproached. For, in addition to being the breadwinner of the family, doing the household chores, mending and darning, reading the *Tehinot,* the book of devotions for women, she was obliged to wait on my father, so as to gain a share in "the world to come," which a woman could attain only through the merits of her husband. By then she was already unwell; she vomited a good deal and could hardly bear to look at a piece of meat. It is common knowledge that countless little Hasidim are started on their pilgrimage through this world "between a yes and a no"—which is ever so much quicker than a twinkling. May every Orthodox Jew be blessed with a share of tatterdemalions and dancers with two left feet! And the more our tzaddikim endeavor to propagate their little would-be saintly sages, the more the common sheep will strive to breed Hasidic lambs to swell their flocks. Could my poor father lag behind? Especially since he was privileged to be the rabbi's adjutant and a dignitary in the rabbi's court!

Thus, I could have yelled my head off; I could have been crippled for life every time I took a tumble; I could have frozen or starved to death in my soiled and smelly rags—all without having anyone take note. Such, indeed, was my miserable lot until, having passed the year of three, I finally came under the tutelage of my father.

2

At my age, my father expects me to be an observant Jew

As soon as I reached the age of four, my father took me
in hand and began to drill me in the tenets of virtue and
tradition. But if you suppose he taught me any of those
stupid precepts with which the German Jews indoctri-
nate their children, such as giving homage to one's parents on awaking and going to sleep, or offering thanks
to their parents after each meal, and so on—well, if that
is what you think, you are entirely wrong. Jews in Poland
regard putting on such fine airs as clumsy and deserving
of scorn. My father's teachings were diametrically opposed to any such social graces: he urged me to be rude
to my mother; my mother, in turn, exhorted me to show
disrespect toward my father; and they both encouraged
me to greet honored guests with rude comments.

At the same time, he insisted on my observing certain precepts which even an elderly Orthodox Jew is not
obliged to fulfill under the Mosaic Law, but which must
be heeded because of tradition. For instance, he taught
me to hold on to my yarmulka at night, so as to keep it
from slipping off my head while I slept. At the festival of

Purim I was supposed to do eighteen somersaults on the table, in obedience to a certain ritual. During the Passover Seder he directed me to join in observing the ritual down to the last detail, and until the crack of dawn. On Yom Kippur, I had to abstain from any food until noon, and to move about in my stocking feet throughout that day. During the Feast of Tabernacles, I had to sleep in the booth even when it was freezing weather; I was adjured to comb my side curls once and only once a week, on the eve of the Sabbath, when I also had to accompany my father to the ritual public baths and have my head completely shaved. And other such virtues.

I shall not dwell on all the good deeds I was expected to perform, but pause only to describe the ritual public steam bath which I had to visit every Friday along with all other pious Jews. That bathhouse dismayed and upset me most of all. Never will I forget those episodes; merely to recall that period of my life is to make me shudder.

Picture for a moment the steamy, reeking Jewish bathhouse then in Poland, to which my father used to take me on Fridays, dragging me up to the topmost step. He would scrub me with a short-handled broom made of birch twigs, dripping with soapsuds, in a room filled with scalding vapor, for a quarter of an hour or longer, as a prelude to plunging me into the mikveh, the pool for ritual immersion. And this was mere child's play compared to the main act of the comedy—the ritual bath itself, long may it flourish! The scrubbing with the birch broom merely caused me physical pain; but the bath itself made me tremble like the leaves of an aspen in the breeze.

Now, it is common knowledge that a child will endure any amount of physical pain, but cannot brook fear. Imagine a three-year-old youngster, accustomed to playing outdoors all day in the sun, being suddenly taken down a spiral staircase, thirty or forty narrow, ramshackle and slippery stairs, leading to a dank, cold, deep waterhole, where a crowd of naked, slippery bodies were slithering and bumping up against one another, all of them belonging to adults and not to children like myself. . . . The least contact with any of these hot sweating bodies made my hair stand on end! But what alarmed me most was the uncanny and forbidding cavern where now and then one would hear a splash and a muffled outcry, like some awful echo from within a forest or from a howling steppe no human being had ever crossed. In this ghastly setting my father would pick me up and throw me into the water. When he finally retrieved me from it, I would be in a daze, quivering all over like a poisoned rat, and groping in that dim atmosphere for my very soul. . . .

Can you, dear reader, conceive of the horrors to which I was subjected? You may say you do, but that can hardly be correct. No matter how much of that scene you may conjure up, it will not amount to even a thousandth part of what I endured on those days! Not to speak of the taste of the bath water and of its stench—or rather, that of the compost pit nearby. In fact, I was so thoroughly cleansed by my father's ritual baths that to this day I cannot rid myself of the dirt that clings, defying the most powerful soap and the purest water! I could describe still other bizarre scenes for you, but I am quite aware that you will see it all as mere entertainment, like a ride on a merry-go-round. But to my father, such practices were the quintessence of Judaism.

Thus I fared for another year, and then it was time to assign me to a heder, the traditional religious school. At first thought I was quite pleased with this new move. As a matter of fact, I had had my fill of being at home, where I felt like a stray dog with no one to look after me. My father was busy soliciting funds for the rabbi's up-keep, and aside from initiating me into his favorite customs and traditions, he heeded me no more than the snows of yesteryear. As for my mother, she had her hands full as the breadwinner of the family, attending to household chores and as caretaker of the offspring—one child clutching at her apron, another being held in her arms, and a third being carried in her belly. So it was that attending heder appeared to me an adventurous move: I would be looked after over there, I thought, and would be brought up as a decent human being ought to be. I had no false illusions about growing up like a child of the rich—but at least I would be on a par with the children of humble but upright citizens.

Then I happened to overhear a conversation between my father and mother, which served to temper my enthusiasm to some extent. It began with my father saying, "Vittye, you can see for yourself how busy I am earning a livelihood. So you had better go over and enroll him in the heder. Now, if it were a matter of engaging a *Gemara-melamed,* an advanced talmudic teacher—well, that would be quite another matter. But to confer with a *dardeke melamed,* an elementary teacher —that would be a bit below my dignity; you understand that much yourself."

"You're right," my mother agreed. "Of course I'll attend to it. But tell me, Yossel—where should I take him? Since there are only two *dardeke melamdim* in town —Nachman 'Slap' and Nehemiah 'Cap'—which one would you say, with all your learning, is more suitable for our child?"

"It would be hard to tell," my father magisterially replied. "Judging by his character, Nachman 'Slap' might be the more advisable of the two."

"But he is bad-tempered with children; and, what's more, my friend Vechna told me just the other day that according to quite a few Jewish worthies, Nehemiah surpasses Nachman in scholarship."

"That may be so; but Nehemiah does not happen to be a follower of my rebbe," my father pointed out.

"What of it?" my mother countered in a wheedling tone. "Even if he is a devotee of the tzaddik of Zodkowetz, he is a Hasid all the same, isn't he?"

"You stupid creature! How ignorant can one be?" my father flung back, losing his temper at last. "Do you put the rebbe of Zodkowetz in the same category with our saintly sage? I've heard our holy tzaddik himself say that the rebbe of Zodkowetz is merely God's clown, since he belongs to the race of blockheads—and, just to prove it, remember that his betrothal took place precisely on the blind night, since he had been circumcised on Yom Kippur. . . . But then you are hopelessly ignorant in such matters."

"How could I know?" my mother said apologetically. "I've seen how people from all over flock to that rabbinical court—so to a simple-minded Jewish woman like myself, it all seems right and proper."

"Oh-oh! So you were taken in by the thought of Jews flocking to that rabbi," my father said sorrowfully. "For that matter, young men are also flocking to the talmudical academies of Lithuania. But does that prove anything? It's only apostasy. Didn't our holy rebbe himself castigate and deplore those yeshivas during his sermon on the Sabbath Shirah, when the Song of Moses at the Red Sea is read? He distinctly put the yeshivas and the rabbinical seminaries in the same category: they are hotbeds of heretics; as for the misnagedim—the rabbinical opponents to Hasidism—in due time they all turn out to be heretics. Apropos of this, our rabbi cited an ingenious passage from Scriptures on this very point, but it would be difficult to expound it to you. Oh, what's the use—you're nothing but a moron."

"Well, what did you expect from an ordinary woman?" my mother whimpered. "Why, you have more sense in your little finger than I have in my head. Go ahead, do whatever seems best to you."

3

The heder

When my mother first delivered me to the heder conducted by Nachman "Slap" (as the boys called him), I
was appalled by the squalor of the setting. Filth was
everywhere; near the entrance were a round cistern and
a moldy slop pail on whose surface floated objects of the
sort that were thrown at Haman's head. The panes of the
narrow casement windows were thickly coated with a
layer of frost etched with various graffiti, including the
Star of David. Some of these were overlaid with a thinner
layer, indicating that they were of relatively recent date;
others were newly and superficially incised. Here and
there a circle had been made in the rime, evidently by
pressing a hot coin against its glistening surface. Water
trickled down from the windows, along the walls, and
onto the muddy earthen floor. Three infants, their skirts
pinned up under their arms, crawled about in the mire.

A long, narrow, rickety table was held by twine and
baling wire; its plank top was gouged, charred, and covered with ink stains. More planks, rough-hewn and studded with knotholes, were set on sawhorses to serve as

benches for pupils of various ages, who sat huddled together with their backs against the dripping walls. The single tattered prayer book that did service as the text for ten pupils was swollen by the damp to three times its original thickness.

At one end of the table, a huge, battered wickerwork hamper overflowed with pots and pans whose residues were being explored by a gray tomcat, while its tail thumped against the head of a small child. Through an open door in one corner there was a glimpse into an adjoining room, where the melamed's wife, her face clammy with sweat, and wearing a greasy cap, was shoving a poker into the oven.

Near the oven, our tutor held the place of honor: having shed the gabardine, he wore only his *tallit katan*, the four-cornered undergarment, whose ritual fringes were yellow with age; the dirty threadbare yarmulka that covered his bald head looked more like a potholder or a mustard plaster than a skullcap. In one hand he clutched a cat-o'-nine-tails, while with the other he scratched his hairy chest, which the unbuttoned and grimy shirt had left exposed.

As my mother and I entered the heder, a strange scene greeted us: while the melamed and his assistant flourished the whips by which discipline was maintained, the older pupils gabbled like a flock of geese and the younger ones sniffed or sobbed aloud. At that precise moment, the teacher's wife rushed in like a whirlwind, carrying a blazing faggot which she plunged into the slop pail. The steam that rose from the pail turned the place into something resembling a Turkish bath. After a few words with the headmaster about enrolling me, my mother was gone, leaving me at the mercy of the "institute."

No sooner was she out of sight than the teacher

addressed me as follows: "See this whip? That's for the little boy who doesn't study properly." And in order to reinforce this point for me, he flicked the whip at the nearest pupil. This initiation over, he yanked me into a vacant seat at the table, and, opening the bloated prayer book that served as the communal text, asked brusquely, "Do you know anything at all?"

"No-o," I whimpered, faltering, and then burst into tears.

"Be still! What is this crying for?" the teacher barked—meanwhile pinching my cheek so that I screamed with pain. Then he set me on his knee and pointed with his ruler to the first letters of the alphabet on the page. When I could not read them for him, the solution was to adopt a new tactic, namely, to promise me that if only I would make an effort to study, an angel would drop me a kopeck from the ceiling. At the prospect of such a reward, I forgot the text and craned my neck to stare upward. The teacher then uttered a series of threats of what awaited one so remiss as a scholar: I would be lashed with iron thongs in the world to come, I would be carried off by the Evil One to the Mount of Darkness, or be sold by elves to the Gypsies; at night I would be haunted by ghosts of the dead and other such apparitions as would make my blood run cold. So it was that aleph, the first letter in the alphabet, seemed to have the shape of a goblin, and beth, the second, that of an iron thong, while the swollen textbook yawned like the very portals of hell.

At that point I went into such hysterics that I had to be taken home. That night I had visions of evils spirits, while corpses armed with iron rattans glowered at me, screaming, "Chant aleph! Chant beth!" For a whole month I lay delirious, suspended between life and death. I am aware that on reading the above, a Polish Jew or

Jewess may smile, attributing to me no more than a wish
to entertain. The truth is that just as I was then terrified
of evil spirits, of the dead and the iron thongs, so all
Polish Jews even now tremble before the thought of such
horrors. What they fail to realize, however, is that they
have inherited this state of mind from their heder days.
That is why they show no mercy to their own offspring:
it does not occur to them to bring up their children more
reasonably, or to spare them from pain and fright. But
how can they be expected to wean their children away
from such a way of life when they still cling to it themselves as though it were ordained by Holy Writ? There
is no lack in Poland of old wives' tales about werewolves
or the dybbuk and so on and on—which is exactly why
newborn children must be protected by all those quaint
names inscribed on the *shir hamaalot* posted on door-
posts and window ledges, and why there are talismans
and amulets in all living quarters and all cellars—to ward
off the evil eye. And the more precautions they take, the
greater the fear they encourage. Thus they send their
children down the same treacherous road that their own
fanatical fathers had led them to traverse.

And it is all nothing but superstition. No elfchild was
ever left as a changeling for an infant; no one has ever
in fact caught sight of a goblin in a cellar; and no one has
yet witnessed the dead worshiping in a synagogue. . . .
When the gravedigger himself steals the shroud from a
corpse, do you think he carries a *shir hamaalot* on his
person? And what does the rebbe's assistant have in
mind when he steers someone into a blind alley late at
night? Certainly no amulets or talismans are to be found
there! And what does the holy rebbe himself think of
being summoned by the sheriff or the bailiff? Indeed,
those officers have no amulets either. Is he deterred by
the possibility of some evil spirit there? If anything, what

he has to fear there is the likelihood of prosecution. Moreover, when a Polish Jew reads in some Yiddish book or a journal about such fanaticism and superstition, he only grins and says, "Well, well, whoever wrote all this hit the nail on the head all right. Isn't such stupid nonsense just what all Jews encourage?" It doesn't dawn on him that he is one of those same Jews—or that he doesn't benefit by it in the least. And as sure as I live, any Polish Jew who reads this book of mine will say concerning one point or another, "He is absolutely right." But it will never dawn on this same reader that he himself is more weighed down than his compeers by all these fallacies and superstitions. Yet he will go right on sounding off as though he were completely innocent. Let me assure you that my present intention is not the mere telling of a fairy tale. My intention is to try to save even one single Polish Jew—if no more than that—to prevail on him to abandon the fanatical ways that have played such havoc with his own life. I want him to be more civilized and better educated—to be more aware of the true nature of the species *Homo sapiens*. If the fathers are beyond redemption, let them at least not undermine the future of their children. But I have wandered a long way from my subject. Let us go back to my heder.

4

The just and learned melamdim of Poland and their assistants

Before long, in fact, I grew accustomed to the heder. From the other pupils I learned more than enough tales of the restless dead and of angels and goblins. Item: one small boy informed me that every night his father went up to heaven to study Holy Writ in the company of the angels, but on waking he would forget everything he had ever learned. Another pupil told me that whenever his father went away on a journey, a demon would appear and start choking his mother. Still another boy declared that his big sister would often trap a goblin in the cellar and pull off its hat, making the goblin pay her to give it back. One pupil insisted that his father could cast a spell on witches that turned their hair gray. Another said that his father could recognize the dead who wandered in limbo—and that these lost souls bribed him not to give them away. And there were still other tales, horrific yet fascinating. Also, I learned by heart a number of folk songs that I found bewitching.

In a word, the heder would have been more tolerable had it not been for the teacher's assistant, a rat if

there ever was one—may he fall down dead! He made my
life miserable. During the study period I had to stand
before him for hours on end, and he would resort to the
whip at the least provocation. And he regularly took
almost the entire lunch I had brought along and ate it
himself. The result was that if I refrained from telling my
mother, I all but starved; whereas if I told her—why, then
he would beat me black and blue. Keeping quiet thus
seemed the lesser of two evils. And I'd rather not tell you
what took place the times we went swimming. This preceptor would dive and then bob up again far down the
stream, where the "white goslings" were bathing. I did
not consider this my business—as long as he left me
alone.

Now, this assistant could not be held solely to
blame. He had arrived at his position through devious
means. All the local matrons, for instance, would take his
side. It is a rather long story, going back to when he was
ten or twelve years old and made a pastime of catching
and killing flies, which he sold to fishermen at the rate
of a kopeck per pound—or for a loaf of bread. The
fishermen recommended him to the manager of the public baths as a likely youngster. In due time he came to
know the gadabouts who frequented the women's section of the baths and of the synagogue. As they contributed their bit to his polish and enlightenment, he
gradually became a man about town. Having insinuated
himself into the private lives of some influential townsmen, both male and female, he had come to know just
when the town's worthies caroused at public expense; he
could tell you which married men were flirting with
which young women during the ritual of tashlikh, performed near a stream, when devout Jews murmur,
"Thou shalt cast thy sins into the sea"; he knew of
women rifling their husbands' pockets at night, and so

on. He had also learned how to pronounce, though un-grammatically, certain Hebrew expressions. Eventually he became a special sexton, whose duties included bring-ing up the rear with a lantern following the ritual slaugh-ter of chickens for the kapparah, atonement, and accom-panying the cantor as he made the rounds to collect for Hanukkah, as well as delivering watercress to the syna-gogues on the eve of the Feast of Tabernacles. Also, he served as the bearer of sad news; he ran ahead of the funeral processions of local nabobs; he perforated mat-zoth with a rowel; he prodded the sluggish townsmen awake to put out a fire; and so on.

In the course of these varied missions he would help himself to a spoon here, a knife there, a candlestick or some other object of that sort; and he knew where to dispose of them, though they brought next to nothing. A local gossip, a stout, shrill Jewess who went every day to the synagogue, carrying the thickest prayer book, served as his "fence." The women all knew that she invariably received direct from heaven the formulas for the nostrums she concocted. She looked forward to re-ceiving the loot and knew how to dispose of it—at a profit, moreover. It didn't take much to gratify the assis-tant: he had a sweet tooth, and in exchange for the booty, this female cossack would make the rounds of all the Jewish households, collecting preserves, jams, jellies, os-tensibly for the sick in the poorhouse. Thus the many-sided honorary beadle was enabled to indulge his appe-tite. Now and then she would speak highly of him to the other matrons, saying such things as, "He may be a bit uncouth, but he's such an honest soul!" or "There's not another person in the world so devout!" and much else in the same vein. Her propaganda hit its mark, and with the support of other women she got for him the position of assistant to the melamed, Nachman "Slap"—and the men could only say "Amen!"

Not to prolong the tale, I struggled with the alphabet for almost half a year, and made no progress. For one thing, my teacher received hardly as much as a copper in tuition from my father. Whatever money my father had promised the teacher was credited to the maintenance fund for the tzaddik, the holy rabbi. But when it came to that, what need had this teacher of tuition fees? He was never, thank God, refused a nip at the house of worship! As you well know, precisely as the Tailors' Guild is bound to come to blows before any day is over, a Hasidic congregation, come what may, is sure to have its quotidian liquid cheer. Pretexts? Reasons? Whatever you like! On one day it will be that the rebbitzin has presented her husband, the rebbe, with a manchild. On another honors are bestowed on the rebbe himself. Or else the rebbe is summoned by the justice of the peace —which calls for a nip to combat depression. Then the rabbi is acquitted—which calls for a celebration, doesn't it? Or the rabbi is presented with horses and a carriage, or his son becomes engaged, or the community of Vorchivka has sent the rebbe a silver rooster symbolizing the scapegoat in the pre-Yom Kippur atonement ceremony, and so on. Not to speak of the anniversaries of the dead, of which there are more in a small Hasidic synagogue than in all other houses of worship! I would have you know that not a few ailing Hasidic Jews might have recovered their health, had they not started visiting the rabbi, and wound up with an *elixir vitae* as a cure. . . .

The whole thing is quite simple: when presented with a note about someone critically ill, the holy rebbe finds himself in a quandary; he rolls his eyes, knits his brow, and heaves a troubled sigh. In this way he preserves a happy medium: if the patient should die, it will appear that the rabbi has been clairvoyant—for did he not roll his eyes mystically, knit his brow, and heave a sigh? If on the other hand, the invalid should recover, why that can be attributed to the intercession of the miracle-working tzaddik: with gestures of supplication he has succeeded in wresting the struggling Jew from the clutches of the Angel of Death. In the meantime, when the messenger returns to report the rabbi's ominous deportment and his sighs, the ailing one is scared witless, and this mortal fear may hasten an untimely end.

However things turn out, a new annual commemoration is scheduled in the synagogue, and my teacher is given another opportunity to slake his thirst. Nor did he ever go without a meal, precisely because he was regarded in the community as indigent—a fellow chronically down on his luck, whom it was a mitzvah to invite to dinner. And on those rare occasions when there was no celebration or comparable event, he could resort to other avocations. During the month of Nissan, Jewish calendar, he would deliver to the prosperous townsmen their supply of matzah baked under strict supervision; during the month of Elul, when women visit the graves of the departed, he would turn up to interpret the Hebrew engraving on the tombstones; on the Feast of Tabernacles, he would furnish a citron and a palm branch to his various patrons; on the seventh day of Sukkoth, he became a wholesale dealer in willow branches, which, incidentally, were gathered for him by his pupils. And in the month of Kislev he molded Hanukkah candles for sale.

In addition to all this, he was an occasional marriage broker; now and then he led some unpretentious congregation in prayer during the High Holy Days, or recited the Mourner's Kaddish for the childless, or chanted psalms of intercession for the rich when they were at death's door, or wrote letters for illiterate women whose husbands were conscripted. He also converted bark into an imitation of snuff and regularly sold it at the synagogue. So what need had he for my father to pay him a tuition fee? So long as he was provided for, what did it matter that his wife and children suffered hunger and privation! To begin with, there is nothing new about a Hasidic Jew's lack of concern for his family.

What's more, my teacher detested his wife—which is a story in itself.

It seems that for several years my teacher was the assistant to an earlier melamed. The predecessor of Nachman "Slap" had a daughter—a rather awkward and unprepossessing creature, dour as the wrath of God, but plump enough to ensnare the heart of the assistant. In plain words, the spell was so strong that in about five months her clothes had become too tight, especially about the waist. Her father saw from the outset where the wind was blowing, but pretended not to. It was only in the sixth month of the pregnancy that he confided in his brother, the mayor of the town; whereupon the two brothers called for an audience with the assistant, and the mayor presented him with an ultimatum: either be joined forthwith in holy wedlock under the Law of Moses, or be conscripted into the army of the czar. Confronted with so dire a choice, the assistant agreed to an immediate wedding.

As it turned out, the father-in-law died a year or so later, and the mayor spared no effort to have the son-in-law appointed to the vacancy so that his ugly duckling of a niece might not starve. The local community was somewhat put out over so unpromising an appointment, but the new appointee lost no time in showing his devotion to the leader rabbi—and the outcome was assured. In Poland, to become a follower of the rebbe in authority is all that is required; such a move atones for all worldly sins. And so, by one stroke of luck, our Nachman "Slap" attained the status of the town's *dardeke melamed*. But as for his spouse, to this very day he cannot endure the sight of her.

To be brief: during the second term I was supposed to master the accents used in chanting the Torah. But in this my success was equal to that of the tzaddik in predicting that I would be born a girl. I howled and panted my way through in school without learning anything. At the end of the term I left the heder of Nachman "Slap" and enrolled in another, where I was introduced to the study of the Five Books of Moses.

5

The new is no better than the old

How can I describe to you, dear fellow Jews, the trials I endured before I so much as set eyes on a copy of the Pentateuch? For all of a month I was subjected to the ordeal of memorizing a sort of declamation concerning the *Humesh,* the Five Books of Moses, which I was expected to deliver at home before invited guests of both sexes. This exercise called for the participation of two other pupils, one of them as my interrogator, the other as the one who pronounced a benediction upon me. Every day we rehearsed this ceremony for three hours, while the interrogator continually tweaked my nose and pushed up my chin, bringing about a permanent dislocation of my Adam's apple. And the other, who was to pronounce the benediction, twisted my head so often that he left my neck permanently awry. But of course all this was worth enduring, in view of the quaint questions that were put to me—for example, "What is the meaning of *Humesh?*" To which my reply was, "Five." "Five of what? Five bagels for a kopeck?" he pursued. "No," I answered, "I mean the Five Books of Moses." "Which of those books are you studying, little boy?" went the next question. "Leviticus," was my answer. "How does it begin?" he asked. " 'And the Lord called unto Moses, ' " I informed him. "Which Moses? Do you mean our blind Moses of the Knolls?" he persisted. "No," was my reply. "It is Moses of Mount Sinai." And so on and on.

The singsong accompanying the catechism was more interminable than the Diaspora. And also we made faces, just like the wife of the synagogue warden while she molds her dumplings, or like the ritual slaughterer of Tiverivka with his knife poised to strike. To be brief —on the eve of the Sabbath designated for this examination, my mother placed on my head a brocaded yarmulka, which she had made over from a bonnet five years ago for the child she had expected—on the strength of our tzaddik's prediction—to be female. I was then escorted by my mother to the sage for a preliminary benediction, just as I felt the urge to perform a bowel movement. So when the sage pinched my cheek and asked, "What is your wish, my dear child?" I answered straight out, "I need to *go!*" Well, you can imagine the scolding and the beating I got from my mother; and if, God forbid, she had told my father what I had done, my life wouldn't have been worth a copper. Now tell me, dear fellow Jews—did I deserve to be scolded and beaten, especially while I wore a brocaded yarmulka?

After the Sabbath meal, the assembled local dignitaries—relatives and friends, along with several clodhoppers who had come to gawk—sat down around the table. My melamed was present, as well as my fellow performers. The tzaddik of Sirevka also attended—an honor that spurred my father to a resolve that he would do his utmost to raise additional funds for the hallowed sage. My mother and her friends, all in their best and wearing the traditional headgear, sat apart in the center of the room. As my two schoolmates and I were climbing onto the table, I slipped and fell off. I might have been badly hurt except that the earthen floor was fortunately knee-deep in mud, thus cushioning the fall. To be brief: the three of us were at last standing on the table, with me in the center, flanked on either side by the interrogator and by the one who was to pronounce the benediction. My melamed was in a state of agitation, since he was both director and producer of the spectacle. My mother and the rest of her sex burst into tears of delight, quite as though I were about to deliver a sermon in the leading synagogue. And after my recital, the table was spread with fresh goodies such as boiled chick-peas, sweet cakes, flat rolls sprinkled with poppy seeds, cider, and noodle pudding, while at the head of the table, within easy reach of the tzaddik, were a bottle of cognac, two bottles of mead, and a fine stuffed goose neck—all of them fit for a king.

In the new school I was introduced to still other wild and freakish customs, such as vilifying one's parents and grandparents, throwing stones at beggars, sticking out one's tongue and contorting one's lips in frightful grimaces, twisting one's eyebrows this way and that in imitation of a corpse. I also learned all about sorcerers, demons, fiends, and goblins, as well as the legends concerning the eyes of the Angel of Death and his vial of poison, and the "paper bridge," and so on. Moreover, I was introduced to the right incantations, exorcisms and magic spells for warding off evil spirits. One of these I remember to this day: when confronted by the Evil One, you are to place your thumb on your little finger and mumble, "Abracadabra!" along with the other Kabbalistic mumbo jumbo. Then betake yourself to God's acre, and raise your voice in a shout of "Hear, O Israel!" stroking your right eye with the left ritual lock, three times over, spitting each time and yelling, "Go back to where you came from!" and then take to your heels. . . .

I remember the melamed's assistant telling us once that if we were to present him with the buttons from our breeches, he would show us a goblin. Having each bitten through the thread that held the buttons and given them to him, we were suddenly confronted by a creature of some sort, wearing a yarmulka and a *tallit katan* devoid of the ritual fringes. When the assistant shouted, "Goblin! Goblin!" and clapped his hands, the odd creature vanished. Let me assure you that we were infinitely delighted. But when I found out the practical joke that had been played on us, using an ordinary cat, I felt both ashamed and profoundly hurt. Still, why should I have been chagrined? There is no great feat in deceiving a youngster. Why, even old men are continually being taken in, yet they are not distressed; neither are they ashamed. If anything, they actually take pride in being deceived, regarding the deception as a sign of esteem. Furthermore, they will even *pay* to be deceived. For the donation of a silver coin or two they are led to believe that the rabbi can capture angels or exorcise a dybbuk, the soul of a malefactor that has taken refuge in a living person; that he can bring down snow and rain; that he dances with the patriarchs during the feast that ends the Sabbath; that he can see from one end of the world to the other; that he wrestles with the Evil One; and finally, that he holds the key that can release barren women from the doom of childlessness. And even though no one ever witnessed any of these miraculous powers—what did it matter, so long as the hallowed sage rolled his eyes and cried, "Welcome, Father Abraham! Welcome, Sarah, Rebecca, Rachel, and Leah! Begone, Satan, begone Angel of Death and Sammael, from my dwelling! Lilith, be off with you from that woman!"

Well, a Hasid is duty bound to play along with the mystification. We youngsters at least had seen a cat wearing a yarmulka, whereas they, the old Terahs, were still totally in the dark. But all my talking is of no avail. How can you argue with a flock of hypocrites or covey of Polish slatterns who engage in every sort of evildoing, but when something happens which touches them vitally, are off like a bolt of lightening to the hallowed sage or to the graves of their ancestors, where they wring their hands and bewail their misfortunes.

I am thinking that by now those hallowed sages are themselves disgusted to the point of nausea by such doings. Indeed, what upright or reputable person could reconcile himself to a way of life that compels him to associate with hundreds of idlers and ne'er-do-wells, of hypocrites, gossips, and horse thieves? And even when the landowner, the postmaster, the tax collector, the leading merchant, or some other local nabob calls on him, does he not recoil from giving out hypocritical pronouncements that cater to each supplicant's stupid or immoral wish? What of their false promises of pseudo-miracles, such as raising the hopes of an elderly Jew that he will shortly beget a new child? Or of the debtor that the lord of the manor will charge him no interest on a loan? Or of some butcher that the next lot of cattle will consist of unblemished kosher animals? Or to a coachman that his blind and starving team will carry passengers as on the wings of eagles—without any expenditure for hay and oats? And what about the promise to the sleigh-maker of snow, and to the landowner of rain—both on the same day . . . and all such miracles? Surely a rabbi is well aware that he cannot thrust his hand into water that is too cold or his foot into a tub that is scalding, and that he dare not face the sheriff. Accordingly, he is bound to go on rolling his eyes and knitting his brow,

sighing and groaning all the while, and to continue outlandish gesticulations and grimaces—all of which must
surely prey on his mind. How can he be content with
leading such a life?

But every rebbe is owned body and soul by the
warden of the synagogue, and likewise chained to his
rebbitzin, who appears to exhort him, "Keep it up, my
husband. Go on hoodwinking the world and refraining
from scruples; go on associating with sluts and drifters,
with informers, sons-of-bitches and thieves—so that I
may flaunt jewelry by the bushel, wear fine dresses and
slippers embroidered in gold!" Alas, in such ways money
is thrown to the winds. Newly married men squander the
dowries of their wives; craftsmen push their luck until it
runs out; trustees steal from widows and orphans, they
dissipate the funds entrusted to them, and make gifts in
order to enhance their credit—until they go bankrupt.
The poor mortgage and sell their belongings, bag and
baggage, in order to raise enough money to visit the
rebbe; the last ruble that had been set aside for medicine
in the event of sickness is diverted to an honorarium for
the holy rebbe, who proceeds to roll his eyes and knit his
brow, to sigh and groan—until the invalid is finally gathered to his fathers. . . . The fact is that people spare no
effort in lavishing money on the rebbe. What all that
Jewish blood and sweat are destined for—and who benefits thereby—God alone knows.

6

In Poland, Jewish children have no trouble learning good manners at the heder—and politics at the public baths

I have certainly strayed from the subject, digressing all the way from goblins to rabbis! The crucial matter I had meant to speak of is my study of the Pentateuch. My melamed taught me in a way that was bizarre: the original Hebrew text was translated word for word into Yiddish. But although I was a little past the age of five, I had already become adept at playing truant from school, and had found a safe hideaway—the public baths. Since the Hasidic flock, including my melamed, lingered at the steam baths until noon, there was no need for me to go into hiding before then; and in the afternoon I had no school and could do as I pleased.

On one occasion, I recall, I found two gaunt fanatics in the steam bath, scrutinizing the *tallit katan* in search of Pharaoh's "third plague." I slipped behind the boiler to avoid detection, and eavesdropped on their conversation.

"You know, Chayim Haikel," one of them said, "The way I see it, a most dreadful calamity is about to overtake us."

"How did you arrive at that conclusion, Baruch Tanchum?"

"The Turk is casting sheep's eyes at the French princess."

"He is? And is the Frenchman unwilling to let her marry him?"

"Chayim Haikel, how stupid can you get? Why, the Turk rules the world. Do you think the Frenchman would disdain the match? Would you consider it beneath his dignity?"

Chayim Haikel was now curious. "Well, what do you make of the whole thing?"

"It is clear that the Austrian emperor has found out and is up in arms over it," said Baruch Tanchum.

"Could it be that his majesty has a hankering for her himself?"

"Who could have told you that? All the same, you've hit the nail on the head. Do you think that the Austrian emperor is a fool? If the Turk is after her, she must be a ravishing beauty."

"So what came of it all?"

"Don't ask such questions! Why, nothing came of it. The emperor of Austria stationed two huge gendarmes with thick red mustaches at the frontier. They had orders to seize the princess if she tried to cross, and to carry her off, with no ifs, ands, or buts."

"Ah, but they were probably asleep at the crucial moment."

"Mastermind, did you ever hear of gendarmes caught napping? Why, they're not human, the devils! No, they beat her within an inch of her life; it was a miracle she got out of their hands alive!"

"Ah, but then trouble is on the way, Baruch Tanchum. Such a thing bodes no good; it's playing with fire."

"So, you moron, at last you're beginning to see what this could lead to?"

"Go on, Baruch Tanchum, tell me the rest; don't leave me hanging."

"Can't you understand, imbecile? All the governments must already have sent cossacks galloping on fiery horses, with instructions to seize the two gendarmes, dead or alive!"

"So, were they caught?"

"Just a minute! It's not so easy to seize gendarmes: people are saying they have disguised themselves as converts to Judaism and are hiding out in the cellar of the melamed of Zlotchev. Meanwhile, all the nations are sitting on a keg of powder."

The story gave me an idea. Now that I thought of it, what good to me was the steam bath, where I could be seen by so many people? What about the cellar of our own house? And so, without further hesitation, I made my way into our cellar and settled there, withdrawing from the world and its turmoil as though into a patriarchal vineyard. But on my third day in this haven, I suddenly heard footsteps: it was evidently my mother coming down to get the jellied calves' feet for the Sabbath meal. I flipped up a pebble almost without intending to —but what a commotion I stirred up! Though it was merely a childish prank on my part, word soon passed from mouth to mouth that a poltergeist had come to haunt our cellar and that it constituted a mortal danger, since it was throwing stones without interruption. My mother lost no time in enlisting a witch to cast spells against poltergeists, and my father brought amulets and talismans from his hallowed sage to ward off the evil spirit. Meanwhile, the term was drawing to a close, and I knew that I would be transferred to another melamed, thus making it unnecessary to hide any longer. And so, the tzaddik of Sirkov suddenly had his reputation as a miracle-worker augmented by exorcising the poltergeist from our cellar.

Yes, as my attendance at the one school came to an end, my father was planning to enroll me in a heder conducted by a *Gemara-melamed*, a teacher of the Talmud. I was by no means enraptured over this new move, but I reasoned that whatever happened, with the approach of the High Holy Days, I would be free of school for a while and could enjoy a breathing spell.

Had I in fact realized what the situation was for me then, I would have had little relish for that so-called breathing spell. As it turned out, I was at the mercy of the elements, continually pummeled and buffeted by the whim of all and sundry. I never had enough to eat. My father saw to it that I could not indulge my appetite, and whenever I was caught sneaking an extra morsel of food I would be soundly thrashed. I slept on the bare earthen floor, using rags for a blanket. My clothes were torn and threadbare; my shoes—bought all of two years ago and previously worn by a child of Shmuel Sirkes's—had neither soles nor heels; and the uppers were split, with the result that my feet were black and callused. Yes, altogether it was quite a breathing spell. But then a child doesn't know any better; when a worm crawls into horseradish, it supposes there is nothing sweeter. As a matter of fact, my mother kept urging my father, "Just look at him, Yossel—don't you think he should have a pair of shoes?" And my father would answer, "You'll have to be patient. When the Feast of Tabernacles rolls around, I'll unload upon the lessee of Kishkewitz my two bruised citrons for thirty rubles, the way he always pays me. Then we'll look into it."

"But Yossel, those citrons are not fit for any benediction," my mother objected.

"It serves him right, the ignorant lout," replied my father. "He shouldn't have allowed his precious son-in-law to patronize the rebbe of Zodkowetz."

From the preceding conversation it was hard to tell whether I would have shoes or not; but there was no doubt that the lessee of Kishkewitz would be sufficiently taken in to shell out thirty rubles for two deconsecrated citrons. And at last my father did say that if I should prove truly devout, shedding tears as I prayed during Rosh Hashanah, it was quite possible that I would have a pair of shoes. His words impressed me, and I decided to take him up on it—crying, after all, is easy enough to manage. And so Rosh Hashanah rolled round bringing with it that faint hope of shod feet. By then I was all of six years old.

7

Tears are of various sorts—only Polish Jews can shed real tears

At long last it was Rosh Hashanah. My father and I were in the synagogue. With the entire congregation engrossed in prayer, I made an effort to weep, but it turned out to be less easy than I had expected. I screwed up my face, I scowled, I squinted and then shut my eyes, I tried still other grimaces—all to no avail. And, in fact, what reason had I to weep? Was I to weep for the lessee of Kishkewitz, about to be cheated out of thirty rubles for two unacceptable citrons? The prayers themselves did not move me to tears. For one thing, I hardly understood them; for another, I gave free rein to my imagination. If I had had any sense at all and had paused to consider the sorry plight of the Jewish people as a whole, or to reflect on the sins committed throughout the year that was ending, I would have grasped my own predicament as well. And then I would have given way to tears, to torrents of them, on any day at all, and without a prayer book in front of me. But lacking in wit and with my heart set on a new pair of shoes, I could not bring myself to cry. I looked around me: the congregation had almost finished the Eighteen Benedictions, yet I was nowhere near tears. So it occurred to me to eavesdrop on those worshipers who were actually crying: perhaps I could learn from them how it was done.

No sooner thought of than acted on. I crept up to the rabbi's lectern. Luckily for me, some Jews lapse into Yiddish as they pray and weep, instead of clinging to the time-hallowed Hebrew of the prayer book. So it was that I heard the rebbe groan, "Lord of the Universe, You well know that Pini, the ritual slaughterer, will not stop short of using a faulty knife. Because I am a simple soul and not proficient in the Code of Laws, whereas Pini is a man of such erudition, is it necessary for him to prosecute and humiliate me at every rabbinical judgment? Dear Lord, I pray you to visit him in the coming year with a fall like Haman's!"

After listening to the rebbe's plea, I was curious to hear what cause the ritual slaughterer had to weep. I sidled over to the lectern of the slaughterer and I heard him tearfully sighing, "Lord of the Universe, You well know that the rabbi is an ignorant lout; that, although he may know a little about Hasidism, he has been able to function as a rabbi for three decades now only with the help of our tzaddik; and that he infringes upon the dietary laws and fosters bastards in Israel with his marriage ceremonies and his bills of divorce. By what right, then, is he entitled to a share in my earnings? Dear Lord, uphold the integrity of the Torah, permit the congregation to rebel and drive him from the rabbinate!"

Standing not far from the ritual slaughterer was the local nabob, a scoundrel if there ever was one. I was most anxious to find out what he was praying for. I edged up to him and listened. "Lord of the Universe," he whimpered. "You well know how loyal I am in guarding Your treasury, so that year by year it should increase and not

diminish. But then You incite against me those mis-
creants, the synagogue wardens, making them ask time
and again for assessments of eighteen rubles for the
rebbe's benefit—yet I am expected not to register the
slightest protest, or I risk losing all my possessions. And
as if I had not given enough, You chastise me in my old
age with a scoundrel of a son, who is such a fanatic that
he is ready to sacrifice his life for the rebbe and the
rebbe's followers. If he had his way he would bring everything I own to the rebbe, reducing me to such dire
straits that I would have to go from door to door begging. Dear Lord, do enlighten that blockhead and cause
him to renounce his idolatry of this rabbi!"

From the nabob I tiptoed over to the son, and heard
him praying as follows: "Lord of the Universe! Alas, that
miser my father is all but senile—but still he clings to his
handsome fortune as a hound clings to a carcass. In
order to obtain from the old rat a donation for the rabbi
—may his life be prolonged—I have to go through fire
and flood. Dear Lord, I pray You, help me by depriving
the old skinflint of his eyesight, so that for Hanukkah I
may be able to give my rebbe a silver menorah with a
three-foot candelabrum supported by two cherubs."

From the young Hasid I moved on to the lectern of
the mayor of the Jewish community. I heard him praying
through his tears as follows: "Lord of the Universe,
where are those miracles and wonders of Yours which
our ancestors had so much to tell of! My father and his
father before him, in their capacity as *khappers,* as kidnapers, were authorized to round up recruits for compulsory
military service once a year; whereas for me the draft
came only once every three years. Also, they would lead
ten recruits off on a single chain, whereas I issue one
chain for each recruit. And whereas my grandfather and
my father in their day drafted the sons of the oldest

families in town, I do my best to recruit only those caught trying to escape, including those who have passports; why, I recruited a father who was the sole breadwinner for his family, the only son of a blind and aged mother, and likewise even a village rebbe; to me they were all the same. I tore up one man's passport, at the risk of going to jail; on another occasion I made a man of fifty into a recruit by plucking all the gray hairs from his head. In short, I adopt any and all expedients to bring them into the army of the czar—simply in order to safeguard my community. But my grandfather—may he rest in peace! —left a row of stores; and my father, of blessed memory, left behind a three-story building that filled a square block. Yet all I have managed to acquire, not without struggle, is a minor house, a flour mill, a luxurious cottage completely furnished, and five wooden stores—plus such odds and ends as a butcher shop and a tavern or two —nothing more. True, I have married off three daughters—may their lives be prolonged—and the sons-in-law are a fine lot—even You, Lord, might envy me such a blessing as that. Not to prolong my plea—dear Lord, I pray Your help by inspiring the secretary of war with the notion of decreeing at least two drafts annually. Indeed, there are more than enough young heretics, those so-called Berliners, to fill *three* draft quotas a year. Let those poor devils, those outcasts, learn to fear God and respect their fellowman. Let them fathom the meaning of 'And, therefore, O Lord our God, let Thine awe be manifest in all Thy Works!' "

On leaving the mayor, I stumbled against an exceptionally large lectern, behind which stood the warden of the burial society. I wonder what is making him weep, I said to myself as I listened to his barely audible words: "Lord of the Universe—yesterday I went to consult the past years' records, and found only fifty-two corpses, not counting abortions and miscarriages. That comes to no more than one a week. And every last one of these departed souls was destitute. So I beg of You, Lord of the Universe, how can I be doing as well as anyone else? Were I, of course, to ask You for more corpses, that might appear contrary to Your wish. So, dear Lord, I ask only that for the new year some five or six of the departed shall be from the well-to-do. You understand, Lord, how it is. Later on, I might ask You to steer in my direction those who are learned and who pretend to intellect: I know how to square accounts with them. There is the doctor, for example: bedridden with a paralytic stroke, suffering endless misery, the devil alone knows why he still hangs on. Dear Lord, please bring down the curtain and deliver him *there*, so he can take the cure at the hot mineral springs that are tended by the sexton of Gehenna. Then he will recover . . . and I shall profit accordingly. . . . And let the prophecy, 'And all wickedness shall vanish like smoke' be fulfilled as soon as may be."

I moved near several other lecterns, one after another, and at each I came upon the kind of weeping that made me snicker or that convulsed me with laughter— but none that moved me to tears. Then, just as I was about to return to our pew, I caught sight of a Jew with his head half-shaved, wearing a drab overcoat with the convict's diamond-shaped badge sewed on the back, beside whom stood a soldier with a rifle. That sight naturally aroused my curiosity. I crept nearer and heard him lament in a voice choked with tears, "Lord of the Universe, You above all are aware that it never occurred to me to forge the squire's name on a promissory note. It was only on the advice of the rebbe's sexton and with the approval of the rabbi himself that I ventured such a step; and what is more, the note was forged by the hand of the rabbi's own private secretary. Now I am sentenced to rot in prison, and no one knows what my last end will be. Ah, but should I not have relied on such a tzaddik, in whom the townsmen's faith is as great as in the Law of Moses? And You, Almighty One, manifest through him Your great miracles and wonders, every minute of every hour. So I pray You, Lord of the Universe, to deliver me from the hands of the heathen, and to let the words, 'And therefore, O Lord, grant hope to those who yearn for Thee,' be fulfilled in my case!"

Suddenly the sexton called out, "Eighteen gulden for *shelishi!* Twenty-five gulden for *shishi!*" For it happened that Rosh Hashanah fell on the Sabbath, when seven worshipers are called up to the reading of the Torah. As they proceeded to the lectern, behold, the warden of the burial society stepped to the rostrum for the honor of *shelishi.* Although greatly distressed by this presumptuous move, I restrained myself from weeping. But as I caught sight of the mayor coming forward for the honor of *shishi,* I could no longer control myself. I burst out wailing, and when my father, along with some of the other Hasidim, inquired what was wrong, I answered— out of embarrassment before the congregation and the fear of the mayor—that the night before I had dreamed of being drafted into the army, that the sight of the mayor reminded me of that dream, and so I was frightened out of my wits. . . . To be brief about it, whether as a result of my tears or because my father—thank God —had unloaded his two defunct citrons on the lessee of Kishkewitz, I was rewarded on the eve of the Feast of Tabernacles with a wonderful pair of new shoes.

8

New squire, new decrees; new year, new transgressions

For a Jewish boy in Poland the year held no pleasanter or more cheerful season in general than the Ten Days of Penitence, and in particular the four days between Yom Kippur and the Feast of Tabernacles. It was vacation then and the teachers had no authority over their pupils; also, during the period preceding Yom Kippur, parents went about conscience-stricken by their numerous transgressions in the year that was ending, and had no time to find fault even with their own children; and in addition, they were especially elated during the four days between Yom Kippur and the Feast of Tabernacles, when old sins had been forgiven and not enough new ones had yet accumulated to need accounting for. There was a long way ahead before the next Rosh Hashanah; meanwhile, new transgressions awaited their turn. For the time being one's lusts could be indulged as one chose —and let the good Lord worry about the future. On those few bright days that preceded the long, grim winter at the dark and gloomy heder, I indulged myself in every way possible, burning the candle at both ends and having a riotously good time to make up for the rest of the year. Item: I molded all sorts of figures out of the wax candles for Yom Kippur; I jumped up and down on the branches of fir used to roof over the tabernacle; I wove discarded palm leaves into baskets; out of reeds I whittled pens and whistles and cigarette holders. In short, I reveled and frolicked to my heart's content—until the Feast of Tabernacles rolled around, and my father again began taking note of me.

Of course, there is no cause for excitement about the afternoon before Sukkoth, when the family ate a leftover noodle pudding and took a nap. But in the evening, the Hasidic flock converged at our house. After Havdalah, the ceremony that marks the end of the Sabbath, they proceeded to troop out again and my father went and took me along. Outside I noticed several Hasidim carrying buckets of water. When I asked my father where we were bound, he told me that we were about to observe a Sukkoth libation ceremony, one that went back to the time of the Temple in all its glory. When we got to the house of Shmuel Sirkes, a young fanatic scrambled atop the tabernacle beside it, and two other Hasidim handed him their buckets of water, whose contents he proceeded to pour through the flimsy roof. Just as the fanatic jumped down and ran off, someone in the tabernacle screamed, "Help! My wife has fainted!" and with no sign of concern, the Hasidic flock strolled off to another tabernacle and another—about fifty, all told—and at each repeated the same performance, striking consternation into numerous households. Just at dawn, the entire crew headed for the the ritual baths. Of course I had great fun during this nocturnal escapade, but it had been spoiled somewhat by the thought that the very next day I would be handed over to the teacher of Gemara.

And sure enough, on the following day we were

visited by Reb Avremel Hirik, the great Gemara teacher. A red-haired fellow he was, with huge brows overhanging eyes green as a cat's and set deep into their sockets and a wart at the very tip of his snub nose. Each of the four furrows on his wrinkled forehead looked as though it could easily accommodate a ritual fringe or two; his nostrils were broadly distended; his upper lip with its pendulous folds had the proportions of a dewlap. With his sparse red goatee and an Adam's apple that moved about like a globule of mercury, he was all in all the image of a scarecrow in a cherry orchard. He made a wry face as he spoke nervously, his right thumb hooked inside his sash while his left hand raked at his goatee. Although he stammered he was fairly coherent. Listen, will you, to this dialogue:

"How are things with you, Avremel?" my father inquired.

"Bah!" was the reply. "How should things be? You do this and you that—and after you've done it all, you find yourself holding the bag."

"How many pupils do you have now at your heder?" my father persisted.

"Who can tell?" the other complained with a wince and a shrug. "It's all in the way you look at it. All of it is in the hands of the Almighty. The Lord of the Universe provides for every living creature. So, in fact, what difference is there?"

"But you will admit my boy to your heder?"

"Your boy? I don't know quite what you mean," the teacher demurred. "Man is a frail creature; all things are predetermined; the Lord of the Universe ordained it all—"

By the time these divagations ended, it had been decided that I should report to my new preceptor on the following day.

You can well imagine the state of mind in which I passed that night. . . . And then I found myself in the new heder. If it was somewhat cleaner than the one of Nachman "Slap," that was mainly because most of the dirt and muck remained in the tabernacle beside it.

As soon as I set foot in the house, the new melamed sailed at me and grabbed my ear, screaming, "Listen, you scamp! Do you think you can behave here the way you did there at Reb Nachman's or at Anshel Buzeche's? Here you'll be beaten within an inch of your life! Do you hear me, you scalawag?" and before there was time to think about it, he had taken two birch rods from under his long coat, laid me across a bench, and proceeded to deliver an advance installment. A fitting welcome to a festival, indeed—and may he find, Lord of the Universe, a welcome like it in the hereafter! But for the time being I had to put up with the situation. That is why, during Simchas Torah, the last festive day, I unloosed a rumpus, as a bull will kick and gore on his way to the slaughterhouse.

The delicious Feast of Tabernacles had departed, as a Lithuanian Jew will do, deserting his wife and children, at the least glimmer of false hope. The festive fur-trimmed hats were now replaced by greasy caps; the striped mohair gabardines now gave way to threadbare kaftans; the fancy traditional headgear worn by the women was replaced by drab bonnets; embroidered slippers gave way to wooden clogs, songs to sighing, joy to sadness; and young women turned overnight into old crones. But I was more miserable than all the rest, since I was doomed to attend the heder of Avremel Hirik. . . .

9

In the heders of Poland

When I arrived at the heder, the melamed was not there, but was still at the ritual bathhouse, or it may have been the synagogue. So along with the rest of the pupils I waited for him until noon. Such was the daily routine; still, all of us did our best to arrive early in the day, since the forenoon was the one bearable part of it. We were never idle, thank heaven; oh, no, for the rebbitzin, the melamed's wife, saw to it that each of us had something to do. One pupil carried out the slops for her, another helped her in the chore of baking bread, a third plucked feathers for her daughter's dowry, and so on. In the winter, my own invariable task consisted of taking out the ashes and clinkers from the oven; in the summer I emptied the cinders from the same oven into the slop pail—a task that explains how I kept so fair and unblemished a complexion the year round.

Precisely at noon the melamed appeared, his face bright red from his ardor at prayer, or simply from the flask of mountain dew, schnapps, that had been passed around at the synagogue. The rebbitzin had just baked buckwheat wafers with poppy seeds, and the melamed directed her to sell them to us at two groschen each— merely to keep us quiet until he had had his own lunch and taken his nap. The little girl spread an exceptionally dirty cloth on the table and served him while he sat down to his meal in solitude, without the rest of the family— as is customary among all the Hasidim. He was in the habit of eating his food while it was piping hot; and his performance as he said grace and wolfed it down—the grimaces, the undulations of his dewlap, the twitching of his nose and eyes, scared us almost as if we had been set upon by a mad dog. Then he stretched out for his nap, his face toward the wall, disclosing his coarse, yellowed linen underwear. At about two he awoke, to display a red-blotched forehead and a nose that ran, dripping down his chin and into his goatee. He got up, loudly cleared his throat and blew his nose, wiped his face with the sleeve of his grimy shirt, swallowed some water, took out his supply of snuff, and sat down at the head of the long table. The pupils opened up the talmudic tractate at the prescribed page—which, like all the others, was so smeared with tallow and tobacco ashes that the Aramaic text was blurred, and it took concentration to decipher the words at all.

Hitting the table with his snuffbox, he began. "Now, children, say after me: 'He rode on the back of a cow.' " The pupils answered in the traditional singsong, with a sound like the cackle of geese being carried off in a cart to the ritual slaughter.

"Quiet! May the Evil One abduct your mothers!" howled the melamed. "Once again: 'He rode on the back of a cow.' " The melamed seemed to mean that Reuben had ridden on a cow's back. It seemed odd that Reuben, eldest of the heads of the Twelve Tribes, should have ridden that way. Some of the class stumbled and were incoherent, and so the teacher boxed the ears of those nearest him. We struggled and floundered thus all through the week that ended on Friday afternoon.

On the Sabbath, when his nap was over, my father sent me to fetch the talmudic tractate so as to check my progress. When I reached the school and asked for the book, the melamed decided to come back with me. Along the way, he told me that whenever I was at a loss for an answer during the examination, I was to watch his lips and his right forefinger for cues, and never to answer without having done that first. . . .

Once we were there, I sat down beside my father, the melamed opened the tractate at the page we had studied in school, and I began with the passage, "He, Reuben, rode on the back of a cow." Suddenly my father broke in to demand, "Tell me, what day is this?" As it happened, Haya Rikkel was to have her *vorspiel** on that very day, and I cheerfully burst forth with this information.

"So your mind is on Haya Rikkel's *vorspiel*, not on the Gemara—is that it?" my father said in a fury.

At that moment I turned to look at the rabbi, who whispered that yesterday had been Fri. . . . I began to catch his meaning. "So today is . . ." prompted the melamed in a barely audible tone. "Today is the Sabbath!" I announced in delight at answering so quickly.

"Nu, but is it permissible to ride on the Sabbath?" my father persisted.

"Of course it is," I answered happily. "Why, I even saw the melamed's boy riding a goat today!"

Very much humiliated, the melamed pinched my cheek, ostensibly in fun, although in fact he very nearly

*Merry entertainment on the night of the Sabbath preceding the wedding

gouged out a chunk, and declared, "Never mind, I shall take care of my son. But you should know that on the Sabbath no one may. . . ."

I quickly understood and declared in the traditional singsong that riding was forbidden on the Sabbath.

"If that is so, how does this Reuben happen to be riding on a Sabbath?" my father wanted to know.

I had not anticipated a question so perplexing. Speechless, I stared at my melamed. He prompted me, but I failed to understand him, thus exasperating my father still more.

"You're a nice little boy—just think carefully before you speak. For instance Reuben was go—' "

I racked my brains for a proper interpretation of the cue, finally blurting out joyfully, "Reuben was a goy!"

"You scamp, you imbecile—what can have made you say that?" my father fumed, and struck me such a blow that I landed under the table. The melamed could only sputter, "It appears you're right, Yossel: Haya Rikkel's *vorspiel* is on his mind. Otherwise, he's got a good head on his shoulders. Let it go until another time."

It was not likely that I would be subjected to another examination. For one thing, the fall with its cold and stormy weather had now set in; for another, my father had already lost a boot when he got stuck in the autumn mud. We did not have as much as a crust of bread. There had been a decline in contributions for the tzaddik whom my father so revered, and as if that were not enough, the holy sage had been called in by the authorities. As a result, examining me was to be the last thing on my father's mind for a while.

But instead of improving, things only got worse. October, the month of Heshvan, having set in, our studies now continued after dark, making our lives miserable. The three-kopeck candle each pupil had to bring to school was usually dirty and broken, since we were bound to stumble and fall in the knee-deep mud a dozen times over before we got there. The melamed would stick these candles of ours into lopsided earthenware candlesticks, encrusted with tallow and burnt-out wicks (the good brass candlesticks being reserved for the Sabbath). . . . It is easy to imagine how dispirited and miserable we became.

10

Only secular schools have afternoon recess;
—in our schools you study until you drop

Picture, my friends, a narrow, cramped, low-ceilinged hut, roofed with thatch, with never a breath of fresh air stirring, where twelve young pupils sit facing one another at a long table containing four talmudic tractates, one folio for every three pupils. As these folios are tugged at and shoved about, the earthenware candlestick topples over and the candle goes out. During the brief intervals while it is burning, it sputters, so that now and then a particle of tallow lodges in my eye—but none of my classmates will try to lick it out as a remedy, since tallow is not kosher.

Under this sort of illumination, which gave less light than the reflection in a puddle of a candle burning in a window would have, we huddled in groups of three, bending over the talmudic volume and squinting at the barely legible print. Also, we had to recite the words in the same dismal and wearisome singsong, which sounded as mournfully at that nocturnal hour as the howl of the wind in the chimney. As we hunched over the folios, the shadows of our heads and the silhouette of our

instructor's grimacing profile did likewise, so that now
and then we might have been ghosts in an abandoned
grist mill—a thought that would make our teeth chatter
and leave us breathless with fear. We would come back
to ourselves only when the melamed had relit the extinguished candle, shouting, "Go on with your reading, you
curs! Why are you quiet all of a sudden? Go on and read,
you vermin!"

When, after so macabre an evening, I had to find my
way home alone in the dark, staggering through the mud
and pummeled by howling winds, I would be beside
myself with terror. For along with the weird tales remembered from the other school, there now ran through my
mind a whole set of new ones, capable of demoralizing
Asmodeus the prince of demons. Avremel Hirik had told
us, as though merely in passing, about digging up a
corpse, and how the straw underneath pricked it as
though with needles, making it scream loud enough to
be heard from one end of the world to the other, yet no
creature except for one black cock and one demented
bullock had been able to hear. . . . And then there had
been his account of the ordeal of the dead malefactor in
his grave—a description of how the Angel of Death split
open the belly of the corpse, plucked out the putrefying
intestines, and thrust them into what was left of the mis-
creant's face; and of how that same Angel of Death im-
paled the corpse by running his spear through the nose,
and after flinging it from one end of the world to the
other, hurled it into Sheol, in whose infernal regions the
evildoer wound up seething in a caldron until he was
thoroughly purged of all sins. . . .

And there were other dreadful tales—of the transmigration of souls, of limbo, where sinners await redemption, of the seven circles of hell, and so on. Also,
as if that weren't enough, it happened that Nachman

"Slap" had died a few weeks before, and there was a widespread rumor that his spirit was now wandering through Sheol. All of these things would rise before my mind while I slogged home at night, especially when I was obliged to pass a synagogue and its cemetery. So there would be times when I got home more dead than alive, and to this day I have remained timid, anxious, and easily frightened; for most of my life I have lived with one foot in the grave.

I struggled along like this until Hanukkah, when for an eight-day breathing spell we studied only until two in the afternoon—and what was more important, we were released from studying the talmudic tractate! Also, we played the game of dreidel. In this the melamed's little boy took part, and it is true that he fleeced all the players of their last groschen—but what could have been more natural, since that great scholar his father slyly tipped him off in advance? As a matter of fact, we were happy to let him win, simply to keep him from telling on us to his father. As we started for home, the talmudist would call after us with a hypocritical laugh, "You might bring along some money tomorrow, children, so that you can play a little, too."

Needless to say, I would have stolen the last copper from my mother in order to play. It was then, in fact, that I became a compulsive gambler, so that even after Hanukkah was over I continued to play with the other pupils on the sly, while we bent over a tractate of the Talmud. And so long as his son was winning, the melamed, after first pretending to be angry, would end by exclaiming with a smile, "Oh, you scamps! Very well, you can go on playing for half an hour, but after that see that you pay attention to the Talmud." To be brief, one by one, I learned all the children's games, and later I actually went on to cards. To this day, I am consumed with a desire to play cards. Yes, indeed, the Jewish virtues in Poland are the prelude to a contrary set of operations. . . . From playing dreidel, one graduates into a card-sharp; from a tikkun, beginning with that sip of brandy after prayers in the synagogue, one turns into a sot; from filching a handkerchief for fun, one goes on to become an inveterate thief; from Hasidic gossip, one degenerates to the status of an informer. . . .

After Hanukkah there was once again the miserable trek home from school at night—but at least there was no longer mud up to the knees. As for new evils, the clods of frozen earth over which I stumbled in my worn boots with their cardboard half soles, and the piercing cold that went through my threadbare clothes like a knife —those were nothing! Every time I tripped or fell over backwards I actually forgot the fear and dread of the night around me. And so far as hard winters were concerned, it was self-evident that a person frozen to death was no longer sensible of the cold.

Before you knew it, February, the month of Adar, came around, when toasts were drunk a bit more often, and people could relax. Now and then I would steal into the public bath and watch the Purim play being rehearsed. After that I would go skating. And soon the enchanting Purim festival itself arrived. A marvelous time! I bought Purim-sweets; I flogged Haman and ran off with hamantashen, the three-cornered pastries filled with poppy seeds and honey, that my mother had baked. I invited the Purim mummers to call at our home for *shalech-monnes,* the exchange of gifts: to Chayim Baruch I gave a candy and a radish, and I received the same sort of thing in return. If any youngster did not immediately reciprocate, I promptly picked it up for myself; and were he to hold back, I would grab his cap.

The Purim players arrived in the evening. An apprentice shoemaker played Ahasuerus; a hospital orderly took the part of Haman; a male clerk played Vashti; and a bathhouse attendant wearing a gabardine and a cap portrayed Mordecai, who was reputed to speak seventy languages but was incapable of simple Yiddish. In short, the event was one of cheer and jubilation. Just after Purim, night studies at our school were at an end. On the afternoon of Shushan Purim, the day that followed Purim, the melamed said that each of us was to bring along five kopecks and a hamantash for the evening feast. Our preceptor was to provide vodka and strong-smelling stuffed derma, and the rebbitzin was to bake buckwheat wafers for us. At the feast, the melamed drank to our health, a *l'hayyim,* with a hearty swig, squirting a drop of the liquid fire onto the extended tongue of each pupil, who was then handed a slice of the putrid derma, which was no thicker than a worn-out gulden. Half a buckwheat wafer was put into the coat pocket of each pupil.

As we were leaving, the melamed encouraged us to appear drunk on the way home. Nu, and what do you think happened? I had always been thought of as a good-for-nothing, and now, as ill luck would have it, while I imitated a drunkard on icy ground, I slipped and broke a leg. Well, perhaps it was preordained. I was laid up for almost a year and a half, and in the intervals when the pain subsided, my father would help me to struggle through a chapter of the Mishnah, or a page in *En Yaakov.* And thus I arrived at my ninth year. There could be no thought of going regularly to school for me. Nevertheless, the community regarded me as an intellectual prodigy and a keen mind—since in Poland the more scornful and impudent a Jewish lad is, the more learned and sagacious the community supposes him to be.

11

*At the synagogue, the adolescent arrives at
manhood*

Quite seriously, my brain—may it be delivered from the
evil eye—functioned so well that it had to be lubricated
now and then with gray salve. And since there was no
teacher sufficiently competent, the time had come for me
to begin attending the synagogue, rubbing elbows with
the ordinary young men who attended it—those who,
after journeying to visit the holy sage on the occasion of
Sabbath Shuvah, had made a side trip to call on a female
sage and who, on returning home, were obliged to consult the physician in private. . . . The lining of my mother's old coat was fashioned into a frock for me; my father
bestowed on me his worn black yarmulka, since on the
eve of Rosh Hashanah the rabbi had presented him with
his old white one. Of course, my father's gift was a bit too
large for me; on the other hand, since my head was
scabby, this was no disadvantage. I also made do with my
father's old footwear. Then, what else was lacking? A few
sparse hairs on my chin and a conspicuous Adam's apple
—those I had no need to borrow from anyone. And so,
dear reader, I could safely attend the synagogue.
Agreed? Which is precisely where I was headed now.

I got there at one P.M. By then most of the worshipers had gone; there was only a handful of young men seated behind the reader's stand near the Holy Ark, where they were having a drink or two. As a matter of fact, it was a toast to a mitzvah: two youthful congregants had bought a flask of schnapps. One of them complained that every now and then while he recited the *Shema*— "Hear, O Israel, the Lord our God, the Lord is one"— he had had a vision of—God forbid—a cross; the other asserted that while spending the night in the synagogue he had dreamt that the gentile woman who was whitewashing the place had aroused his desire. That was why they had purchased the bottle: to ward off evil spirits and improper thoughts. . . . Of the other young men, one had a pipe in his mouth, a sign that he was just about ready to settle down to his prayers; the other two, with their prayer shawls draped about their shoulders, toyed with their ritual fringes in the same way a city councilman fingers the tassels of his silk robe while a poor townsman tearfully pleads with him to charge no more than ten rubles for a six-month passport. They paced the floor absorbed in disputing two contrary points of view. Feeling very much snubbed when they ignored me, I was so curious that I decided to listen in on their conversation, in the hope of learning something as well as of noting the habits of the synagogue's steady customers. So I withdrew to a nook near the stove and kept my ears open.

The older of the two was addressing the younger. "Froika, believe me—in this the mother-in-law is entirely innocent," I heard him say. "Everybody knows that Helka, the attendant at the ritual bathhouse, is a kosher Jewess, and good-natured enough. But no rose is without a thorn, and the woman is a complete bitch. If you want to know how I know this, I'll tell you. She worked as a domestic for Reb Shmuel Sirkes. Now you probably know all about Reb Shmuel's teacher—may his name and memory be wiped out! Well, Froika, what more can I tell you?"

"I don't quite know what you're talking about. Did she, God forbid, sin with the teacher?" Froika asked dumbfounded. "Gedaliah, you ought to be ashamed of yourself! How can you even speak such words?"

"God forbid!" Gedaliah replied. "Did I say that she misbehaved with the teacher? I meant something else. As a scribe, I am often called upon to fasten mezuzas to the doorpost of a wealthy Jewish house. Once I had the occasion to perform this service at the home of Shmuel Sirkes—and to witness something about Helka that was not at all fitting for a Jewish woman!"

"And what did you see that was so bad, Gedaliah? I must know what it was—"

"That was so bad, you say?" drawled Gedaliah. "No use concealing it, though my heart bleeds for you. But why conceal the truth? I will tell you, Froika, exactly as it happened. About a year ago I was at Reb Shmuel's to attend to a mezuza, when lo and behold, I found the darling teacher bent over a heretical work while this beauty of yours was stirring the coals on the grate, weeping as she did so. I don't know what had gone on beforehand, but as I came in I heard her saying, 'I am the only one to suffer such a miserable fate. I thought that for several years as a domestic I might marry someone halfway decent, so that I wouldn't have to struggle to keep myself alive. But it turned out that my mother had married me off to a fanatic and a bigot, who is also a clumsy oaf and a lazy bench-warmer at the synagogue, unfit for the world around him. Now I must carry the burden; I must spend a life of misery to look after him, so that he may perhaps toss me some crumbs of consolation—promise for the hereafter, a promise of honoring me with the merit of his fervent prayers, and of his prancing about at the court of the rebbe. My life is ruined!' And then she burst into such a paroxysm of sobbing and wailing as I had never heard, even during the *Unethaneh Tokef* on Yom Kippur. So, Froika, her criticizing the ritual baths will no longer surprise you, eh?"

"For pity's sake!" Froika protested, sounding heartbroken. "But I know, all the same, that she doesn't exactly hate me—"

"What do I care about your vanity?" Gedaliah answered with disdain. "Really, such talk is disgraceful for a young Hasid. What does it matter whether she loves or hates you? Either way, it is contemptible. I tell you, Froika, that one is not for you!"

"Then what do you advise me to do?" Froika asked in despair.

"What is there to advise?" Gedaliah exclaimed. "Don't Jews have a way of dealing with an erring woman? I know that if I were saddled with such a creature, who stood in the way of my faith, I would not remain under the same roof with her for a moment. . . ."

"I don't quite understand you," Froika whimpered, as one might plead with a bandit. "Does she interfere— God forbid—with my life as an observant Jew? It's true that she objects to my daily immersions in the mikveh, that she frowns on my wearing a *tallit katan* with ritual fringes that reach down to my shoes, and that she resents my shaving my head like a convict's. But, Gedaliah, is she to be called to account for such trifling things?"

"So that's the way it is, Froika! You *are* in a bad way, and yet you still don't realize it," Gedaliah declared. "So you're still not sure whether all this has anything to do with the Law of Moses and of Israel? What is Judaism if it is not this? But of course it is clear that you have gone far astray—in which case there's no point in discussing the matter further."

"Whether or not I have gone astray, one doesn't divorce his wife over such a trifle," Froika insisted with some heat. "Gedaliah, you seem to forget what is stated in the holy Gemara—that for the sake of domestic harmony one may disregard even the Mosaic Law, not to mention ritualistic trivia."

"Trivia?" Gedaliah cried, his face contorted with disgust. "Nu—today she disapproves of your ritual bath; tomorrow she will frown on you for chanting hymns; the day after that she'll be against your rabbi; and so on, until she's driven you to haggling over a peck of grain in the marketplace. . . . Yes, indeed, you're in a bad way."

"How can you say it's so bad, Gedaliah, knowing that there are always two sides to a coin?" Froika urged, brightening. "Why, the Mishnah itself states that the Torah is even-handed in its treatment of the subject: haggling over a peck of grain is a stepping stone on the way to becoming a merchant. Are there not some respectable merchants among the Hasidim? Lord of the Universe, may I live so many prosperous years! Just look, for instance, at Reb Shmuel's son-in-law. I'm sure Reb Shmuel would be perfectly happy to provide for his maintenance for life, yet as you know, the young man keeps his nose to the grindstone and is forever buying up grain from the landed gentry. Yet in his leisure moments he pores over a talmudic tractate, and he is held in high esteem by the Hasidim. I don't like to delude myself, Gedaliah: but is it sensible to be a perpetual bench-warmer, roasting potatoes in the synagogue? Luckily, the mother-in-law still provides room and board; but she is no longer young. So what does the future hold in store? Listen to me, Gedaliah—I'm sure the women are not to be envied their lot either. If you think of it, the life they lead among us is a miserable one. As for their sharing in the world to come, won by our prancing about in our underclothes at the rabbi's *melaveh malkeh*, when the Sabbath Queen is ushered out—well, I'm not so sure about it. But however it may be, a man's wife and children are entitled to food, shelter and clothing of some sort—after all, people cannot go around naked. And a wife is not likely to find any comfort in either ritual baths or *melaveh malkehs!* No, I swear!"

"Ah, so, Froika, you obviously are treading on the heels of the Berlin mob, becoming a maskil, one of those people of the Haskalah, the so-called Enlightenment," Gedaliah said with a scowl. "The husband to sweat and slave, while his wife stays at home like a duchess! . . . Nu, nu—and perhaps you might also hire a maidservant for her, so that she won't have to dirty her hands at the cooking stove—eh?"

"Ah, if I but had the means, of course I would hire a servant for her!" Froika returned excitedly. "Does not the holy Gemara state, 'Man should love his wife more than himself?' What's more, Gedaliah, our rabbi is a righteous and saintly tzaddik, is that not so? He is most certainly not one of those Berliners, *lehavdil*—to distinguish between the sacred and the profane! And yet, does he not treat his wife as though she were an empress? Lord of the Universe, that I might live only to see my wife enjoy even a thousandth part of the worldly pleasures that an empress claims as her own!"

"Oh, oh!" Gedaliah yelled out with all the derision of the Lord of Mischief himself. "Scoundrel! Villain! Reprobate! You dare compare yourself to the rabbi, and your reigning beauty to the rebbitzin? How could you, heretic? I'll fix your buttons for you!" And he now raised such a commotion in the synagogue that those present soon had Froika pinned down on a table and were beating him black and blue. And from then on, I worked my way into the good graces of the humble congregants and became their leader and guide.

12

I become known due to my actions in the synagogue, and matchmakers beat a path to my door

I was given my first assignment by an older youth of eighteen or so, who suddenly called me over to ask if I knew where Traina the Gossip lived. On being assured that I did, he gave me the following instructions: "You are to go there. First you make sure no one is in the house but her daughter, and tell *her* she is to bring some apples to the synagogue immediately. If her mother happens to be at home, you are not to say a word about apples, but are to get yourself out of the situation whichever way you can. Now, do you understand?"

"Of course I do," I replied. "If Traina herself is there I'll ask her to conjure an evil eye for my mother."

"Very good!" he exclaimed with a sly grin. "You've got a good head on your shoulders. Get moving, and don't spoil anything." After I was outside of the synagogue, he caught up with me and whispered, "When you see her heading this way with the apples, you are to stop off at the dayyan's—the rabbi's assistant—and ask him for me when the prayer you say against a drought is supposed to be recited. Step lively, now, or the rest of the crowd will be here and there won't be enough apples to go around."

I hurried off on my mission; after escorting the girl to the synagogue with apples, I went around to the dayyan's. When I returned to the synagogue, some fifteen minutes later, the girl was gone, and the youth who had sent me on the errand was hopping about as excitedly as a tailor's apprentice. He was fulsomely cordial toward me, as though I had just saved him from kidnapers.

Soon I was on good terms with all the young men who hung about the synagogue and who gladly called for my services whenever they were faced with a difficulty, even though it were the task of Sisyphus; and they were always well pleased with the way I carried out my errands. Whether it was a question of ripping the gabbai's prayer book to shreds, or of reducing the Talne melamed's lectern to matchwood, or on a Thursday evening when the young men were studying the Talmud, and the theft for their refreshment of pears and melons from the gentile women who sold them was necessary, or occasionally throwing somebody's clothes into the ritual baths, or tying together the prayer shawls of the worshipers as they stood reciting the Eighteen Benedictions— whatever the assignment might be, and no matter how urgent, I was always ready for it. But one thing I shall always be sorry for, since it could not be undone. One Thursday evening, the youthful clique at the synagogue banded together in a practical joke on the elderly Laibtzi Reb Naphtalis, because he would not tolerate having the young fellows talk during the service. So at midnight, when old Laibtzi regularly came to the synagogue to pray in memory of the destruction of Jerusalem, the plotters had me put on a robe of white linen resembling a shroud, cover my head with a hood and a prayer shawl, and then stand beside the pulpit, motionless as a corpse, with a shofar in my hands. As soon as the old man opened the door and entered the synagogue, I was to blow the shofar and then lunge at him. The plotters put out all the lights except for one tiny oil lamp behind the cantor's stand, and the moment old Laibtzi crossed the threshold I carried out my part. The old man lost consciousness and sank to the floor, and we all took to our heels. It was not until morning that he was found by the first worshipers to arrive and a doctor was called to bring him around. But he merely lingered on in a state of shock for more than two months, and then was gathered to his fathers.

Still, why should I berate myself over that, knowing that stranger things have taken place at the synagogue without so much as a word getting out. In the meantime, I had acquired status in the synagogue, and the youthful clique were very much pleased with me. Besides, I was now eleven and the matchmakers were already converging on my father. One proposal reeked all the way to heaven: the bride, a nine-year-old girl, was blind in one eye and had not a kopeck by way of dowry. The matchmaker declared, however, that all this was compensated for since the father of the prospective bride had inherited from the eminent tzaddik Gordin a well-worn pair of slippers for which venerable Hasidim had offered him thirty pieces of red gold, but that he had scorned all such offers. One of those slippers, the matchmaker went on to explain, the father of the would-be bride was willing to put into escrow for a dowry, while the second would be pawned to buy a trousseau and pay the wedding expenses—simply on condition that the prospective bridegroom undertook to redeem it, and promised never to sell the pair of slippers for any sum whatsoever. My father was ready to agree, but this time my mother was adamant in resisting him: such an engagement, she vowed, would take place only over her dead body.

Another matchmaker likewise came with an offer from Troskevitze: a girl of eighteen or possibly nineteen, who came of a patrician family but likewise had not two coppers to rub together. She had, however, a wardrobe fit for a queen! Item: she had inherited from the rebbitzin of Kototchov a quilted jacket fastened with frogs and a striped windbreaker, and also she had acquired a brocaded vest from the sluttish wife of an itinerant maggid. But all this sumptuary splendor was available only on condition that my father attended to the tailor's bill for altering all these things to her size—in exchange for which I would be presented by the presumptive bride's father with Rabbenu Tam's phylacteries, which had been handed down by the scribe of Drelivke of blessed memory. My father was greatly pleased with this match, but he simply could not lay hands on the cash to pay for the tailoring.

One day while I was at the synagogue, engrossed in a game of checkers, my younger brother came in, breathless, lugging our father's long gabardine coat. I was to put it on and come home, he informed me, because a matchmaker had come, along with an examiner who was to test my scholarship. I had to comply—there was no escape—but the good Lord only knows how I managed to drag myself back with that long coat on. With every step I took, I looked more and more like a turtle with its flippers extended from under its shell. I arrived home after a good deal of exertion, and on entering I heard the examiner ask my father, "Is this your boy?" "Yes," my father replied. "He is, eh?" barked the examiner, then turned to me to ask, "What talmudic tractate are you studying now?" I was no more ready with an answer to his question than the peasant soldier who slipped and fell into the tabernacle while he clambered up a ladder intent on committing burglary in the attic, and was asked, "What are you looking for?"

Racking my brain, I managed to recall what I had studied some four years before. With my heart in my throat, I answered that I was studying the Sabbath tractate.

"Let me see that tractate," he commanded. As I set out dejectedly to fetch the Gemara from the school, I overheard the matchmaker berate the examiner for badgering me so—a remark that I took as a great encouragement in my predicament. And when I returned with the Gemara, I looked at the matchmaker with the eyes of a milksop. (At the time I didn't yet have the sense to perceive that the matchmaker was anxious not so much to help me as to be sure of his fee.) The examiner opened the Gemara I had brought, and at random selected a baffling Mishnah. Seeing that I was uneasy, the matchmaker broke in on my behalf, "Now say after me, 'A stove that was stoked with straw and kindling—' "

No sooner had these words been spoken than the examiner retorted with a question so complex that the matchmaker was dumbfounded. Then my father intervened, and the three of them fell to disputing and contradicting one another, emphasizing their arguments with jabs of their thumbs upward and downward, and forgetting me entirely. The examiner jabbed his thumb upward, asserting that this or that was the "essence of the Mishnah!" My father, on the other hand, turned his thumb downward, declaring with a gasp that "in such a case the issue has to do with. . . ." And the matchmaker used both thumbs while he called on heaven to witness that his contention, which was diametrically opposed to that of his opponents, was correct—and so the bridegroom was in the right. In the midst of the uproar, I put in a few words of my own, and was dubbed a "gifted boy." And so a betrothal was arranged. The sum of fifty rubles was promised as a dowry: half of it to be put in escrow with a third person immediately after the wedding, and the rest to be paid after the circumcision of a son, God willing. . . . After this I was showered with presents such as Abish's fur-trimmed hat—which, as the whole world knows, was able to crawl about on a table by itself, all of eighteen years following Abish's demise. (Scoffers called it a living relic of the "third plague" . . . but who pays attention to such heretics?)

I was also the recipient of a worn sash of time-yellowed white silk, an heirloom of the eminent maggid of blessed memory. And I was handed as well my prospective father-in-law's pedigree, testifying to his descent from authentic holy sages for fifty-two generations. There was hardly any mention of the bride; nor were any other vital issues touched upon. And so, providentially, I became betrothed to a girl in Krokodilevka. The marriage was postponed for two years or so to coincide with my Bar Mitzvah, when I would wear a prayer shawl in addition to putting on phylacteries.

13

The nagging title of bridegroom—I become important and now earn my keep

At last I was an adult! I now belonged to the company of those upright grown-up youths who had sown their wild oats and enjoyed all their rights and privileges: carrying the Six Orders of the Talmud from the synagogue to the tavern as a pledge for a bottle of vodka; or walking around with a cigarette in my mouth while the worshipers were absorbed in the *Kedusha*—the third blessing of the Amidah prayer; or tossing a sooty rag from the chimney straight into the face of the shammas; or tripping up some young fellow while he put on his phylacteries, so that one of those would drop to the floor and he would have to fast in expiation or redeem his fault with half a gallon of hard schnapps; or dipping a skullcap into water and then rubbing the face of some local worthy with it; or, under cover of darkness, laying a booby-trap consisting of a pail of slops and an oven rake near the synagogue door, directly in the path of the dayyan; or strewing the heads of elderly congregants with thorns and nettles during the mourning on Tisha be-Av; or tossing the splintered willow twigs at a banner on the east wall of the synagogue on the seventh day of the Feast of Tabernacles; and many other such prerogatives. By now I had also turned to good deeds: every Friday, along with another youth, I made the rounds of the town to collect alms, which we turned over to the leader of our group to dispose of as he saw fit.

One thing, however, I am sure of: on certain days when we were short of liquor, such as Purim Katan (the 14th day of the first Adar in a leap year), the Second Passover (on the 14th of Iyyar), Zoys Hanukkah (the last day of the Feast of Lights), the 29th day of Kislev, the 15th day of Shebat, Lag be-Omer, the 20th of Sivan, the 15th day of Av, and so on and so on, it was the leader's custom to buy liquor with the alms we had collected. He was likewise generous with those funds in such times of dire need: as when the fellows broke a window or caused other damage to the synagogue during a free-for-all; or when some irate vendor made a scene at the synagogue and insisted on being paid for the melons and apples that had been stolen from her at night; or when the Fast of Esther had arrived after the Minhah prayers and the megillah that had been pawned at the tavern had to be redeemed without any further excuse; or when a gentile woman offered a *tallit katan* or a yarmulka for sale in the marketplace; or when other scandals occurred, like near-blasphemy or casting the evil eye. . . . That is how I whiled away my time, with boisterous merriment, until Rosh Hodesh Nissan, the first of the month of Nissan.

On Rosh Hodesh Nissan we, the golden youths of the synagogue, got ourselves small spades to winnow the shocks of wheat for *shmure matzah,* the "guarded grain." The Jews would bring their little sacks of grain ears, tagged; and each of us would try to winnow at least one potful of *shmure* sprouts every day. During the last two days it was my turn to tackle the dayyan's two pots of grain, at the rate of a groschen a stalk. I pulled out a hundred and fifty-four stalks, so that he would owe me a hundred and fifty-four groschen, and with them ran cheerfully to the dayyan's house to draw compensation. As soon as I had told him the number of stalks I had, he snarled, "Little rascal, are you trying to cheat me? Nu, count again!" After I had counted them once more, he had me do it over again and again a dozen times, shifting the stalks from hand to hand each time, with the number dwindling as a result until the final count had been reduced to fifty stalks or thereabouts; and even then he tried to palm some stalks to cheat me out of a few more groschen. I greatly resented this and was on the point of telling him what I thought of him when the door of an adjacent cubicle opened and out popped a huge, towering fur hat, in whose shadow lurked a face hardly more than the size of a fig. "Who's that?" I asked the dayyan, and he told me that it was a great-grandson of none other than the saintly Baal Shem, the Master of the Good Name and founder of Hasidism, who was making the rounds to raise funds for the marriage of his only daughter to an accomplished young man who was the grandson of the renowned Rabbi Melech.

This prodigy now approached and said with a twisted smile, "Listen to me, my dear Reb Zemach. There's no need to quibble with this young fellow when he claims to have winnowed a hundred and fifty-four stalks. After all, you are one of the dignitaries in the eyes of the Holy One; it is quite clear that Providence itself is protecting you from so much as a crumb of leavened bread at Passover—and there is even a hint that this applies exclusively to you! Oi, dear Father in heaven! Oi, oi, oi—it tallies according to the gematria, the numerical value of its component letters: thus, *zemach* means sprout, and Zemach is truly your name. Moreover, the word *zemach* contains the letters of hametz, the leavened bread that is forbidden during Passover. Oi, oi, oi—the might and grandeur of the Lord! The Lord Himself protects Zemach from even a trace of hametz. Reb Zemach, you have acquired great honor because of this young man! Therefore, Reb Zemach, reimburse him what you owe him and he, in turn, will contribute twice eighteen gulden toward my dowering of the bride." I was delighted by this timely hint, and the dayyan, nonplussed, had to pay me in full. I promptly donated some of my earnings to the distinguished guest and took off so enraptured by those few coins that just in front of my house I ran straight into a wagon shaft and was knocked senseless. When I came to, I saw a ramshackle carriage with a scarecrow of a nag standing next to our house. And just then I heard my mother calling me. "Itzikel, Itzikel—come in this minute!" She told me that the carter had come from Krokodilevka to convey me to my prospective bride's for Passover.

"That rattletrap out there?" I asked. At that moment an old Jew holding a whip came out of my father's alcove and said sarcastically, "Hello there, bridegroom. Did you say something about a rattletrap? It sounds as though my vehicle is not to your liking. But if you knew the trouble of getting here in this foul weather! It is lucky the melamed's wife expired, or I wouldn't have even this rattletrap!"

"What has it to do with her?" inquired my mother.

"It has a great deal to do with her!" the old man returned. "Because she was—may my words be forgiven! —a hussy: she never wore the ring of a married woman; she always flaunted her own hair; she never gave her children real Jewish names but preferred such things as Marcus and Fifi and Liza and Clara and even gave one of the little urchins the name of Victor. And she had other such virtues. . . . Luckily, as the Everlasting willed it, she expired all of a sudden, and there wasn't one merchant who would sell the white linen for her shroud; why, even sackcloth was too good for the likes of her to be buried in, they said. And so her dear husband was obliged to hire a carter to come here looking for a linen shroud, and your in-law-to-be took the opportunity to pick up your bridegroom-son and bring him to Krokodilevka for the holiday. So, now you see just what sort of rattletrap this is! In fact it is a—"

But at that moment my father called me to his alcove, breaking into the old man's monologue.

14

*One would go through fire and water to
visit a person who writes such eloquent
Hebrew*

Going in, I found my father engrossed in a letter, which
he put down, seizing me by the sleeve. "There, have a
look at the Hebrew letter from your prospective father-
in-law—may his life be a long one!" he began. "I felt
utterly ashamed at having to send anyone like you to
such an erudite scholar, such a luminary in the realm of
the Talmud, knowing as I do that you are so ignorant and
dull-witted that you cannot write even one Yiddish line
correctly—"

"How can you blame me, father?" I protested, chagrined. "If you had engaged Yekel as my teacher I would
have known as much as any of the boys."

"Yekel, you say?" my father exploded. "And have
you turn into a crackpot like him? And have you sport a
shock of shaggy hair, and come to the synagogue on the
Sabbath with polished high boots and your shoulders
draped in a prayer shawl no bigger than a girl's scarf—
eh? Or possibly wear your trousers long and your ritual
locks short, plus a dog collar around your neck? You
prefer Yekel, do you, you good-for-nothing?"

"Well, then, you might have taught me how to write yourself," I said.

"I might have?" my father fumed. "Do I claim to be a writer? My ancestors were no writers! But whatever a Jew needs to know, they learned by themselves, they were self-taught, and I was the same. So why didn't *you* master writing by yourself, eh?"

Perhaps you, sirs, could have found an answer to that bewildering question. I had none. As I stood there gaping like a clay figure he yanked me over to the table and cried, "Listen, you loafer! Let me at least read his letter aloud, and it may be that you'll draw a moral from it and try to apply yourself to your studies a little!" And he proceeded to read aloud a letter so astounding that I still remember it word for word down to this very day. And indeed it is meritorious to publish so priceless a document, one that will enable those so-called intellectuals, the enlightened ones, to perceive how others without an instructor or even a book of grammar can attain to eloquence in the holy tongue of Hebrew—in fact, the Hasidim could teach its elevated style and flawless orthography to the pretentious upstarts of scholarship! Here, word for word, is the letter as it read in Hebrew interspersed with Yiddish:

By the grace of God, Portion Zav, the holy Congregation of Krokodilevka.

To my future relative by marriage, the Great Scholar of the Torah, and God-fearing Yossel, may his light shine forth! I send herewith a horse and wagon and a carter for which I paid one and a half birds, i.e. rubles, so that you may know that I am not parsimonious where my daughter's future bridegroom is concerned. Please send him, the bridegroom, to me immediately, but let him bring along his bedding, since I do not have any to accommodate him. And don't forget to send with him the fur-trimmed hat of Reb

Abish of blessed memory, since without that hat he would be a laughingstock. Moreover, kindly stand the elderly bearer of this message to a good drink of schnapps, by way of a treat.

These are the words of your future relative by marriage, who wishes you and your wife and the rest of your household all of the very best, and a kosher Passover.

Shraga Feivish, son of Shemariah Katz, of blessed memory.

"Now that is what I call Hebrew!" exclaimed my father in a transport of delight. "It staggers belief how well a man like that has mastered the language!"

So I had to get my things together for the journey. There was not a box, a sack, or any other container in the house. What was I to do? But my mother—may her life be long!—hit upon a novel solution: she brought up from the cellar a barrel that had been recently emptied of dill pickles, into which she packed the bedding from the baby's cradle, along with my festive wardrobe (which ought by now to be familiar to you) and various other odds and ends, and I was ready to set out on my journey. But we nearly forgot the one essential thing: the round fur-trimmed hat! "Where has that hat gone to?" my father cried in a frenzy. "Oh, the hat," my mother said, trying to soothe him. "I was just going to look for it." "Yes, yes, don't forget to bring along the hat," the carter joined in. "Well, mother, so where is the hat?" I badgered. "How long will it take you to find the hat?" growled my father. "As if I didn't have enough troubles, now I have to worry my head off about an old hat," my mother complained. "I saw it just a while ago—and now it is vanished into thin air!" "Could it have crawled off all by itself?" the carter asked. "After all, it was Reb Abish's hat!"

The hat was here, the hat was there—the hat was

nowhere. The word must have been repeated fifteen times; and had the Baal Shem's great-grandson been present, he would surely have observed that according to gematria, the numerical value of the component letters in shtreimel, the word for hat, repeated fifteen times over, was the equivalent of "hat-salvation." And I would have told him that repeating it fifteen times over would make it into "the salvation of a round, fur-trimmed, louse-infested hat."

And then, without warning, the hat began to crawl out of the oven, and my mother was obliged to confess that the day before yesterday she had covered a pot of buttermilk with it. My father then gave her a talking-to she would remember to her dying day. So at last the shtreimel likewise found its way into the barrel, and I was off to visit my future bride for the Passover holiday.

On the way, the old man became quite a comrade. "You may not believe it, my dear bridegroom," he said, turning to me, "but I happen to be a person of importance in Krokodilevka; the entire community thinks quite well of me. You are smiling, my dear bridegroom? You regard me, do you, as an ordinary carter? But if you knew the role I once played you would look at me in a different way. I would have you know that in my prime I served as estate manager for the duke of Shmirevka, and carried great weight in the Jewish community. At twenty I married the daughter of a tax collector of Krokodilevka, and a dazzling beauty she was. But the Almighty punished me —she had no children, and this childlessness cost me a king's ransom, for there was hardly one holy sage we didn't call upon about her sterility, and I paid every one of those rabbis handsomely—especially the tzaddik of Zodkowetz, who promised us a child year after year— only there was nothing solid in all his promises. Very probably the sage must have seen in his mind's eye that the time had not yet arrived; anyhow, nothing worked. Here I was, a Jew well over thirty, still with no child in sight, and my wife and I pined for one. We braced ourselves and journeyed to the tzaddik of Zodkowetz; but this was for the last time, since we had made up our minds not to leave him until he had at last produced a child for us. . . .

"When finally we gained audience with the saintly rabbi, I presented him with fourteen times eighteen rubles—my very last savings—for a *pidyon.** And then my 'better half' and I both wept, pleading and imploring, 'Holy rabbi, we will not depart from here until you have given us a child,' as we prostrated ourselves before him! Bridegroom, did you hear what I have told you? We ourselves at his feet, just like this—" And in his excitement he tumbled from the driver's seat and became entangled in the harness. It was only through some miracle that he escaped being trampled by the old mare or crushed under the wheels. By sheer luck the nag availed herself of the opportunity to halt in her tracks; and after the carter came to and I had helped in extricating him from underneath the cart, the conversation was halted, while I fell asleep, exhausted by the incident.

*The fee paid to a Hasidic rebbe for counsel and intercession with the Almighty

15

Life and death are in the hands of the rebbe—as long as sanction is given by the synagogue warden

I was jolted awake when the wagon wheels struck a stone, and the carter went on with his story. "Yes, bridegroom —that is the way we humbled ourselves, and the Everlasting at last took pity on us and the holy rabbi told us to rise. Casting his penetrating glance first toward my wife, then toward Khlavne, his gabbai, who stood at the other end of the table, the rabbi at last addressed me. 'Now listen to me, Lemel. I see in the mirror of illumination that the virtue of compassion is doing its utmost to reach me, but a difficulty has arisen because of the *pidyon.* Oi, oi, there is some hindrance up there in the world of souls.' At this point he rolled his eyes upward in a way that dismayed us as we watched his hallowed face. 'Yes, yes—the *pidyon* is still short by a half twice eighteen, along with a new silver ruble. True, true! The aggregate will total 298, which in gematria equals *rachamim,* mercy. Oi, oi—the silver ruble will mitigate the severity of the Law. Yes, yes, that's the way it works! Therefore, Lemel, you had better add twice eighteen with a silver ruble on top of that, so that the virtue of compassion may prevail over the letter of the Law, and your *pidyon* achieve its purpose."

"After hearing these prophetic words from his sainted lips, I hastened off to the house where we were staying, and the rabbi, meanwhile, told Khlavne to escort my wife to the rabbi's private chamber so that she might say prayers of penitence until my return. At the inn I found a few more valuable objects, including the fur-trimmed hat which Reb Abish of blessed memory had himself given me as a talisman, while I was still a bachelor, to help me find favor with the duke of Shmirevka; and this talisman proved a rather costly gift—though Reb Abish of blessed memory was himself worth a king's ransom. And in fact I managed to pawn these additional valuables with the innkeeper for the sum of twice eighteen plus a new silver ruble, and then I hurried back to the rabbi. This took me two hours or so, and upon returning I found my wife in a drowsy state and barely coherent. I immediately surmised that the rabbi must have put her to sleep so as to transform her barren soul into a fertile one. And I was right! As I put down the additional *pidyon,* the rabbi seemed to be in a trance, but then he suddenly opened his eyes, seized my hand and exclaimed, 'Lemel, go home! Your wife—God willing—will conceive!' You hear that, bridegroom?

"And true enough—within nine months my wife gave birth to a baby girl. . . .

"The fact that I had beggared myself for the sake of a child and have had to live from hand to mouth ever since, and the further fact that my wife was in poor health from the day she gave birth—all those things I had endured without protest for the sake of the child. But there was something amiss: the child herself became a source of concern. I was aware that I had forced the rabbi's hand in getting this child, and I was always apprehensive over the matter. And we were even more worried as the child grew up to be unusually beautiful. Sure enough, as she matured she began to manifest certain airs and traits such as no Jewish child in Poland would be capable of. For example, when she had just turned five, I remember that someone asked her out of curiosity, 'Kroindele' (she had been given that name by the rabbi, after the old rebbitzin of blessed memory)—'Kroindele, darling, which would you prefer as a fiancé—the cantor or the doctor?' She answered without hesitation, 'Pfui on the cantor! I'll take the doctor.' And bear in mind that the cantor was an ardent follower of our rebbe. Now you will understand why the child always had me wondering. As she grew older it was still worse. She would join the boys at their games or mimic the faces the women make while absorbed in cutting dumplings; or she would poke fun at her mother's wig in the presence of others, saying that another woman had a prettier hairdo; or she would openly make fun of the Hasidim, calling them clodhoppers and oafs, and indulge in all sorts of outrages, improper in any Jewish child but still more so in a girl. Now and then I would even speak to the rabbi about it; and Khlavne would join in, as concerned as though she were his own daughter. . . .

"And the rebbe would reply, 'Lemel, be patient; there is a time for every purpose under the heaven. Her impertinence is due to her beautiful face. Wait until the Lord performs some manner of miracle to deprive her of her self-conceit.' I realized only too well that her sauciness came from her stunning beauty, and this hurt me to the core. Of what use was an exquisite vessel if the wine it held was sour? And she was going from bad to worse!

"So by the time she was ten she had blossomed out like a rose, and her beauty was enough to take your breath away; and at the same time her mischievousness had become unbearable. Just imagine her telling us, her parents, 'That young duke is so handsome, no girl would get tired of kissing him!' Now you can understand what we were faced with. Woe is me that I, her father, should have to tell you all this. However, I am telling it all long after the event. Just bear with me a while and you will understand the miracles of the Almighty, as expounded by our tzaddik—may his life be long! Only listen: one day she became ill, and on the third day she was running a very high temperature. We tried every sort of household remedy, but none was of any help—she was being consumed by fever. Well, finally I called in the doctor, who declared after examining her that she had smallpox and was now critically ill because of being neglected for three days. As soon as I heard this, I hastened to the rabbi of Zodkowetz. I presented the sage with a *pidyon,* and after informing him of the medical diagnosis I wept. For a while, the rabbi stood lost in thought, and then suddenly he said, 'Listen to me, Lemel! Providence has shown me the word *aish,* fire, followed by the words, 'thy glory has faded.' Oi, oi, Lord of the Universe! *Aish* means smallpox, according to gematria. Lemel, you face two alternatives: she is either, God forbid, to be consumed by fire, or she is to be deprived of her beautiful face—"

" 'Rebbe,' I answered in fear and trembling. 'Whatever happens will hardly matter so long as she stays alive.'

" 'If that is so, you have met the test and, God willing, your daughter will recover,' the rebbe declared. 'Go home at once, Lemel. As soon as the smallpox is at its worst I will dispatch Khlavne to Krokodilevka with my sovereign remedies, as well as a special talisman that was bequeathed to me by my grandfather of blessed memory. With that he, Khlavne, will rout all the demons and goblins and deliver the child from all the powers of darkness.

Then he, Khlavne, will put this amulet of mine about her neck. But you must see to it, Lemel, that while Khlavne proceeds to hang the amulet about your child's neck, no one else is present. Farewell, Lemel, and may the Almighty restore the child to health!'

"When I got home I found my daughter running a very high fever. I gave my wife an account of my consultation with the rebbe, but said nothing of the child's being fated to lose her beauty. Three days later, even the doctor was certain that she was no longer in danger, and warned us to make sure that she kept her hands away from her face, so as not to leave it pockmarked. The moment the doctor left, up bobbed Khlavne, the rabbi's gabbai. I remember distinctly that when Khlavne entered, my wife became confused and upset, and came close to fainting. She apparently had a premonition that her child would come to grief. Anyhow, after Khlavne had recited his spells and exorcisms and had taken out the rebbe's amulet, my wife and I withdrew into another room just in time to hear our child give an agonizing wail, followed by Khlavne's murmur of 'Quiet, my dear child!' (On hearing these words my wife fainted.) 'Instead of your beautiful face the good Lord will bestow on you a kind heart.'

"My wife was somehow brought around, and my daughter recovered. But she emerged from the trial pockmarked like a sieve and looking like the wrath of God. However, she had been transformed into a person almost as righteous, kind and devout as the late rebbitzin after whom she was named. Now, my dear bridegroom, what do you think of Providence? Now let's get off the cart for the Minhah prayers, and then I'll tell you the rest."

16

The father is handsome, the grandfather even more so—but in looks the bride surpasses both

After the prayers we climbed back into the ramshackle cart and the driver continued.

"My Kroindel had already turned fifteen and still there wasn't so much as a whisper about a marriage. For one thing, alas, she was unsightly; for another, I didn't have a copper to provide her with a dowry; and third, the scoundrels and heretics—may the names and the very memory of them be obliterated!—had spread the malicious falsehood that my Kroindel was not my daughter at all, but the offspring of Khlavne, the rabbi's warden. . . . Now, bridegroom, what do you think of the blasphemy and brazen malice of such heretical scum of the earth? And now, everything came out right, for when I complained to the rebbe about those blasphemers, he scolded, 'Why do you eat your heart out, you fool? There is a saying that if you hear dogs barking, there is a village near. Precisely because dogs are barking, your daughter will be held in high esteem by our dignitaries, and God willing, she will find such a fiancé as to arouse the envy of man and God. And then the saying, "Not a dog shall whet his tongue," will be proved true in your case. Go home and be patient for a while—your daughter's betrothed will come directly to your house.'

"The devout and righteous Khlavne—long may he live!—also comforted me, promising on his word of honor to keep after the rabbi, and assuring me that the Lord would be merciful. But four more years passed, my Kroindel was nearly twenty, and still there was not a glimmer of hope for her marrying. I was beginning to have my doubts about the faith of the sages—heaven preserve us!—when suddenly luck came knocking at my door. Only listen—you'll hardly believe your ears. Sick at heart, I had at last gone running to the rebbe to reproach him for breaking his promise to me. No sooner had I crossed his threshold, however, than he turned and said to me with open displeasure, 'You seem to be slipping, Lemel. Heaven help us, you've become a man of little faith! Once and for all, I have told you that the predestined betrothed will come directly to your house. Are you trying to tempt the Lord? Your sorrow, however, will atone for your folly. What's more, you had better hurry, for your daughter's betrothed is already waiting. . . .'

"I was bewildered by the prophecy of so holy a sage and dared not ask how I was to recognize the destined bridegroom. As I was about to leave, Khlavne, who had seen me to the door, told me in the name of the tzaddik that on Friday my daughter's betrothed would be at the steam baths of Krokodilevka—and that I would recognize him by his shout of 'Steam—let's have more steam!' On approaching him I was to utter the words, *'Bemazel tov'* and he would grasp their significance since according to gematria, the numerical value of component letters in the phrase would be the equivalent of the letters in *lamed vav*, the proverbial Thirty-Six Righteous Men on whom the continued existence of the world depends.

And he would have me know that the betrothed was one of the *lamed vav* tzaddikim . . . 'Farewell,' he said. 'Go home and use your head! . . .'

"And that is how things turned out. On Friday at the public baths I recognized the young man; but no sooner had I uttered the words *'Bemazel tov'* than he flew into a rage and exclaimed, 'Oh, so the tzaddik has given me away! Well, that's the last straw! He put a shtreimel on my head; and now you want to put a *kroindel** on my head. But I will have you know that I won't marry your daughter without Reb Abish's own *mitzel*. The names of the three kinds of headgear—shtreimel, *kroindel*, *mitzel*— lend gematria to the letters that make up the phrase *mitznefet bad kodesh*, fur-trimmed priestly headgear. . . .' Bridegroom, you can readily imagine how befuddled I was in the presence of such a righteous tzaddik. I was left speechless, and dared not invite him as my Sabbath guest. And, indeed, how could an uncouth and sinful fellow such as I compare with a person of such sanctity and enlightenment? Nevertheless, it was he who tugged at my sleeve and said, 'There, I will be your guest for the Sabbath. If for the Lord of the Universe it is right and proper for me to become your son-in-law, then it is right and proper with me as well. But be careful not to betray my identity to anyone. For in doing so you would jeopardize your life and the lives of your family. . . . Hurry, from one end of the world to the other the Heavenly Voice is already chanting the Sabbath hymn *Lechah Dodi.'*

"We went home to celebrate the Sabbath feast, and on the day after the Havdalah rite that marks the end of the Sabbath the ceremony of betrothal took place. But soon afterward my wife—may she rest in peace—returned her kosher soul to the Lord, thus bringing a long

---

*A coronet; also used as a girl's name

and embittered silence to an end. May she intercede for all of us in the world to come!"

"So," I said, "you are the bride's grandfather?"

"Indeed, I am," the old man answered, beaming. Then he explained, "I went through such details because I see that you are still a youngster and may not find the bride exactly to your taste. . . . Therefore you ought to know your future mother-in-law, and your future father-in-law in particular. If such a holy man would settle for something besides a beautiful face, then you need not be squeamish about the lack of beauty. And did you suppose that the letter to your father was really written by your future father-in-law? It was not at all. Until the proper time, he will not reveal himself for anything in the world. That revelation will be at the hands of Providence. Why, that letter was actually written for him by our rabbi himself, a fanatical Hasid. You understand?"

At that moment we arrived in Krokodilevka.

To the adage, "Who is rich? He who rejoiceth in his portion," the Gemara adds the comment, "He who has a washroom near his table." Since my prospective father-in-law lived close to the public baths, he was indeed close to riches. . . . The interior of his house was not much different from the school of Nachman "Slap," except that the ceiling was about to collapse and that almost all the windowpanes were broken and stuffed with soiled pillows. There was a glimpse of a huge pot and of the bottom of a trough for kneading bread. Suspended from several hooks in the central rafter were a cradle, a shtreimel that had seen better days, and a palm branch with citrons, left over from the last festival; there was also a little sack of *shmure matzah*. The round water trough and the slop pail were placed beside the door leading to the alcove. My prospective father-in-law, in rather shabby clothes, extended his hand to me, and his pockmarked wife gave me a nod, her bluish lips contorted in a piteous smile. The rest of the household also greeted me in one fashion or another; could I be otherwise than elated over entering so affluent a household? Only one thing was missing: I was anxious for a look at my future bride. I glanced about the room but failed to catch so much as a glimpse of her. The grandfather, evidently reading my thoughts, observed, "You are probably looking for your bride. There she is, right in front of you. . . ."

I was struck dumb, and stared open-mouthed. Imagine if you can: I myself was no more than a head higher than a dog, but next to me she might have been a bat next to an eagle. If I had had eyes in my elbows I might possibly have looked her straight in the face. Did I say her *face?* Since her head, set between two humps very like to a camel's, was of a size to have gone through the eye of a sacking needle, what sort of a face could she have? But at this point the grandfather intervened. "Well, Tseitele," he asked—although the word "gnome" would have been a more fitting name—"and how do you like your bridegroom?"

"So long as he is to my father's liking, nothing else matters," she answered in a voice like the squeak of a door and then vanished into the kitchen. Her high voice and her abrupt disappearance reminded me of all the stories about the hobgoblin living in a deserted flour mill that haunted the heder at night. I stood there speechless, not knowing what to make of things. I saw myself as this book of mine will be seen by a Jew from abroad—or even by some Jewish aristocrat from Odessa—who, on being told of the doings of a Polish Hasidic rabbi, is horrified and supposes the talk to be of some werewolf with horns along the back of his neck. He will laugh along with all the other enlightened Jews. But he won't have the slightest idea of why he is laughing. It will be like the laughter of the Jewish woman of Strizhevka at the sight of a drowned man. In all sincerity, dear reader, whose good deeds allow such creatures to exist! How can non-Hasidic Jews beget children without the rabbi's miracles? How can they live without talismans and amulets? How can they carry out their secret dealings with country squires except through the rabbi's intervention? How can they come to good fortune and prosperity if they never help themselves to *shiraim*, the leavings of a Hasidic rabbi's meal, of which his adherents partake as a matter of honor? I simply can't understand how an ordinary Jew can get along without a bit of ecstasy and Hasidic fervor. Who but a Hasid can savor the sweetness and spiritual delight of a Hasidic tarantella? Or of scratching one's chest while rubbing one's back against a warm oven, and touching the tips of the rabbi's fingers, and so on and on? Ordinary Jews will probably look down their noses at my book. But, my dear Polish Jews, for you it has a quite different meaning! True, on the one hand you will revile me, and the extreme pietists among you will pronounce me anathema both in this world and in the world to come, not hesitating to condemn my dazed soul to search through eternity for my bones after my stinking remains have rotted away. . . . On the other hand, some people will pronounce blessings upon me and sing my praises, and still others are likely to present me with *pidyonot* as they implore my prayers on behalf of the tzaddikim and Hasidim and gabbaim, and the rebbitzins, and zealots of lesser rank, the *hevra borsht*,* and so on and on, so that they may be cured of their ailments, physical and emotional. . . . Amen!

*Literally, "beet soup crowd," that is, poor people

17

A Passover with a Torah—a veritable miracle; and, by way of dessert, a pinkas *with regulations*

At the ritual baths on the eve of Passover, I became convinced that my prospective father-in-law was not only a *lamed-vavnik,* one of the Thirty-Six Righteous Men for whose sake the Almighty keeps the world going, but also an occultist. For as the two of us left the anteroom to cool off, in a flash he had gone out by a side door and begun peering through a latticed partition. Not until a few days later did I learn that on the other side of this partition was the women's section of the baths. . . . But it was naturally hard to fathom the mind of such an occult tzaddik. Anyhow, the Passover was fit for a king, with the house so tidy and spotless, that you could pick up a millstone off the floor. And why should it not be spotless when it was so spacious . . . knock on wood! Just imagine a chamber with an adjoining alcove that was no doubt as roomy as the biggest tabernacle ever put up in Poland during the Feast of Tabernacles. And, indeed, how large was my prospective father-in-law's family? Besides him and his spouse there were only his two married sons with their wives and five small grandchildren, my fiancée, her

younger brother and sister, the old grandfather and I.
And how much space did they need? Besides, there was
the kitchen with all its facilities—i.e. an oven. And as for
all the good things to eat and drink during the holidays
—oh, my!

On the eve of Passover my prospective father-in-law
made the rounds of the well-to-do Jewish lessees in the
area with the rabbi, collecting the donations to provide
for the needs of the poor during the Passover. Throughout this mission, the rabbi would help himself to two or
three turkeys, possibly several geese—but not too many
—a dozen chickens, and just a few sacks of potatoes.
Since it was only natural that my future father-in-law
should emulate his rabbi in filching as much as possible
of the latter's share to supplement his own foraging, on
his return home a good deal of effort was needed to get
the commodities into the house—and I can assure you
that my future father-in-law was more of a Samson than
a *lamed-vavnik*. It would be hard to picture the way all the
members of my fiancée's family gorged themselves
throughout the Passover festival—but at the end they
could hardly put one foot before the other. And as for
the raisin wine, there was enough and to spare: my prospective mother-in-law was reputed to be the best maker
of raisin wine in Krokodilevka. A pound of raisins at her
hands would yield more than five pailfuls of crystal-clear
water! All the men assembled in the house ate *shmure
matzah*, while the women ate only the ordinary matzah.
And although on the eve of Passover all the consumers
of *shmure matzah* in Krokodilevka, including myself, actually took castor oil to purge ourselves of hametz, the
food that is ritually unfit for Passover, the oldest son of
my future father-in-law still could not restrain himself:
on the very first day of Passover he snatched a matzah
knaidel and made off to the privy to eat it. He almost

choked on it, but luckily that Man of Righteousness, his father, arrived in the nick of time, and by taking out his amulet and exerting his thaumaturgic power, kept him from the hands of the Angel of Death. . . .

On the seventh day of Passover, my prospective father-in-law took me with him on a visit to his rabbi so that I might pay my respects. And on that day the rabbi delivered himself of a homiletical allegory such as I shall remember to my dying day. Only listen and marvel: "Passover may be likened to a bridegroom who before the wedding ceremony passed through the houses of the Israelites to receive their good wishes and, of course, their sundry gifts and contributions. And the *kalah,* or bride, is in the order of matzah, a term that is in the order of kuchen, or cake, a term of endearment, and is also not unrelated in sound to *kochana,* which is Polish for 'beloved.' The nuptial tie of bride and bridegroom begets children, who may be likened unto bitter herbs—a reference to the children of our day. Because of our manifold sins, our children fall away from the traditional custom and cause agony for their elderly parents. And the preacher particularly stresses that 'we ate bitter herbs.' Also, why do we eat garlic for the sake of children of our day? It is well known that according to the Gemara garlic is to be eaten on the eve of the Sabbath. But since the children of today grow up to be goyim, then why should garlic be consumed for their sake? The answer is to be found in the phrase, 'Because the Egyptians made our ancestors eat garlic, to arouse their concupiscence and turn them into breeders of slaves.' As it is written, 'the garlic and the onions.' That is why we must keep up this practice—to commemorate the exodus from Egypt. . . . And the preacher alludes to the passage, 'with mortar and bricks, all the tasks that they ruthlessly imposed upon them.' It applies to the current generation, in which the children practice idol-worship 'with mortar and bricks' along with the white collars that derive from the ancient conspiracy of Egypt on the order of 'donkey' and Laban the Aramean. But we pray to the Holy One, blessed be He, that we shall be able to atone thanks to the three hundred holy sparks that inhere in the abomination of Egypt, as is known to those able to fathom the knowledge of the Almighty. That is why we place the bitter herbs opposite the egg, to atone for the sin of the egg, which in its turn is symbolic of the exodus of the Israelites from Egypt. . . ." I ask, can any of you pseudo-intellectuals and enlightened ones boast a treasure so priceless? Hardly! . . .

The day after Passover ended, a group of young men, one of them carrying a large volume under his arm, called on me to say that since, God willing, I was about to settle in Krokodilevka (evidently a matter to be proud of) they were inviting me to join their fellowship, known as *Hevra Osur Ledabair be-Shabbos,* the Association for the Prohibition of Common Speech on the Sabbath. I accepted immediately, and they conveyed to me all the rules of membership as embodied in the constitution of their association.

"It is written in the holy *Zohar,* 'Even as God is exalted in the heavens, so shall He be praised here below.' His essence being more fully realized during the Sabbath, we the undersigned have all therefore resolved not to utter secular words on the Sabbath. For the exaltation of the wonders of God is carried out quietly. As the Ari says, we can embrace God only in secret. And whoever transgresses the above regulations is unfair to those who wish to reach God.

"The Regulations are as follows:

"1. No secular words are to be uttered between the

time of the lighting of the Sabbath candles and the Havdalah service that concludes the Sabbath—even should such utterance mean the saving of human life.

"2. If by chance some secular words are uttered during worship, because of zeal, it shall behoove the utterer to expectorate and then proceed to utter a few sacred words, such as the name of the Almighty in the holy tongue.

"3. At the ritual baths on the Sabbath, there is really no need for speech in the holy tongue, so that total silence is to be observed—with the exception of course, of the term 'mikveh' and one or two others of a ritual nature.

"4. Even the familiar forms of names, such as Nochumtzi, Itzik, Hershke, Yossele, Mekhtzie, Kraintzi, Golda, Zissel and the like, are not to be uttered on the Sabbath; only their formal equivalents in the holy tongue are to be used.

"5. Indispensable communications are carried on by manual signs. Only in an emergency may such interjections as 'Eh?' and 'Nu' be uttered.

"6. All Sabbath dishes, such as farfel, tzimmes, kugel, chicken livers, must be designated by their counterparts in the holy tongue.

"7. If a goy should ask a question, he is to be told in the holy tongue that 'common speech is forbidden on the Sabbath.' Should he become belligerent, however, he is to be told in the holy tongue, with a finger placed against the lips, 'Villain, this is the Sabbath!'

"8. All members are duty bound to communicate to one another the Hebrew translations of abstruse Yiddish words.

"9. It is best to avoid speech on the Sabbath even in the holy tongue, and to resort, at need, to sign language. For instance, in referring to the term 'under-cantor,' it is best to saw at the throat with the edge of one hand and to cup the other on the rectum.

"10. But one is permitted, and is even obliged, to respond to the rabbi in ordinary Yiddish, since the meaning of Sabbath is that 'truth is everlasting' and that justice is the foundation of the world."

As I was leaving, my bride's father handed me a large shabby satin bag. "My child," he said, "since you are about to be married, I am presenting you with this phylactery sack which I inherited from the eminent Reb Gad, who in his turn inherited it from his great-grandfather, who in his turn assured him that an uncle of his had personally purchased it from a distinguished holy sage."

I accepted the splendid gift with gratitude, and began the trip home in the same ramshackle cart that had brought me to Krokodilevka. But my bride's grandfather was now replaced by a gentile driver, and when we arrived all hell broke loose, with the driver insisting on being paid for transporting me, since he swore that my father-in-law had not done so. As for my father, for one thing he was poor as Job's turkey, and for another he objected strenuously to the effrontery of the Man of Righteousness. In the end Reb Abish's hat was pawned on condition that the pawnbroker would also attend the wedding and compel the bride's father to redeem the pledge.

So at last the gentile carter was paid off, and preparations for the wedding began.

18

It is time to marry off the thirteen-year-old boy—then he will be an upright member of the community

So what do you say, my dear readers? Do you consider it high time for me, a lad of thirteen, to be married? Yes or no? You seem to hesitate; are you trying to make up your minds on the question? Well, my friends, I am as smart as you are, and I can guess the reason for your silence. You are probably thinking, "Look at who's being entrusted with a wife!" Isn't that so? Well, first of all that is completely wrong, if you'll pardon my saying so. For you are well aware that I've been wearing my father's shoes for the past few years: it follows that I've shed the juvenile moccasins. And your looking askance at me doesn't worry me a bit—so long as my fiancée, thank God, is enamored of me. Just ask her, and she will tell you that all the so-called genteel folk are not fit to shine my shoes. And here is the proof: she personally told her grandfather that she was in love with my shadow. . . . You may think it a joke, but I can very well believe it. Just try watching a Jewish fanatic as he strolls on a bright windy day. You will be amused to see how he contrives to cast his shadow; how his plaited side curls and goatee flutter in the wind; how the skirts of his kaftan swoop like the wings of a swan; how the tassels of his underwear flap against his thighs; how at each step the heel of his slipper throws a separate shadow a yard long, with the sun throwing patches of illumination between; and how each time the heel touches the ground again, the ritual fringes along the front of the *tallit katan* get caught in the slippers, while those along the back prance in the wind like the spindle legs of some huge, grotesque crane. This silhouette is cast in every detail by the shadow. Nu, could one not become enamored of so lovely a figure? Now you understand that it was even easier to fall in love with my shadow, since it was small in stature and the shoes and cap I wore were oversized, and thus only the shadow of my figure could be seen. Nu, of what account is your ridicule? You may object, perhaps, that I am unable to support a wife. Ha, ha, ha! You make me laugh. That is the least of my worries. Of course, those who are educated in the secular schools, and who therefore fail to observe the customs and traditions of their parents at home are concerned, being actually convinced that they will have to support their wives and keep their noses to the grindstone to provide luxuries for their families. However, we Hasidic children are brought up at home, and we observe, thank God, how parents in all the Jewish communities of Poland conduct themselves, so we have an inkling as to who is the provider in the family. Take my father, for instance: he devoted his life to the rabbi, and my mother was the breadwinner. What, you ask, was her line of business? Why, what business did she not engage in?—whether it was making dumplings, or conjuring up the evil eye, or administering home remedies, or uttering spells, or baking matzah, or darning stockings, or serving as a waitress or as an attendant in the women's ritual baths—and the rest came from the gro-

cery stand. In addition to which she had household duties, suckling and rearing children, cooking, darning and
mending clothes, heating the stove, and emptying the
slop pail. And when, on his return from the synagogue,
my father failed to be served with food immediately, my
mother would be raked over the coals. And still she
would receive him with open arms, fawn upon him and
pay him homage, serving him the choicest part of the
meat and fish, and a white loaf, while she herself would
be content to exist on what was left over. I knew how
husband and wife managed in Poland. So what was there
for me to worry about? I knew that my wife would exert
herself to the utmost. And if she should become ill for
a while—why, that was no calamity either. Was there not
a holy sage in the next town? So one would repair for a
time to the rebbe and the *hevra borsht*, letting the wife and
the children fend for themselves until things straight-
ened out. We have an Almighty Lord who sustains all
creatures, from the maggot to the bison; I don't have to
be their provider. What, am I correct? And anyhow, why
should I ask your views concerning my wedding? I am
well aware that according to you, I could remain a bachelor another five or six years. . . . But what of the holy
Gemara, and the other edifying books, which are the
advocates and champions of marrying at the age of
twelve or thirteen? That seems to carry small weight with
you. If you deprecate the one, I can just as easily snap my
fingers at the other. I can make fun of your ridicule of
me. I will be married at the age of thirteen—and you can
call me whatever you choose.

And so the wedding garments are already being tailored for me. Lord of the Universe, may so grand a wardrobe be vouchsafed to all fine young Jewish men: two
shirts and trousers made of coarse Turkish linen; a cloth
kaftan for ordinary wear and a mohair coat for the Sab-

bath and other holy days; a quilted windbreaker and a robe fashioned from my mother's wedding cloak—for which the sleeves, there being not enough fabric, were pieced together out of my father's satin winter trousers, which the rabbi had given him as a wedding present. Also, a Bershid *tallit katan* and chamois slippers. On the Sabbath morning preceding my Bar Mitzvah I was dressed in this attire and escorted to the synagogue. I remember to this day that when I was invited to honor the Torah, and was about to pronounce the traditional benediction, the reader of the Torah asked me, jokingly, "Do you know how to recite the after-meal benediction?" In my confusion, instead of pronouncing the benediction pertaining to the Torah, I proceeded to recite the one pertaining to the meal . . . and the congregation burst into laughter.

But I got through it all somehow. One thing, however, I shall not forget to my dying day, and whenever it comes to mind, I feel endless distress and mortification; my life becomes gloomy as the grave. The day before my wedding, my father had me put on my new clothes, and then, accompanied by the shammas, make the rounds of the wealthy and the other local notables, ostensibly to make my farewells, but in fact to solicit wedding presents. The clergy and other worthies of Poland had engaged in this practice since time immemorial; and my father followed suit. Cursed by the day when I was born —on the eve of my wedding I went through hell on earth! For one thing, as soon as I entered a wealthy household all the women and girls would roar with laughter, leaving me crushed and humiliated. For, along with the propriety of so splendid a custom as leading the bear about, there was my grotesque image as a bridegroom; and at so comic a sight, nobody could help laughing till his sides split. And if one local nabob or dignitary refrained from laughing in my face, he would say with a leering grin, "Have a nice journey!" And I had to hold on, biding my time, up to my ears in misery, until he deigned to produce a wedding gift of some sort. Now and then, out of pity, someone would shove an object into my hand, while a dozen others asked impatiently, "Well, what are you waiting for?" . . . And what about my trudging through the marketplace in my finery, accompanied by the shammas, while all the clerks and shopkeepers and ordinary bystanders stood in the doorways, pointing their fingers and jeering at me? Do you have any conception of what that could mean? Believe me, running the gauntlet of a thousand lashes is preferable to the humiliation of that experience. Beware, you Polish bridegrooms; don't let anyone trick you into making the rounds on the eve of your wedding day for ostensible purposes of leavetaking, even though it means forfeiting your life. Do not submit, my brethren, or you will never be able to rid your mind of the inhuman disgrace and ignominy. If I could obliterate it by dying, I would gladly do so. But that is a thing of the past, a moment of idiocy that cannot be repaired by all eternity.

So the wagons are all set to carry the guests to the wedding. Aside from my parents and kinfolk, the party is to include Reb Avremel Hirik, the synagogue sexton, and several ardent followers of the rabbi, as well as the pawnbroker, who is involved in the controversy over the hat. . . . The group had a final drink and climbed into the wagons.

19

The prowess of the Jews, inherited from the days of Egypt—a confrontation—land and order—true flunkeyism—enduring faith

Jews in general, and Hasidic Jews in particular, don't give a tinker's damn about anything when they are on their way to a wedding; they don't give a damn about anything at all. You take just one Jew with a sense of his own importance, and he will become the biggest frog in his own small puddle, a hard taskmaster and even a despot over those lowlier and weaker than himself. Now imagine a quorum of Jews getting together! They are noisy and blow off steam; when they meet with a muzhik trudging along the highway, it is they who will twist a corner of his kaftan into a pig's ear before he can do it himself to mock the Jews; or on meeting a peasant cart they will knock off a wheel or cause some other mischief. Or when the peasant is hauling his farm produce to market, he will be unceremoniously relieved of it and called a few names into the bargain. In a word, the crowd is feeling playful and indulging in every sort of prank.

Abruptly as a flash of lightning, their ears are smitten by the jingling of harness bells, followed by a shout of *"Stoy!"*—the Russian for "Halt." At the mere sound of those bells and that cry of "Halt," the would-be men

of importance, heroes and pranksters all turn into jel-
lyfish and sycophantic grovelers. The previous leaders in
the demonstration of brute force now shiver in their
boots, their teeth rattling like castanets. They now look
so harmless you'd think they couldn't hurt a fly, and so
innocent, you'd suppose in all the world they owed only
their souls to the Lord and a few quarts of milk to the
dairy woman.

The vehicle bearing two Russian officials—one with
a red collar, the other sporting only a cockade in his cap
—came to a stop and Red Collar barked, *"Otkuda ee kuda*
—Where you from and where you bound?"

"What did he say?" my father asked, bewildered.

"Never mind what the uncircumcised dog of a Jew
is babbling about," Avremel Hirik advised, but not without trepidation.

"Fellow Jews, prepare to do penance!" cried the
shammas in a voice full of terror.

"Nu, da, a passport u vas yest—Well, now, have you got
passports?" Red Collar brusquely demanded.

"Now we're in for it!" Avremel Hirik murmured
under his breath; then, turning to face the interrogator,
he implored in a fawning mixture of Polish, Russian, and
Ukrainian, *"Panye, nashto nam prashport, yak mi sam tutochke*
—Sir, what need have we of a passport when we are here
ourselves?"

In a fury, Red Collar howled, *"Stupai k'tchorty, zhidov-
skaya khara, ty etakaya! Takoi parkhati zhid stroyet mnye uly-
botchki! Siyu minutu tchtobi bil mnye passporty, a to ya vas—
kotory mezh vami starshy*—Go to the devil, with that Hebrew snot of yours! A scruffy Jew, making up to me like
that! I'll have those passports this minute, or else—who's
your elder here?"

"Fellow Jews, pray the Almighty—we're lost!"
gasped the pawnbroker, who was trembling all over.

"*Ty starshi*—Are *you* the elder?" asked Red Collar, pointing at my father.

"Gevald—help! Avremel, what is he saying?" whispered my father, looking more dead than alive.

"Quick, get out the rabbi's good-luck charm," Avremel, pale as a ghost, replied in a barely audible voice. "Probably he wants to know where you're going."

"Ah-ah-ah"— meekly, and with a servile grin, my father ventured to address Red Collar—"*Panye, nye znaye yak meni yekhali? Meni yekhali na vesselye*—Sir, you didn't know where we were bound? We were bound for a celebration."

"*Akh ty tchutchelo gorokhovoy!*" stormed Red Collar. "*Ty na svadbu yedesh? Ah zhenikh gdye?*—Ah, you confounded garden-patch scarecrow! Bound for a wedding, are you? Then where is the bridegroom?"

My father gave him the beady-eyed look of a mouse caught in a trap, with no idea of what the question was.

"*Khossen, khossen*—the bridegroom, the bridegroom!" said the official with the cockade.

"Ah, the *khossen, panye,* the *khossen! Vot on*—there he is!"—and he pointed at me.

Though I was frightened out of my wits, Red Collar now only shook with laughter: "*Tak eto tvoi zhenikh? Otlitchno! Ah gdye yevo metricheskoye svidyetyelstvo?*—So that's your bridegroom? Very good! And where might his birth certificate be?"

Once again my father looked about him with a shrug of bewilderment, until the official with the cockade called out, "*Metrika! Metrika!*"

"Ah, ah—*metrika!*" said Avremel Hirik, venturing in an ingratiating tone to address the official. "*Yai bog, panye, ye tam v'tlumik! Ot yak ya mayu boord un paios*—As truly as there is a God, sir, it's in that bundle! As truly as I have a beard and ritual locks!"

"*Otkroitye vash zhidovsky khlam—posmotrim*—Open up your Jewish ragbag and we'll take a look!" Red Collar ordered, pointing to the bundle.

"We're in real trouble, fellow Jews!" whispered the shammas.

When the bundle was untied, Reb Abish's hat was the first to crawl out, and Red Collar laughed as though he could hardly contain himself. Then he clapped that hat onto my head, pulled it down over my ears and said to me, "*Eto dlya nevesty*—is that for the bride?" Nearly prostrated with fright, I was actually in tears until Cockade said to Red Collar, "*Im kyem toot imyet dyelo! Ostavtye etikh dikarei; pust sebye yedut k'tchartu na kulitchki! Brrr—gadost etakaya!*—What is this we're bothering ourselves with! Leave these savages alone; let them go to the devil out here in the middle of nowhere! How disgusting it all is!" At that, Red Collar flung down the hat, spitting as he did so, and climbed back into the carriage.

As soon as the harness bells had faded into the distance, the Hasidic party began intoning a new melody, "May the Rabbi's Merit Shield Us!"

"So why should they not retreat?" the shammas asked in perfect seriousness. "Why should such a goy not shrink from Reb Abish's hat?"

"I only wonder why he was laughing so hard," said the pawnbroker.

"Laughing?" my father broke in. "The laugh was on the wrong side of his face! And the proof of it is that the hat almost crippled that vile hand of his; if he hadn't thrown it down, he would have been minus a hand!"

"No wonder," said the shammas, "that he was clearly about to give up the ghost—may the Lord preserve us! He was already foaming at the mouth so that he could barely spit—"

"That is right," my father joined in. "He was lucky

that the official with the cockade saved him from disaster just in time."

Another bumpkin, who had remained huddled in the cart, frozen with fear, suggested, "It may be that the other one is a gilgul, a transmigrated soul, of the old tzaddik's house slippers, may his memory be blessed!"

"Why must it be from one of the slippers?" exclaimed Avremel Hirik. "He's not worthy of that. From the old man's tobacco pipe, perhaps—"

"Avremel, have you any idea of where the old man's pipe came from?" asked the shammas. "You must understand that after his demise the old man's father of blessed memory—he was the eminent maggid—was led by the Archangel Michael to Gehenna to eat every one of the lost souls down there. But since the great maggid of blessed memory could not carry out his mission without the *lulke-tzibbuk,* the likeness of a pipe was fashioned for him. It had a long stem turned out of Aaron's staff, and its bowl was a conceptualization from the soul of the pious Riveleh, who was in need of a *tikkun neshomah*—a means of spiritual assistance—because a Hasid had once chanced to glimpse her in the nude as she was on her way to the river for immersion prior to the midnight service, thereby inflicting undue torments upon a future Hasidic saint—even though she was unaware of all this herself. But you know that the Holy One, blessed be He, deals very sternly with the tzaddikim. Anyhow, the maggid, of blessed memory, satisfied the tikkun by means of the pipe; and on the following night he returned the same pipe to the old man, of blessed memory—and incidentally, Michael returned the pipestem, now once more a staff, to Aaron as a matter of honor. Now you see how remarkable a pipe it was."

"Although I had not been aware of this story," said Avremel Hirik, deeply moved, "it goes without saying that the garments of the saintly old man, as well as his carriage and horses and appurtenances of any sort—all things in fact—are the conceptualizations derived from souls—"

"You have discovered America!" my father broke in. "It is common knowledge that once on the holiday of Lag be-Omer when he rode into the country to practice archery, his white horse—may it rest in peace!—reared up on its hind legs to prevent the old man from aiming the arrows toward the east. And the old man, of blessed memory, informed the people then and there that the soul of the steed's sire was in the east and was clamoring for a *tikkun neshomah*, for a means of spiritual betterment. It was only because the old man obliged the steed that it settled down so that the ancient could aim his arrows eastward. . . ."

In this fashion, for the rest of the journey the Hasidic elite continue to wrangle over where the gilgul, the transmigrated soul, of the official with the cockade might have originated. In the end it was unanimously agreed that he was indeed the gilgul of a callus that had been trimmed from Reb Abish's foot and that had an unmistakable resemblance to the official's cockade. And so at last the Hasidim arrived in Krokodilevka.

20

All the fair sex, believe it or not, are
favorably impressed with me

On reaching the city limits we caught sight of a wagon,
drawn by two nags, that had come out to welcome the
bridegroom. The vehicle was jammed with Jews of all
ages, who were singing, cheering, clapping their hands
and shouting themselves hoarse. And like a small boat in
the wake of an ocean liner, behind it trailed a cart drawn
by a blind mare and loaded with women; clustered all
over the cart, like flies about a festering sore, were a lot
of boys and girls, all shabby and down at the heels.

The younger men took charge of me. Next came the
processional circuits of the marketplace before the wedding ceremony, with the bride circling the bridegroom
seven times. Well, to be frank, the fair sex were certainly a
mixed lot: washerwomen, scrubwomen, serving wenches,
chambermaids, scullery maids, gadabouts, tatterdemalions, and even gentile hawkers all came running to witness the charming spectacle of which I was the center.

The procession was preceded by half a dozen musicians: one using a tub for a drum and two rolling pins as
drumsticks, another clashing two pot covers as cymbals,

a third sawing on a fiddle that had cost all of twenty kopecks when it was new, a fourth blowing into the neck of a bottle in lieu of a trumpet, a fifth banging his ears to imitate a cello, while a sixth whistled—shrill as a fife —through two fingers stuck in his mouth. It may be that I have failed to identify the instruments properly, but regardless of that such music could hardly have emanated from any others. The married women and girls were all feasting their eyes on me, all longing for a child or a bridegroom such as I. And the proof of it is this: they immediately cast an evil eye so that I began to yawn.

Long life to the Jewish women of Poland, who avert their eyes from long trousers and short jackets! They are not like those supposedly educated grand ladies who take offense at any disrespect, or are put into a fury when one of our young men, and he a paragon of virtue, happens to reach inside his unbuttoned shirt and scratch his chest, or to blow his nose onto the floor, or to yawn in a lady's face or, God forbid, he should happen to spit on the train of her dress. Or if, on some rare occasion, he should happen to say anything crude. Then he is labeled an ignoramus, a vulgarian, a savage. The grand ladies prefer polite, flowery talk and eloquence; they relish compliments, as if they belonged to the nobility and were not daughters of Jerusalem. Indeed, thank God, our Polish women are able to put up with anything; they can take it. You can scratch to your heart's content or spit, or blow your nose, or stand on your head—and not only will they remain unperturbed, the fact is that the more uncouth and vulgar a man's behavior is, the more he will appeal to her. She would not exchange his knobby Adam's apple for the swanlike throat of the most exquisite gentleman.

And aren't things really better that way? Indeed, why should one have to be forever on tiptoe, wary of

committing a social error or uttering some impropriety?
Gentlemen, indeed! When you think about it, who but
these same half-baked clowns and rakes, these debauchees and breakers of the law are responsible for promot-
ing the belief that the female is superior to the male?
These scoundrels declare that the female is a gentle being and appreciates the esthetic things of life more than
does the male; they likewise propound the notion that it
is the female who influences the spirit and guides the
emotions of the male in courtship, and that all men are
therefore duty bound to pay homage and give honor to
women—to be gallant and gracious and accommodating.
Nu, what do you think of such moralizing? Our ancestors, mind you, had a bit more wisdom than these modern pillars of society, and they looked on women as cattle. The statements of the holy Gemara concerning those
creatures run along much the same lines. And for this
very reason, our ancestors' womenfolk worked like
slaves, and would not have dared show themselves in any
masculine assemblage—let alone, God forbid, intrude
upon the discussion.

Anyhow, who pays the slightest heed to those traditional ways of life, and our wives will dance attendance
upon us, minister to us, venerate us, and be suitably
grateful. As for you half-baked scribblers, do not suppose that your writings will carry any weight with the
Jewish women of Poland! They won't in the least, believe
me—even if you point out to them a thousand times over
that they are doomed to a life of misery with their husbands, that they are looked on as of no account and that
even the most insignificant, the laziest and most unat-
tractive husband is lord and master over the loveliest, the
finest and also the unluckiest of women, and can hold her
in contempt. The life of women passes like a cloud, devoid of either happiness or comfort, and she must swal-

low the cup of her misery. And so, with all the rest of
your various fancies and illusions.

You may even write *A Polish Girl*, but you'll merely
be riding a balky mare on a wild goose chase and tilting
with windmills. For the Jewish women of Poland will only
declare, "Once and for all, we'll go on making bricks
without straw, we'll do the most menial tasks, we'll endure insults and humiliations, and still go on serving our
husbands as breadwinners and worshiping the ground
they walk on! For we cherish a *tallit katan* and a protrud-
ing Adam's apple more than we care for all the spruced-
up coxcombs and because a small share in the world to
come earned by our Hasidic husbands through their
prayers, their ritual baths, their *melaveh malkehs*, their
merrymakings at the rebbe's court, are far dearer to us
than the worldly pleasures offered by the fine gentlemen!"

At last we arrived at the palatial quarters where the
bridegroom and his in-laws-to-be were to be housed. In
fact, those quarters were not a bit less luxurious than the
elementary schools I had attended, or the home of my
bride's family. But the furnishings were different. In the
center of the room a noodle board that rested on a
kneading trough served as a table; a discarded door laid
across two trestles served as a bench; an old shawl belonging to the bride's mother doubled as a table cover,
on which cake and schnapps—both worthy of a king, of
course—were laid out. Mildew bloomed on the lower
surface of the inside walls. I sat on a small tub turned
upside down, and the guests sat on the makeshift bench.
They had hardly drunk their first toast when there arrived on the scene a man who was stone blind. He carried
a shepherd's staff; a black sash encircled his belly, and a
cap with a cracked visor sat on his head like a worn-out
yarmulka; the high boots he wore were too big for him

and were falling apart. He had the face of a drunken butcher. Leading him by the hand was a fifteen-year-old ragamuffin, whose expression suggested a veteran of fifty. There were cheerful cries from the guests: "Quiet, quiet! The badchan is here!" The badchan, adept at improvising humorous songs, was the traditional entertainer at weddings. For all his blindness, he managed to reach for the bottle, poured himself a tumblerful and swallowed it without blinking, wolfed down a hunk of cake and announced, *"Raboisay,* gentlemen! If you'll quiet down, I'll compose a few rhymes in honor of our bridegroom. Let's hear you, masters—tune up!"

And standing beside the table, in a lugubrious voice he began to chant.

21

Nuptials and a synagogue—a feast of the soul—and let the Polish-Jewish badchanim do the moralizing

The Badchan's Chant

Bridegroom, my dear bridegroom,
Listen to what I say:
Your Yom Kippur is today—
It is your day of doom!
But for your sins, I calculate you've paid,
And have now atoned by the Holy One's aid.

Bridegroom, my dear bridegroom,
To the Holy One lift up your head,
Let your heart be laundered by the tears you shed,
And your wedded bliss will bloom.
To be a bridegroom means, you well know,
That with time your wealth will grow.

Bridegroom, my dear bridegroom,
Though you wed while the world is burning,
Your sons will be men of great learning,
Despite predictions of unending gloom.

Wisdom arrives, my son, with the passing years,
And so, for now, please lend me your ears.

Bridegroom, my dear bridegroom,
Give homage to beauty and respect to the soul,
So the Lord will keep you unharmed and whole,
And guide your offspring from cradle to tomb.
If your happiness with others you share
You'll prosper and never fall prey to despair.

Bridegroom, my dear bridegroom,
Today you are king and your bride is queen—
For what do the words beloved bride *mean?*
They mean, for one thing, a prolific womb.
Many daughters and sons will bear your name;
Their beauty and wisdom the world will acclaim!

Bridegroom, my dear bridegroom,
Now comes the end of my song:
The Lord protect you all your life long,
But before I leave this grand bridal room,
I beg you earnestly, hear my plea,
And if I'm rewarded fittingly,
I will pray for you and your bride-to-be.

As you stand beneath the canopy,
I'll pray for all your progeny,
And also for your family,
I'll even toss in this company,
And personally guarantee
My prayers are first quality!

The truth is that the badchan caused me to weep in despair over my wretched lot. I regarded my wedding day as the eve of Yom Kippur rather than as Yom Kippur itself. But on Yom Kippur eve, while the guests were feasting, for the afternoon Minhah prayers I would be having to recite the *Vidduy*, the confession of my sins, and put on a shroudlike robe of white linen while my parents pronounced a blessing over me; whereas today, I was to become a kapparah, to be offered up for the sins of my parents, as a matter of course, just like the chicken that is sacrificed on the eve of the Day of Atonement. And likewise my bride was to become my kapparah, my own expiatory chicken—the sole difference being that on the eve of Yom Kippur the chicken is *white*, whereas my wife and I wore *black* . . . But no kapparah whatever would have been likely to redeem the two of us. . . . As for my being spared the traditional stripes of the *malkot*—well, to begin with, the small boys were sure to contribute their share of pinching and sticking pins in me when I found myself under the bridal canopy, so as to make up for that omission. Moreover I was already feeling so whipped that there was no further necessity of beating me. To be brief, they proceeded to drape me with the white linen robe, buttoning and fastening all its bands and strings. An ox has to be tied up for the slaughter, but among Polish Jews a juvenile bridegroom faces it voluntarily. A single nod from his Polish Jew of a father, and there is no need for chains or irons! As the bride was about to be veiled for the ceremony, my prospective father-in-law noticed that I was wearing an ordinary cap. "What's going on here?" he shouted. "Where is Reb Abish's shtreimel?"

"The shtreimel?" rejoined my father. "And did you pay the carter that time?"

"Fool!" retorted the father of the bride.

"Moron!" my father responded. As one word led to another, they both fell to swearing like troopers. Finally the guests prevailed on the pawnbroker to release the shtreimel with a promise that he would be remunerated out of the wedding presents, so that the wedding could proceed.

The women for their part were also in an uproar,

snatching at each other's wigs. My mother was in a rage because she had not been presented with a white blouse, as was the tradition, before the wedding ceremony, and the bride's mother was in a fury because her daughter had not been presented with a fur jacket. To make a long story short, I stepped into the women's section and caught a glimpse of my beauty—the last one before the slaughter. . . . In her bewildered state as she sat there with eighteen women busy primping her and arranging her pigtails, she looked like a fly trapped in a spider's web. If I had not thrown the veil over her face at that moment, I would probably not have survived to take part in my own wedding. The attending women showered me with hops as a sort of leaven for encouraging the dough my parents had concocted to rise. And then we were being escorted to the bridal canopy.

All of a sudden, there we were in front of it. I was somewhat baffled to realize that we were not being taken to the synagogue for the ceremony, but I supposed that the bride's father knew what he was doing. It didn't dawn on me for some minutes that we were in fact standing close to the synagogue. Try, if you will, to visualize a small ramshackle structure, roofed with moldy thatch full of gaping holes, its walls of clay cracked and peeling, propped up by rotten planks. Some of the panes in the three front windows had been pasted over with paper and with strips of a mothridden curtain that had once hung before the Ark where the Torah scrolls were kept, and other panes were missing altogether. The south wall bulged like a pregnant woman who appeared likely to miscarry any day now, and there was a breach in the eastern wall through which you could glimpse a crumbling corner of the Holy Ark—out of which the shammas would scoop the dry rot to be used in the rite of circumcision. Well, and how is that for a synagogue?

Suddenly, as I stood there befuddled, there was a staccato burst of handclaps and the sound of voices from inside the synagogue, a noise that shook the place to its foundation.

When my father inquired the meaning of the commotion, he was told that the Hasidim of nearby Nachmestrivka had bought their rebbe a silver samovar, for which they had paid two hundred rubles, that in the evening the gift would be taken to the sage, and that meanwhile they were having a nip of something in the synagogue as they saw off the delegation to their tzaddik.

And so, my friends, ought not our fellow Jews of Poland live to see the advent of the Messiah? Where else in the world would you find such people, who would sacrifice so much for their tzaddikim? Living in direst poverty, in cold and starvation, down at the heels and out at the elbows, with a house of worship falling into ruins —yet to buy a silver samovar for their holy sage they could and did find two hundred rubles. He was, after all, a divine personage, and deserving of a certain homage. Indeed how could a synagogue compare with a holy sage? The entire prestige of the synagogue rested on the prayers offered within it. But did not the sage himself personify prayer? Did not the great Reb Hillel, when his aging rebbitzin became pregnant, tell her that she was carrying two scrolls of the Torah? (By which he meant two sons.) In fact, she gave birth to a girl, and a deformed one at that. But what of it? It stands to reason that a Jew should be more in awe of delinquency in paying taxes than in awe of the synagogue, since implicit in tax delinquency is the fact of having to face Red Collar—whereas the necessity of paying in the world to come for your fun here is still far off. Moreover, the Jews of Krokodilevka will submit to having their last pillow and featherbed hauled to the police station, as well as to personal arrest, and still they fail to pay taxes! For how can they raise money when they are destitute? Yet they will move heaven and earth to raise twice eighteen rubles as a *pidyon* for the holy sage, and an emissary will be delegated to deliver it in the name of the community. Whereupon the sage—may his life be prolonged—prophesies that the local tax collector will be dismissed from his post. And the prophecy comes true: the old official is removed from office; the only catch is that the replacement turns out to be a thousand times worse than his predecessor, and the havoc he causes in the community is more calamitous than the destruction of Jerusalem. But the Jews go right on being delinquent in paying taxes, for what can you do when there is not a single crumb in the bread box? And if all your efforts and pains succeed in scraping together a couple of hundred rubles by pawning the last featherbed is blood money like that to be shelled out for taxes, or a donation for the synagogue, or the poorhouse, or a Talmud-Torah for poor children, or to help the ailing and indigent? Now, I ask you: are all these projects of greater importance than presenting your own rabbi with a silver samovar?

You seem to be extraordinarily quiet. Very well: let the Nachmestrivka Hasidim rejoice in their rebbe's samovar; let the synagogue walls continue to bulge; let the invalids, the women in childbirth, the cripples, the widows and orphans go on suffering as before.

And in the meantime, under the bridal canopy, let me contemplate my own tragicomedy.

22

Mazel tov, fellow Jews! You've had your fun! One more outbreak on the old abscess

Well, and now the groomsmen had completed the traditional circuits around the bride and groom under the marriage canopy—while I went on standing there like a blockhead in paradise. The rabbi had performed the marriage ceremony; the precentor had already recited the traditional document in Aramaic setting forth the obligations of the bridegroom toward his bride; I had already placed the betrothal ring on the bride's finger and had pronounced my own death sentence by uttering the words, "Behold, thou art consecrated unto me with this ring according to the Law of Moses and Israel. . . ." Everything seemed to be moving smoothly ahead. And then the bride stepped on the toes of my right foot—a portent that she would rule the roost after the nuptials. That was all I needed, as though I weren't already miserable enough! Actually, her doing it was superfluous. It is common knowledge that every Jewish girl in Poland who stands under the marriage canopy is fully aware and even wishes wholeheartedly, as she steps on her bridegroom's toes, that as a consequence of this act her husband will walk all over her for the rest of her life. But for some reason or other, the ancient superstition continues to be observed. Then, last but not least, with the same foot the bridegroom shatters a glass—the traditional token of mourning for the destruction of the Temple, and the destruction also of juvenile newlyweds, who by the thousands, alas, spend their lives in wretchedness and perhaps bequeath that same lot to their posterity. For this the Jews have no memento—a fact which, however, I have also overcome. "Mazel tov! Congratulations!" you hear people saying all around you. Thus the Jew forever relies on good fortune, drifting with the current and eating the bread of idleness. He seems oblivious of the statement by the Gemara itself, that Israel is unlucky—but if you make an effort, the Lord will help you.

So at last we are being escorted from under the marriage canopy, arm in arm for the first and only time in our lives. . . . Mazel tov! Congratulations! The young Polish boy has now become a young Polish man. The guests move their feet to something like a flourish of trumpets. Now the in-laws pay homage, doing the cossack dance in front of the house with abandon, as behooves two elderly but fervent Hasidim. And all the women looking on cheer and applaud the two God-fearing zealots as though they beheld the Divine Presence hovering about them. At the entrance to the house we were welcomed with a twisted loaf of white bread, apparently to signify that we, like the loaf, would never be parted until, overcome by the force of circumstance, the grave swallowed us up.

We were ushered into the house and given a seat of honor, and then "golden soup," traditional at weddings, was brought in. But when I attempted to dip a spoonful to end the day's fast, there turned out to be neither soup nor gold—the Hasidic guests having lost no time in helping themselves and having left not a drop.

Then they proceeded with the royal wedding banquet, with the appropriate musical accompaniment. When the meal was over, the badchan scrambled onto the table, and placing a huge platter in the middle to contain the wedding presents and donations of money, called out, "Attention, my friends! I will entertain you with a pun or a jest to accompany each present!" My father-in-law pulled out a deed to half his property and tossed it onto the platter. The badchan's invitation, "Trot out your wedding presents, relatives of the bridegroom and the bride!" was met by a stony silence. But the badchan persisted, "Oi, you aunts, uncles, grandfathers, grandmothers, friends of the bridegroom and the bride! Get change for a kopeck and let's have your wedding presents!" Finally, the nabob of Krokodilevka stepped forward and hurled six copper pieces worth five kopecks onto the platter, with such force that it cracked. The damage evoked the ire of my mother-in-law. One word led to another, and my mother was annoyed; then my father turned resentful, and the sour looks and sulking spread to my father-in-law and the guests. In the rumpus that ensued over the poor showing in the matter of wedding presents, the pawnbroker snatched the fur-trimmed hat from my head and took to his heels.

You can imagine the fiasco the wedding had turned into, and above all my chagrin. Had it not been for Hasda, the ritual slaughterer of Krokodilevka, the affair would really, God forbid, have been a calamity! But there, sudden as a bolt of lightning, Hasda was overturning a slop pail on the earthen floor; then he was taking off his gabardine and his trousers, keeping on only his underwear, and urging the rest of the guests to unbend. Next, with a yarmulka that must have weighed two pounds, given its accumulation of dirt, sweat, grease, et cetera, he was whacking the old women and small boys to start them applauding and cheering, while he and the other guests kicked up their heels and danced with abandon. He raised all our spirits—a blessing on him! That is what I call a real ritual slaughterer—as opposed to Pini, one of that office who wears polished boots and a stylish cap, who sports a tidy beard and earlocks and is, moreover, proficient in reading and writing. Indeed, the Evil One would appear to hold undisputed sway over Pini. As if for spite, he is well versed in the laws of ritual slaughter, is exceedingly hospitable, will stop at nothing to help a fellowman in need, is esteemed by officials because of his fine record, and is most upright and conscientious in his dealings with others. Well, what do you say about such an Evil One? Why, the rabbi persecutes him even in public; but it happens that the ritual slaughterer is more scholarly than the rabbi, so that occasionally he exposes the latter's deficiency in rabbinical wisdom, and then the rabbi has to keep his mouth shut. Alas for such a spiritual leader, so fervent a Hasid, to be surpassed in scholarship—*O tempora! O mores!* Now our Hasda is no great shakes when it comes to ritual slaughter, nor is he anything to boast of as a scholar. But I would not trade him for eighteen ritual slaughterers of the likes of Pini, who is no match for Hasda in certain of his mannerisms or his ingenuity. Why, Hasda's tippling, his hilarity, his whacks with the yarmulka by way of enlivening the occasion, as well as his ready wit and banter— all these delighted and enthralled the gathering. He directed the "Sabbath dances" like a master choreographer. Urging the badchan and the musicians to go on, he pulled out his oversized bandanna, gave the bride one corner of it to hold while she passed the other corner to each guest, male or female, in turn, according to the Orthodox tradition. The guests dropped copper coins onto the platter, and the money was used to replenish the dwindling supply of vodka.

Some of the guests, tired and drunk, fell asleep wherever they happened to sink down; others started to drag themselves home. My in-laws exchanged meaningful glances. Some relative remarked, "Well, enough's enough! The bride and the bridegroom have fasted today; time for them to take a little rest!" When, at a signal, the musicians struck up the music for the "Mitzvahdance," the groomsmen took me in charge, the bridesmaids gathered about the bride, and we were steered toward a dark small room—the bridal chamber. The nuptial couch consisted of a sleeping bench, and beside it was a roughhewn three-legged stool. Hush, my friends —my attendants are whispering something in my ear. Good, night, my dear guests! As for me—a miserable lifetime dawns. . . .

23

If it is ordained by God, it is a thing of beauty

And now, my dear readers, since you are already familiar with the story of my life from birth to marriage, and are already aware of what a good sort I am, I may as well tell you the rest. Let the world learn how young Jewish males fare in our blessed Poland—and also acquire a useful lesson or two about life. Bear in mind that when I was still a mere runny-nosed boy, people observed certain performances of mine whose ingenuity and finesse were beyond human comprehension. And the impressiveness of those displays increased as, praise the Lord, I became a full-fledged adult. When you think of it, do you know of many youngsters in Poland with gifts adequate to describe their Jewish milieu so masterfully and in such detail as I have done? And by the way, I haven't told even a tenth of what there was to tell. Can there be many Jewish mothers in Poland who have experienced in the ninth month of pregnancy the miracle of having a girl child transformed into a boy inside their own bellies? How many youngsters have been privileged to see with their own eyes a goblin wearing a skullcap? How many

youngsters can have been so eagle-eyed in noting which
yeshiva students were carrying on behind the oven and
in the attic of the synagogue? To say nothing of Reb
Abish's self-propelled fur-trimmed hat, a thing so
miraculous as almost to be an eighth wonder, following
as it does so closely upon the seventh. And who, after all,
had inherited it? Who was lucky enough to marry the
daughter of a *lamed-vavnik*, one of the Thirty-Six Righteous Men on whom the existence of the world depends?
It was I! Who informed all the world of such wonders
upon wonders as my father-in-law's epistle and the rabbi's Torah, or gematria, the Kabbalistic numerology of
the Baal Shem's grandson, or the minutes of the Association for the Prohibition of Common Speech on the Sabbath? Or the song of the blind wedding jester? Again it
was I! And as far as the students are concerned—needless to say, I am to be weighed in one scale against the
gold in the other. Those fellows pride themselves on
wearing student uniforms with silver buttons. But what
of it? What is so great about being tricked out like a goy?
To be attired like an authentic Orthodox Jew, and to be
at the same time of exceptional charm, is a much greater
accomplishment—one that I had mastered in a way
uniquely my own! Indeed, at the age of nine I had already been dressed like a Hasid of seventy. So judge for
yourself. Who is more to be respected among Jews, and
even among goyim: one such as I, who clings to the
hallowed garb of my ancestors, dating back to the beginning on Mount Sinai, or one of those who emulate others? Take a look at the illustrations in the oldest of holy
books, or at the antique portraits such as those the patriarchs have handed down from one generation to another, and note the appearance of Moses and the other
Jews in the exodus from Egypt! Most likely they were
clad in long coarse smocks and caps with visors. Indeed,

is not Mordecai, the chief minister, portrayed wearing a high fur-trimmed hat, a long kaftan, white linen underwear and slippers? And what of King David or even King Solomon, the multimillionaire in all his glory? Are they portrayed in fedoras and Prince Alberts? Heaven forbid! No, they are shown in the same traditional costume as all the other Jews. Of course, theirs were tailored from costly fabrics, their shtreimels were made of Russian sable; their long robes of imported silk or camel's hair, and their underclothes of softest linen, their slippers of the finest morocco leather. Well, all this may be taken for granted when it concerns sovereigns and high potentates —yet everything is traditionally Jewish. And by the way, the attire of a Hasidic rabbi—may his life be long!—is in no way inferior to that of the kings of Israel. They were sovereigns on earth, whereas the rabbis are sovereigns in heaven. A ruler derives his wealth from his own subjects, whereas the rabbi derives his from the world at large. And how could it be otherwise? This is not what I was driving at, however; I wish to prove merely that Jews have been wearing the same traditional garb since time immemorial, and that it is worn by Polish Jews to this very day. It follows that the Lord of the Universe must have shown this hallowed garb to Moses on Mount Sinai, and enjoined him to cause Jews to wear it to the end of time, when the world crumbles into dust! And it follows that the garb of Polish Jews must foster even greater saintliness than the Ark of the Covenant; for God showed the model of the Ark only to Moses, and Moses in his turn, out of six hundred thousand Jews was barely able to find one Bezalel, one single, solitary, lonesome Jew intelligent enough to put an ark together—and as a matter of fact, since the time of Moses and Bezalel no synagogue has contrived to follow the authentic design because no Jew knows what it was. Whereas this hallowed garb was manifested by God to all Jews alike, so that in every generation there are, heaven be thanked, quite ordinary Jews—tailors, cobblers, hatters—who can copy this style in meticulous detail. Is it not a crying shame that there should be young Jewish rascals who thrust aside such saintliness and such things of beauty? And they actually glory in their ludicrous attire! Even the blind can perceive that whoever exchanges the hallowed Mount Sinai garb for bobtailed coats and visored caps, at once forfeits the image of God and has his Jewish identity extinguished forever.

I am thus a splendid young fellow indeed. Is this not so? For I am the equal in proficiency in many languages of those uniformed scholars. I may even outwit them. Of what use are many languages when you can achieve your purpose with one that for eloquence surpasses them all? A fig for all their knowledge of languages, as compared to a single utterance of Avremel Hirik! Armed with Avremel's eloquence, I shall outdo their mastery of seventy languages. You recall those golden words of his. And are they not a piece of divine oratory?

But since I am so fine a lad, how does it happen that my mother-in-law looks askance at me and puts on a sour face? Ask her for a reason and she will offer no explanation. She seemed to have borne a grudge against me ever since the wedding feast; she is resentful because on disappearing with my bride that night into that dark little room, I was so dog-tired that I fell fast asleep on the kitchen table and slept there the whole night through. For this she made fun of me in the presence of all the town's busybodies; and although I already carry on in the same fashion as all other young married men, she remains set against me. At first my Kabbalistic friend would likewise frown and whisper to me, "It's a disgrace that a young Hasidic man should be so ignorant of marital

relations." But in time he ceased to mention this ignorance and became friendlier. My mother-in-law, however, was still disgruntled and remained so. She was most
impatient to have her daughter produce a grandchild;
she was not satisfied to have grandchildren only from her
sons. I put up with her and did all I could to please her
to avoid unpleasantness. But there was one thing I could
not endure: I was driven to distraction by the aphrodisiac
prescriptions she brought me, hidden under her apron,
before I went to sleep at night. All my pleading was of
no help; she would stay until I swallowed the concoction
—only to vomit it up a minute later. Every night she
brought some new cure-all, and I would swear that she
had already sapped my virility. If my readers had been
eavesdropping as she lectured me every time I swallowed
one of her concoctions, they could have gathered the
pearls of wisdom that fell from her mouth. But in fact she
was undiluted poison; you would have had to be tough
as leather to listen to her.

Let me give you a sample of one of her lectures so
that you can understand what a witch she was.

24

Don't fool yourself—you'll never be free as a bird! There is no escape—you'll be a father yet!

"So, Itzikel, you think your mother-in-law is a wicked woman? Let what I wish you be returned to my own heart! What can I say to you since, alas, you are only a young billy goat! What I wish you and my daughter Tseitel—may she outlive my bones!—may that wish be realized in me, Lord of the Universe! And so what if Traina the Gossip gives in to the carnal appetite of her son-in-law? Yet who is to be envied more—you or he? What do you say, Itzikel? Because Traina, after all—may she forgive me—she came from a very humble family, for all that she is so well-to-do now. Her father—may God not punish me for these words!—her father worked all his life as a butcher in a slaughterhouse—may he intercede in heaven for all those who wear high boots! Whereas my father—may his life be long—in his younger days was a coachman for Reb Getzeleh, or Reb Getzikel, of blessed memory!—I am not worthy to mention that holy name of his. From my wedding day down to the present he has been held in high esteem by the community—may no evil befall him.

"And what of Shmaryah—I refer to your father-in-law, may *his* name be blotted out! If only he wished it, the world would beat a path to his door! Is it not common knowledge that he is one of the Thirty-Six Righteous Men? But what is the use! He is such a ne'er-do-well, of no use on earth! And when you think of it, what is man? Alas! Merely a sieve! No sooner is he full of years than his whole life goes leaking out of him. Why, even a dumpling in boiling water has more substance than he. And as for woman—may I live to hear the shofar herald the advent of the Messiah, but this is the truth!—I heard the saintly Reb Getzeleh himself declare that a woman could be compared to a pot of beans: today she is full and shoved into the oven, but on the morrow she's empty again and back on the shelf. . . . So what is it you suspect me of? You may say what you wish about a woman—and not in vain, for she can talk anyone deaf and dumb—yet all the tzaddikim stem from her. So she does, after all, carry some weight with the Lord of the Universe, whose name I am not worthy to mention. But the main issue is, where does a woman hail from? Of what use is good wine if you put in a vinegary cask? Does man live by bread alone? See what Bahya, the great and saintly sage, writes in the *Tzenah Urennah** about attaining paradise, only by begetting good children. And so, Itzikel, listen to your foolish mother-in-law and do her one more favor—drink this decoction! Why, really, there's nothing to it! And what do you think is in it? There's no poison in it, God forbid! That pious old woman Zissel told me today that a few years ago she heard from Dvossi's own lips about a similar incident, in Little Ketarer. At that time the saintly sage of Zilshtuv, of blessed memory, urged that a few simple ingredients be mixed together and cooked

*The Yiddish version of the Pentateuch adapted for women

in a small pot—it has to be really small. There you have
the whole secret. And yet you suppose that it contains
God only knows what. Old Dvossi, of blessed memory—
may she intercede with the matriarchs for all of us!—was
a miracle-worker. And it's not surprising. A righteous
Jewess who made the rounds of all the tzaddikim whose
names I am not worthy of mentioning—and mastered a
thousand and one cures and incantations! It's a wonder
her head didn't burst open. And indeed—may we all
soon be redeemed!—her conjuring of an evil eye and her
exorcising all manner of sickness induced by evil spirits
were little short of miraculous. So, Itzikel, why are you
suspicious of me? Do me one more favor and swallow at
least a spoonful!"

Whereupon, taking hold of me like a wrestler, she
whipped the cup from underneath her apron and poured
the filthy mess down my throat before I quite knew what
she was up to. It all reminded me of the eager young
heretics who on encountering a pious, provincial Jewish
lad enlighten him by shoving a hunk of gentile pork
down his throat.

Our Hasidim don't engage in such mitzvoth! Ask
anyone in Poland whether a local Hasid is eager to thrust
a piece of noodle pudding into the mouth of a German,
or to shove frozen calves' foot jelly into someone's
trouser pockets. God forbid! It's true that Polish Hasidim are most eager to perform mitzvoth—but of another
sort. Their hearts are set on good works that are indispensable, on matters of life and death: such as using false
pretenses to deprive someone of the lease to an estate
for the least disservice to a Hasidic rabbi; or incriminat-
ing someone on a trumped-up charge for the sake of a
coquettish gesture from the rebbitzin; or setting fire to
someone's roof to amuse a rabbi's child.

And what about such mitzvoth as blasting a young

wife's reputation by the slander that she has given birth to a bastard, merely because she refused to wear the sheitel, the hideous wig that married Jewish women put on to conceal their own tresses, or to anathematize someone for trimming his beard; and so on. And what about the mitzvoth that Polish Jews perform *leshem mitz-vah,* for the sake of the mitzvah itself—such as perjuring oneself, or resorting to sleight of hand with the double-bottomed measure, or a heavy thumb on the scale, all of these *leshem mitzvah.* . . .

Alas, a Jew must somehow find the means to perform numerous mitzvoth, without which one is not deemed to be an observant Jew. A Jew is duty bound to contribute an offering to the rabbi and rebbitzin, and to stand drinks for the congregation. Then, too, there are the contributions for heating the ritual baths, for a custodian for a white chicken as an expiatory sacrifice on the eve of Yom Kippur, and for a Sadagora shawl; one must invest in various amulets and talismans and charms; and so on. And where is all the money to be obtained? There is no problem for a spoiled and corrupt Hasid who will filch a silver candlestick from the rebbe's table, or steal a string of pearls right from the rebbitzin's neck.

Such exploits are not always successful, of course. But are they not all undertaken for the sake of a mitzvah? This has to do with the preservation of authentic Judaism —so what if a few individuals suffer as a result? Must one not take into consideration that to injure a single individual may benefit scores of others who are more in need? As, for instance, when a Hasid deprives a misnaged of a business deal through false pretenses, or some Hasid forges the signature of the local squire to be a financial instrument, and so on? As a result of such acts the rebbe and his entourage can enjoy the finest accommodations, and hundreds of pilgrims to the rabbi's court can avail themselves of a free drink. The rebbe gets his tithes, the rebbitzin and the children receive presents, and the gabbaim have their palms greased. And in the background there is always the Great Beauty, the Reigning Belle—a mere word or a flirtatious coquettish gesture from her, or even a venial little transgression. . . . With the goyim in authority, it may save the rebbe and hundreds of his followers from imprisonment or perhaps even exile to the bleak wastes of Siberia. Now such mitzvoth are worthwhile: no one's Jewishness is undermined thereby, yet numerous Jews are benefited. But you cannot say this of such an act as shoving gentile pork sausage down a Jewish throat: that condemns a Jewish soul forever and renders the Jew an apostate.

But this isn't at all what I was about to tell you. Just listen to what a witch is capable of. True enough, she accomplished her objective. In due time, her daughter began to manifest the familiar symptoms of pregnancy. But now, believe it or not, my mother-in-law proceeded to make life miserable for me. She cursed and railed at me, I was denied food for days at a time, and finally I was turned out of the house. My dear friends, did I deserve such treatment? I found myself at an impasse: the dragon posted herself at the door and barred me from entering. So what does a man do when he is evicted by his in-laws? There is no alternative but to make his way to a rebbe and a *hevra borsht*. So I snatched up and bundled together my few belongings and set out on foot to the court of a rebbe. What I heard and saw there during the first day I shall now delineate for you, with such wisdom as to engrave my story on the memories of generations yet to come.

25

Homiletics and pyrotechnics—let the people wake!

I arrived at the regal court of the rebbe at noon on Friday, and I would swear under oath that it might have been the annual fair at Berditchev. The court swarmed with Jews, men and women, young and old; noise and confusion filled the air; people were dashing about insanely, like poisoned rats. The entire scene was pandemonium: thumbs jabbing, hands gesticulating, arms flailing, elbows jostling, ritual earlocks shaking, people stepping on one another's corns, smoking, spitting, casting aspersions, pushing back their skullcaps, unbuttoning their long gabardines, loosening their sashes to let the ends sweep the floor: a packed undulating mass of humanity whose uproar was louder than a dozen flour mills grinding all at once.

I stood there stupefied, unable to grasp what was happening around me. My head swam, and I was all but fainting with vertigo. Suddenly, an appalling noise of shrieks and sobs reached my ears. Looking around, I made out the figure of a poor browbeaten Jew being pushed from behind by a wild-looking, disheveled

woman with her face twisted up and her entire body
jerking as though with convulsions. While she propelled
her companion forward she kept crying, "To the rebbe!
To the rebbe! Hurry!" Puzzled and dismayed by the
spectacle, I turned to a Hasid standing near me and
asked in an unsteady voice if he could tell me what it was
all about.

"Ignoramus!" the Hasid exclaimed, turning to look
at me with a hoot of derision. "Tell you what it's all
about? What, you never heard of a tzaddik? Where do
you come from? The backwoods somewhere, I suppose.
But before you came here you must have heard something of our saintly rabbi—all the miracles and wonders
he has performed, which were enough to astonish not
only this present world but also the world to come. No
other tzaddik ever attained so many revelations of the
Divine Presence as he has done! So now, young man, do
you understand what it's all about?"

I stood there like an idiot, gazing meekly at him
without a word to say. He must have been affected by my
humility and confusion, for now his tone became kind-
lier. "Nu, I can see that you are an honest lad, only not
quite dry behind the ears. Just pay attention, now, and
I will make everything clear in a very few words, since I
must hurry to get ready for the prayers before the Sabbath service."

This golden opportunity brought me beside myself
with joy, as the Hasid proceeded. "The woman became
ill about four years ago—a thing like that could happen
any day, everybody feels a little off now and then. She
tried some quack remedies and the trouble seemed to go
away. But then before a month went by she was having
fits: her body would shake all over, she'd laugh and cry
by turns until finally she'd fall into a faint for fifteen
minutes or so, and afterward she would wake up as

though nothing at all peculiar had happened. But the spasms got to be more and more frequent, she grew haggard and depressed, and within a year she appeared to be losing her mind. At least that is what those Berliners, those so-called enlightened ones—may their names and their memories be wiped out!—kept saying. Only it wasn't unsoundness of mind at all. What her parents and her husband, along with the relatives and local Hasidim, all failed to comprehend, was that it was almost certainly—"

"A dybbuk!" I exclaimed, smug as a clam in its shell at high tide. (A dybbuk, for the benefit of you ignoramuses, is an incubus with Jewish trappings—the soul of a dead sinner that has taken up residence in the body of a living person.)

"Brilliantly deduced!" the Hasid responded, beaming. "It has to be a dybbuk—how not? So then the woman's family called a conference, and decided that her husband should bring her to our saintly sage so that the dybbuk could be exorcised. No sooner said than done: her husband came with her to our town and steered her to the rabbi. As soon as the rabbi, with his piercing eyes, had taken one look at her, he knew his visitor was in the worst sort of peril. You understand what that means? But in order not to frighten the husband, with pretended calm the rabbi tried to reassure him. 'Don't lose heart. The Lord of the Universe is all-powerful! I'll give you an amulet, a *kamea*, to take along with you. Once you are safely back home, put this *kamea* around her neck, and without doubt the Almighty will have mercy on her and restore her to health. Oi, oi, oi—alas, she is greatly in need of compassion.'

"You understand the meaning of those last words of his? So the couple returned home—and now listen and marvel. The minute the husband, adhering strictly to the rabbi's instructions, put the *kamea* around his wife's neck, she began to babble in a voice containing all of the tremolos and falsettos of a cantor vocalizing the liturgy. Whoever heard her had no doubt that she was possessed by the dybbuk of a cantor who had transgressed during his lifetime on earth, or else misbehaved at his prayers, and whose soul was apparently being ostracized in the other world. Presumably the outcast soul had been groping for a refuge until at last it found one by entering the body of this Jewish woman.

"Her fits became more frequent, and with each one the dybbuk's voice would demand, 'Take me at once to the person who gave me this *kamea!*' Well, the poor woman was plagued so unmercifully by the dybbuk that eventually she had to be brought again to our rabbi.

"The spiritual leader recognized her the moment she arrived at the rabbinical court, and addressed the dybbuk directly. 'I command you to tell me at once who you are and how you entered the body of this woman!'

" 'Oh, rebbe, I am ashamed to mention my name in public!' cried the dybbuk in a piteous voice. The rabbi then ordered all out of his chamber, except for his two personal synagogue wardens, and once again commanded the dybbuk, 'State this very minute who you are!'

" 'But there are still two strangers in this room!' pleaded the dybbuk.

" 'Fool! You happen to be lodged in a woman, and how can a woman be left without a chaperon?' howled the rabbi.

"Whereupon the dybbuk smacked his lips—although some Berliners, some enlightened ones—may the names and the very memory of them be erased!—contend that it was the Jewess who smacked her lips, since a soul has no such equipment. But who gives heed to those mockers? Now the incubus began a loud wail. 'Woe is me, that so hallowed a sage is commanding me to reveal my identity in public! All my life I served as a cantor in the great synagogue at Tarebarevke, and with my chanting and prayer I invariably moved the congregation to penitence and real tears, for truly I prayed to the Lord with the greatest fervor and devotion. And if only one of all the angels whom I called forth by my prayers had extended a helping hand, I would not be enduring such torments in this woman's belly. . . . But it seems the Lord of the Universe wished to subject me to temptation, for I was saddled with a demon so wicked that I could not subdue him and so—heaven preserve us —I was caught in his toils! And to add further to the disgrace—woe, woe to my poor soul—the transgression would have to occur in the synagogue vestibule, of all places. It was the synagogue warden's cook—may she never win redemption—it was that impudent woman who made me a sinner both in this world and the one that was to come. And now because of her I must roam through the underworld for God only knows how long.'

" 'But did you sin voluntarily or under compulsion?' the rabbi asked.

" 'Oh, rebbe—the Lord Himself knows I acted under compulsion!' the dybbuk wailed. 'My fine appearance was my downfall. She became a frequent visitor to the synagogue, this brazen woman did, after she took a fancy to me. And one day at dusk, just before the prayers, but while the synagogue was still empty, this wicked creature appears in the entry, all decked out, and asks me to come with her to the synagogue warden. As I am about to start out she grabs my arm and begins raising a rumpus, shouting, "Don't think you can play with me the way Joseph did with Potiphar's wife!" I ran outside, shouting that this woman was trying to seduce me. Suddenly I found myself in double jeopardy, as worshipers began coming toward the synagogue. And then suddenly I was seized with passionate desire. Woe is me, woe to my sinful soul—I was trapped, I could not withstand the temptation.'

" 'Did you, for this grave sin, at least do ardent penance all your life?' persisted the rebbe.

" 'Woe is me!' wailed the dybbuk. 'From that moment onward she had me under her thumb. I was now oblivious of my very life, and indeed I died that same year. When I reached the other world, the celestial tribunal ordered me to purgatory for an entire year; after that, I was commanded to inhabit the realm of chaos, where sinners await redemption, still unaware of my condition as a corpse. . . . For three years I drifted about, enduring agony, in this condition. Then I was notified from up there of my state as a corpse and of my situation in the realm of chaos. By then I was in terror of facing the world of the living, and went to hide in a cemetery, in the midst of the little children's graves, still searching for a place of refuge.

" 'One day this Jewess appeared in the cemetery, on a visit to the grave of her child, and since she happened to be menstruating at the time, I was given celestial permission to creep into her body, and to find shelter there from the miserable realm of chaos and all those demons of destruction that had been continually persecuting me.'

"Coming to himself as though from a trance, the rebbe called out, 'In the name of our saintly patriarchs I command you to depart from this woman at once and take yourself off to where you belong!'

"The dybbuk did not answer a word.

" 'In the name of all the saintly sages, I command you to depart from this woman!' cried the rabbi again, but still the dybbuk was mum. Did you ever hear of such impudence? A third time, the rebbe roared with the voice of a lion, 'Dybbuk, I command you in the name of the saintly Reb Kakhtzi Sirkover'—here, you understand, he was referring to himself—'the high priest of righteousness, to depart at once from this woman and take yourself off to where you belong!'

"On hearing the rebbe's name, the dybbuk was frightened out of his wits and fell to pleading. 'Rebbe, since nothing is concealed from you, you know that I myself would wish to escape from so abominable a place. But what can I do when a dreadful angel is posted as a sentry before this woman, barring my way?'

"The rebbe now addressed him in a mollifying tone. 'Just go out of her, and I will pray up a *tikkun olam* for you, so you can be freed from all sin through the transmigration of your soul.'

"Now the dybbuk wailed, 'Oh, holy rebbe, the Angel of Destruction and swarms of evil spirits are on the prowl everywhere, and the minute I am outside, they will snatch me and tear me to bits, like a lot of wild animals.' The Berliners—may every name and every remembrance of them all be wiped out—poke fun at this, jeering over the idea that a frail female body could offer protection to a dybbuk against evil spirits and the Angel of Destruction —but after all, what do such vulgar blockheads know about anything? Anyhow, after finally losing all patience, the rabbi shouted, 'Come out! I command you to come out of there, impudent and worthless being!'

"At this the dybbuk displayed his evil nature by declaring, 'I will go since you decree it, but on one condition—that I be allowed to break one of her limbs for a quid pro quo.'

"At this the rebbe screamed to his gabbaim, 'Get this sinner out of here! He died unrepentant—the celestial tribunal will not permit him to repent any longer. Redeeming him is a hard question!'

"Do you comprehend the vision, the sagacity of our hallowed tzaddik? Hard, yes—but *not* impossible.

"And so for almost a year this woman and her husband have been maintained in Sirkov at the rebbe's expense, and every day the dybbuk compels his victim to visit the rebbe in the synagogue, where she sobs and wails before the Holy Ark on behalf of the cantor's wicked soul, in the hope that through the merit of the holy sage it will be redeemed along with all the other souls in Israel, and taken once again under the wing of the Divine Presence. Well, this may not be a total penitence, but a day will come. . ."

The Hasid had related all of this to me with such vivacity and fervor that like him I lost sight of a fundamental point: in sober fact, this rebbe had thus far failed totally to exorcise the dybbuk. And likewise I became infected with the Hasid's enthusiasm, and proceeded to recount the miracle to others a hundred times over, adding new exploits and embellishments with each retelling. For all of us, there is that shiver of excitement, that glow of devotion as we seek to attain the celestial realm. But to this very day not a soul, it would seem, has yet paused to take stock of just what constitutes the divine miracle of attainment, or whether it amounts to a prize worth aiming for.

26

*The life beyond is a realm of milk and
honey, replete with all sorts of pleasures—
the life here offers at best little more than a
slug of schnapps and an oaten wafer, and
is replete with nothing but humiliation and
shabby intrigues*

I groped my way through the regal court of the rebbe on
my way to the rabbi's private suite. I found the huge
outer chamber almost bare of furniture but swarming
with Hasidim, young and old, including women and children, all being herded and jostled toward one locked
door. There was noise and cursing and confusion, as at
a horse fair, much spitting and clearing of throats, and
a mighty blowing of noses; and from the moment the
door was opened, the rebbe's synagogue wardens let go
with their fists and began to curse like troopers. In the
melee that ensued, youthful Hasidim were knocked
down with absolute impartiality as to age and sex; even
impoverished scholars and Men of Righteousness were
not spared by the wardens. Priority was given, of course,
above all to the nouveaux riches and wealthy lessees of
the postal and other services, the tax-farmers, contrac-
tors and communal and other favorites holding similar
posts. Along with the rest of the ordinary people, I
managed somehow to squeeze in through the open door,
and although I came in for my share of blows, they were

worth putting up with because I found myself at last in the anteroom leading to the rabbi's study. There were several chairs, but these were reserved for the pillars of the community. Along the east wall, not far from the study door, a rudely constructed sideboard held various items of food and drink intended for the gabbaim and other members of the rebbe's entourage. Two of the gabbaim stood guard at the closed door to the study. One of these, a ruggedly muscular sort, did not leave his post for so much as a second; the other, who had a potbelly, a bulging red neck, and huge paws, wandered off now and then, generally in the direction of the buffet. This was none other than Mekhtzie, the rabbi's right-hand man, and chief of all the gabbaim.

As I entered, I noticed Mekhtzie at work stowing a smoked fish onto a shelf of the sideboard. When I edged my way toward the study door, with the suddenness of a bolt of lightning Mekhtzie administered a blow to my chin that sent me reeling, and then went on fussing with the fish. As soon as I pulled myself together, I went over to Mekhtzie and handed him a two-kopeck coin—which amounted to all the money I had in the world. He grinned, took another swipe at me, and then let me into the rabbi's study.

How can I describe to you, dear readers, the awesome impression made on me, a young zealot from nowhere, by one glimpse of the grandeur and luxury of the rabbi's inner sanctum? You would then readily understand what a pauper feels on suddenly finding himself in the royal palace! The rabbi was seated on a white armchair with gilded back and legs, upholstered in red velvet. Standing before him was a handsomely carved taboret containing a silver coffee service. The rebbe himself was dressed in silk and velvet, down to his shiny slippers, which were trimmed in silk brocade. All the doors and windows were draped in artistically embroidered cashmere cloth; the rich furnishings were all upholstered in silk and velvet; there were mirrors in gilded frames reaching from floor to ceiling; the floor was covered by a lustrous Persian rug; a chandelier with three tiers of candles was suspended from the ceiling by chains of bronze. In one corner was an ornate bed with eiderdowns covered in blue silk; vases and quantities of bibelots in silver and gold were displayed in etageres along the walls.

At that moment the rebbitzin happened to be standing in the doorway leading to the bedroom, and her jewelry stunned me still more than Mekhtzie's blows—and possibly even more than a streak of lightning on a pitch-dark night would have done. A long string of pearls hung about her neck; her blouse and her traditional headdress were studded with emeralds and rubies, she had a gold ring on every one of her fingers, and the diamonds in her earrings flashed like nighttime beacons. Here, in short, wealth, glory, eclat, distinction and all imaginable worldly pleasures were on view at once. I shook the hand of the rabbi and rushed out to the courtyard, where I sighed almost with relief after witnessing so overwhelming a spectacle.

Once my agitation had subsided, I made out the rebbe's house of study in the courtyard. Entering, I found a vivid contrast to the rabbi's study. The crowd here was made up of unkempt vagabonds, down at the heels and out at the elbows, their faces sallow and emaciated, their heads shaved, beards and ritual earlocks disheveled, smoldering eyes set deep in their sockets, as is usual in victims of tuberculosis. They were all worn out, beaten down and used up—yet they seemed oblivious to their condition, and went on working themselves into a state of artificial enthusiasm by taking sips of

brandy or reading legends concerning the lives of tzaddikim in general and of their rabbi in particular, or doing
Hasidic dances, or hearing an account of some new miracle, and so on and on. Here, in short, were souls without
bodies, the shades of insubstantial ghosts aimlessly flit-
ting, hurrying and scurrying as they danced attendance
on a chimera in an idiotic paradise. They served this
chimera and ministered to it; for its sake they sacrificed
themselves and were hopelessly degraded.

As soon as I entered, I was stupefied by the buzz and
agitation. One group of congregants—ancient, middle-
aged, and young—were milling about by the east wall,
while another, heading toward the exit, moved in the
opposite direction. Yarmulkas were pushed back, prayer
shawls were draped about heads or had slipped off and
were trailing on the floor; one worshiper ran with the
phylactery that is placed on the forehead clutched in one
hand and an oaten wafer in the other; another scurried
with the leather strap of an arm phylactery trailing on the
floor; still another was bent over a volume of the *Zohar*,
all the while nursing a tumbler of schnapps underneath
the lectern; not far from him a swaying devotee with
prayer shawl over his head, was trying at the same time
to down a mouthful of food; some rocked, others rested
their heads on lecterns, slapped their hands against
walls, or snapped their fingers; some were smoking pipes
or cigarettes; one zealot was trying to extract a bandanna
from his neighbor's pocket, while another was busily
knotting the ritual fringes of two worshipers' prayer
shawls together while they recited the Eighteen Benedictions. In one corner was a knot of congregants engaged
in debate, which had so stirred some youthful worshipers
that in their fervor they were gesticulating like windmills.
There was what amounted to a pyrotechnical display of
grimaces and twitchings. Someone was intoning, "All

hearts will rejoice and the heart will be gladdened,"
while someone else chanted, "They were slaughtered in
the northern sector of the Temple." Still another exhorted, "Seek not to hide yourself," and a fourth prayed,
"May the false gods be brought down." A fifth, however,
spoke loudest and clearest of all: "Hey, what about my
commission as middleman?" So it went. The sum total
was deafening.

I withdrew to a corner, put on my prayer shawl
and phylacteries, and was about to begin praying
when it came to my attention that a door in the south
wall was slightly open. At the time I did not yet know
that in this synagogue the rabbi maintained a small,
secluded place of worship which no one else dared
enter. At first I was merely interested in having a look
inside, but then I became captivated by the neat, well-
kept chamber with its splendid Ark, its silken curtain
and ornate table covered by an embroidered cloth
with gold fringe, not to mention a gilded armchair
upholstered in red velvet. Consumed with curiosity
and totally unobserved, I slipped into the secret
chamber, where my attention was at once drawn to a
beautiful bookcase filled with luxurious editions of talmudic tractates, gilt-edged and bound in morocco
leather. Cautiously, giving way to an irresistible urge,
I opened one of the folios. But—wonder of wonders!
—whichever folio I opened, the pages somehow stuck
together, as though just lately delivered from the
printers and as yet unsullied by the eye of any reader.
Then it occurred to me that this must be another
miracle wrought by the rabbi, to prevent outsiders
from peering into his holy tractates! I was about to
slip guiltily from the room when I noticed some written sheets on the floor. I supposed they had fallen

out of one of the tractates, and assuming them to be one of the rebbe's esoteric commentaries on the Torah, I was naturally eager to read them over. But they turned out to be the itinerary of a journey by the saintly sage. On the following pages the entire text is given verbatim, along with a few commentaries of my own.

27

The itinerary of the rebbe's fund-raising tour—the rebbe's table, the white loaves on it, and the marvelous tales concerning it

Itinerary was the title of the log of the rebbe's journey, set down entirely in his own handwriting.

Itinerary

> *On the third day after the reading of the weekly portion of the Law (sidra Va'etchanan), I shall set forth, because of my needs, on the following itinerary.*
>
> *From here I go first to milk that dry cow, the lessee Moshka Torba, "The Sack." If he gives me eighteen birds,* I will promise him and his spouse a male child, but if he gives me any less I will only promise him a girl. And if he gives me nothing, then, I shall ruin him. Also, I do not forget to take from him the cow he milks for silver, his silver canister, which I can put to much better use.*
>
> *From "The Sack" I go on to the lessee of the postal service, to take his spotted horse, which shall be a companion for me, and also take from him twice eighteen birds by way of a contribution. From the postmaster I go to the city of Stukelka [Rattle] to apprise the local nabob of what I know about him.*

*I.e., rubles

From the nabob I make a journey to the congregation of
Vetzeeoni, amid much acclaim, and there I give the local rebbe his
reprimand: why did he fail to visit me on Sabbath Hanukkah?
There I expect to garner a hundred birds. From the rabbi of
Vetzeeoni I make my way to Merinow, where I hope to bag no less
than a thousand birds and also to acquire a carriage from the local
millionaire.

From Merinow I journey to Tchulent [Prunes and Potatoes]
and to the congregations of Weisbral and Pilowitz—and should
realize about three and a half thousand rubles from them both.

And it may be that I shall go on to the congregation of Altov,
where I received the title of maggid [preacher]. Then I proceed to
Krokodilevka and blast the community there: Why did they contribute only two hundred instead of two hundred and fifty birds
to me, as we agreed? And from there I make my way to Zodkowetz
to give my good brother a little talking-to. Why does he arrogate
to himself the right of covering the territory reserved for me? Also,
I shall have the sheriff there dismissed from his post, and I am the
one who knows how to go about it. Everyone will accept this move
on my part as a notable miracle. And I shall come home again.

Estimate of Proceeds from the Tour

From "The Sack" I should receive twice sixty eggs, one sheep,
a full tub of butter and two ducks, plus a gold coin. From the wife
of the lessee of the postal service I shall have to take a loaf of sugar.
As for the wife of that dry cow, the lessee at Stukelka, I shall have
to take two ducks, two hens, and two rubles from her knotted
handkerchief. From the wife of the tax-farmer in the town of
Vetzeeoni I shall take eighteen gold pieces and the ring from her
middle finger, because of a certain incident which, except for
herself, is known to me alone. From the prostitute in Tchulent I
shall extract eighteen rubles, as well as the valuable stickpin which
the Talne Hasid filched from the contributions and gave her before
she would kiss him, as I learned from her own lips. From the
informer in Pilowitz and the pimp in Altov (I am before the

willows by the streams)—*I shall obtain some religious articles, which I need as much as I need a hole in the head. In all the towns I visit I shall scourge both the living and the dead, as surely as my name is Shliomka*—

After perusing this document, I was able to judge the conceit of the tzaddik of Sirkov, owning up to the audacity of a Shliomka. And with a hopeless impracticality, I yearned to be worthy of arriving at the status of this Shliomka! And I felt, though it had been a premonition, that there would be a time for all things! From the rabbi's sanctum I went back to the synagogue, once all the Hasidim had departed, and I said my prayers.

Going out into the courtyard, I discovered a throng of Hasidim, young and old, taking white loaves from the kitchen maid. I elbowed forward but it was no use: the kitchen maid would not so much as look at me. At that time I didn't yet know how to deal with the rebbe's maidservants. But as things turned out, the Hasid standing next to me got a second loaf from the kitchen maid (by what means I don't know) and by mistake, as he was about to put it into his pocket, thanks to the jostling of the crowd, slipped it into mine instead. Hurrying back into the synagogue, I discovered that, along with the white loaf, a silver needlecase and a necklace had also found their way into my pocket. Whether these had been taken from inside the kitchen maid's dress while the Hasid snatched the white loaf, or whether she had offered them to him voluntarily as a keepsake, I could not be sure. It was not until later that I got to the bottom of this mystery.

Dusk was closing in. The congregants had now all returned from the ritual baths and recited the prayers for Sabbath eve, and the huge table was being set for the Sabbath feast. You should have seen the wealth of luxurious furnishings they put on the table: the thirty-six candelabra, each holding from three to ten candlesticks, the twelve gold-plated vessels, the two silver goblets, the three porcelain bowls and the four porcelain tureens, the ten dozen silver spoons and forks, not to mention all the fine crystal and porcelain tableware.

Thus you can understand why there were so many retainers at the court of the rabbi—the ever-present fear that some Hasid might be tempted to make off with one or more valuable objects. After the table had been set, there was the wait by the assemblage for the rabbi to appear and recite the *Kiddush,* the benediction over a cup of wine. The wait was not so very long—no more than four or five hours. Everyone supposed the rabbi to be engaged in private devotions, or in poring over some talmudic tractate, or in communing with the celestial world. Eventually I learned that the rebbe simply took a nap every Friday at dusk to recover from the strains of greeting the scores of visitors and pilgrims who came thronging in from the provinces for the Sabbath festivity. And, indeed, how was a nature of such spirituality as the rebbe's to contend with the hustle and bustle of scores of guests in one day, and then go on with a festival lasting almost until dawn? Of course he needed a bit of rest—though who knows whether it was really rest as he slept the sleep of an exalted soul, especially before the coming of the Sabbath Queen. . . .

However that may be, through the hours of waiting the various cliques among the guests were engaged in discussing every sort of wisdom, both religious and secular. Thus one group argued about the carob-pod, about nightmares and the Lost Ten Tribes, and about the River Sambatyon, which is exceedingly turbulent for six days of the week but invariably is at rest on the Sabbath; another set bandied words over the rabbi's dappled horse and spotted citrons; still another coterie was logic-chopping over the legend of the great Maimonides, who is supposed to have dismembered a human body and then put it into a tun of wine—out of which the dismembered man, six years, five months, four weeks and three days later, had emerged alive and hale, sound of limb and mind, and full of vinegar. Others spoke in whispers of the rebbe's niece, and of Rahab the harlot, and of the financial wizard of the region. But to me the most interesting group was a cabal off in one corner, absorbed in esoteric obscure queries and conundrums. I edged toward them and kept my ears open; and what I was able to fathom, my dear sirs, I now share with you word for word. You may laugh all you will, but I assure you once again that such profound thinkers as one finds among Hasidim in Poland are not to be matched elsewhere. I shall give here their arguments concerning steam and electric power, and then I am sure you will agree with me. Moreover, I should like the common people to learn as well something about the telegraph, about locomotives and steam engines generally—subjects no one could expound to them as lucidly as can our Polish Hasidim. They began by discussing whether a ghost can give birth to twins. Then they went on to catalepsy until finally they came to the telegraph. Only listen: you will be certain to sit up and take notice.

28

Jews unearth clues proving that all discoveries and inventions are mentioned in the Torah, and although it is all utter nonsense the fools persist in their folly

The Hasidic Telegraph

"It is obvious!" an upright Hasid declared with a sour face. "No doubt you understand many things. But I tell you frankly that all worldly knowledge comes from the *sitra achra,* from the camp of the devil, and there you have it! That goes for this telegraph thing too. The Evil One who rules over our world because of our many transgressions, and a Jew who is free of worldly lusts (such, for instance, as our rebbe—may his life be long!) can play, that the sage of Bratzlav—heaven preserve us!—strayed from the path of righteousness. Why, then, do you babble such nonsense? Listen, it's common knowledge that the Evil One always prevails over the Holy Spirit. But neither will the Evil One ever be completely devoid of the sparks of righteousness, since Jews have dealings therewith and thus replenish its holy sparks. As for what the telegraph itself symbolizes—well, I can explain it for you very simply: the moment a Hasid touches his doorknob, he becomes conscious of everything that has happened or will happen to him from his birth to the day of his death. The same is true of the telegraph—you have only to touch it and it will reveal to the man at the other end everything it has on its mind, because while this is happening both sender and receiver are impelled by the same purpose and joined by the same evil spirit. So what is there that is so hard to understand—what is there that is so baffling?"

"Pardon me, but you talk like an idiot," one of the rebbe's valetudinarian Hasidim responded. "Consider what you just said: if the telegraph is like our rebbe—to make the distinction between the sacred and the profane —then the transmission lines would have to run between the doorknob and our rabbi's armchair."

"Ai, ai, ai!" cried an ardent but emaciated youth, quivering with excitement. "You must be growing senile, if you'll excuse my saying so! That's precisely what we are driving at: whereas the fiend and the Evil One must have a foothold, the Holy Spirit is independent and self-sufficient. You seem to have forgotten how our rebbe had to struggle with the dybbuk in order to exorcise him from the woman of Vetzeeoni, and how the dybbuk pleaded his fear of the demons and the Angels of Destruction who were right there waiting for him to emerge from the woman so they could seize him and send him packing, far beyond the seven seas. Now you can see for yourself that the fiend must have a foothold, be it no more than an afflicted Jewish woman, as long as it is a base of some sort. That is why the telegraph must have transmission wires—to afford a foothold. And here's the proof: the lessee of the postal service at Stukelka told me he had witnessed with his own eyes how a wire snapped on a telegraph pole, and the fiendish dybbuk was suddenly deprived of all its power until the loose ends of the wire were connected again. Now, can all this electric business be compared to our rabbi?"

"Oh, you blockheads!" chimed in another unkempt Hasid. "You're woolgathering; you've all missed the point. Actually, the telegraph is a very simple contraption. The whole thing follows the ways of nature: when the wire is shaken at one end it is bound to vibrate at the other end as well, and so one communicates with people on the other side of the world—"

"Hold on!" broke in still another fanatic. "You are arguing to no purpose. All you have to do is simply to pick up the Book of Psalms, and there you'll find the whole telegraph business in minute detail. The Book of Psalms goes on to say, 'And he shall be like a tree planted by the rivers of water, that bringeth forth his fruit in his season; his leaf also shall not wither; and whatsoever he doeth shall prosper.' There's the whole telegraph business for you! So why squabble over such absurdities? That goes for the telegraph as well as the locomotive and all the other mechanical devices. Doesn't the Song of Songs mention the chariots without horses? And how would one drive without horses unless there were steam engines? And Holy Writ goes on to say, 'The coal provided steam.' *Nardi* undoubtedly implies steam—how could it not? And, indeed, they covered the distance from Tzorur to Ein-Gedi in one minute—so there you have all that railroad business in a nutshell."

While this discussion was going on, the rabbi came into the synagogue and began to chant the benediction hallowing the Sabbath. The rebbe's wife and his daughters and daughters-in-law, each one of them bedizened with every sort of jewel from head to toe, and all of them (with the exception of the rabbi's wife, since she was already showing her age) dressed in the latest fashion, so that it was hard to believe they were even Jewish. After the benediction the rebbe took the seat of honor, and was flanked by his sons-in-law. Then came the uncouth relations, the overfed lessees and other fat cats; the

lesser rebbes and dayyanim, along with ritual slaughterers and associated synagogue hangers-on, came last. All
the ragamuffins and members of the *hevra borsht*—bathed
and spruced up for the Sabbath, each one clutching a
white loaf—climbed onto chairs for a better view.

As soon as everything appeared to be in order,
Mekhtzie sprang up, clambered onto the table in his
stocking feet, and proceeded to reshuffle the seated
guests. First of all he ordered a visiting rebbe from a
small town to move back and let the wealthy lessee of
Stukelka have his place. The visiting rebbe hesitated,
looking beseechingly at the rabbinic host in the hope of
an intercession by the latter "for the honor of the
Torah." But although their eyes met, the host managed
to shift his gaze from that of his guest as though nothing
had happened, and Mekhtzie howled at the chagrined
rabbinic visitor, "Move on, you upstart! Have you no
manners? Barging in like that! Where did you think you
were—back on the farm?" When the visiting rabbi lingered, still daring to believe that the authority of his
rabbinic host must prevail, Mekhtzie grabbed him by the
beard and sent him reeling with no choice but to take his
departure. But the host continued to appear as though
engrossed in thought, and said nothing. Well, perhaps
the small-town rebbe had some sin to atone for. How
else is the incident to be explained? And Mekhtzie went
on with his task: those he considered *deserving* moved up,
and those he considered *undeserving* were shifted to the
rear. He swore at some, raised his fist at others, and still
others he tossed out bodily. One elderly dayyan from
some small town had his fur-trimmed hat snatched off
and flung out of the window. The host, however, continued to sit immersed in thought, even when Mekhtzie
yelled loud enough to wake the dead, "You impudent
bastards, you are humiliating our rebbe!" But how, after

all, can mere death be compared to the exaltation of a rabbinical soul?

Before long a huge platter of stuffed fish was placed on the table, and the saintly rebbe dipped his fingers into the steaming mess (the tzaddikim eat with their fingers, so that nothing may interfere with food as a means of spiritual improvement), and gormandized for a quarter of an hour. The Hasidim standing on the chairs and benches in the rear tried to get to the front by climbing onto the backs and over the heads of those between them and the table; one put his feet into the side pockets of the zealot ahead of him, tearing his gabardine. I kept my eye on the rebbe and saw that he was reluctant to part with the platter before him; I also saw that he kept dipping slices from his white loaf into a glass of schnapps. To this day I cannot imagine what he was trying to do.

The moment he lifted his fingers from the platter, the congregants in the front row made a dive for it, shouting like a lot of coarse peasants scuffling in the street over a leaky keg of vodka. A free-for-all ensued as the noisy zealots jostled, tearing at one another's frayed gabardines, bloodying noses, snatching morsels of the fish and gulping them down with such an ecstasy of enjoyment that the morsels might have been a panacea prescribed by the Angel Raphael himself against every pain and calamity. But why should I deliver myself of such nonsense? Of what importance is the Angel Raphael's panacea as compared with a morsel from a saintly sage's *shiraim*, leavings, which for the Hasidim it is an honor to consume? And so the same scene was reenacted with the serving of the noodle soup, the meat, the potato pudding, and dessert.

When the meal was over, the rebbe rolled his eyes upward, leaned his head against the back of his throne, and began humming a familiar melody that seemed to stir the hearts of those assembled to their very depths. Before long some of the Hasidim had picked up the melody and joined in the chant, twiddling the thumbs they had stuck inside the sashes of their gabardines, and swaying with faces aglow. There was soon a jarring and raucous cacophony of rasping voices. The rest of the congregants hummed in accompaniment, snapping their fingers or drumming on the table, or they whinnied and growled, adding another note to the grotesque spectacle.

But suddenly the tzaddik raised his head and blinked his eyes—and the assembly fell into a silence so deep that you could hear a pin drop. This was a signal that the tzaddik was about to hold forth on the Torah. Consumed with expectancy, the congregants riveted their eyes on their spiritual leader, holding their breaths as though in anticipation of a message from beyond this world. And the saintly rabbi uttered words that tugged at one's heartstrings and inspired one with the fear of God.

Allow me to quote his sermon word for word.

29

The rabbi's sermon is a miracle, the rabbi's wine is a marvel, but the rabbi's youngest son is the eighth wonder of the world

"Ai, ai, ai!" the rebbe began in the voice of a man on his deathbed. "Ai, ai, ai! A Jew must always keep one essential thing in mind, namely, the reason why God made the Jews is simply that a Jew must remove himself from all earthly desires, from everything that smacks in the least of the domination of the physical. Yet to attain this state a Jew must humble himself to an extreme degree, yea, even the degree of total self-abnegation, in the sense of *mah anu*, of 'What are we?' But he must do this in such a manner that he himself does not know that he is nothing. For as soon as a man acknowledges that he is nothing, he becomes something which, God forbid, may lead to pride, to disdain of humility. Thus we read of Father Abraham, 'And his concubine was Reu'mah,' as though Reu'mah had been spelled with an aleph—in a mystical intimation of the interchangeability of an ayyin—which leaves us with *reu mah*, 'Behold, I see what I am, and that I am something.' And this is precisely the point: it is a humility that is rooted in pride, and that leaves a man in the position of one who takes a cleansing ritual bath even while he clutches some loathsome reptile.

"Out of such humility, out of such boastfulness about *beholding that one is something*, there follows, 'She bare also Tebah, and Gaham, and Thahash, and Maachah,' which is to say that this humility gave birth within him to evil desire, even as Holy Writ declares, 'He maketh a slaughter of the disloyal,' a slaughter among those who by their pretended humility falsify the worship of the Creator. And evil desire brings about Gaham—which explains the vehemence of the verse, 'In sin did my mother conceive me.' And this brings about Thahash—that is to say, hypocrisy because of the reference to the many-colored coverings of the Tabernacle. And it all ends with Maachah, which means a scraping off and a reducing to dust. For such humility is *Maach-Yah*—that is to say, it erases the name of God. Consider the letter heh, which in itself has no substance whatever; yet how it shows the true humility of God, blessed be He; for the Almighty created the whole world with it, as the saintly sages put it: '*Behibaram* means *be'heh braam*, He created everything with a heh.' This is precisely the meaning of 'He raiseth the poor out of the dust' which is the opposite of 'He bringeth down to the grave,' so that in due time, the proud one loses himself in the things of this world and becomes devoid of all aspiration.

"Ai, ai, ai! Such worship is an abomination. It is the worship of the misnagedim—it is worship for the worship's sake. This is the meaning of 'the blessings of those who enjoy,' that you worship the Creator for your own pleasure. A man prays, he studies, he observes the mitzvoth, because he finds pleasure in so doing. Then these brazen curs think by such study and prayer they dress up the Almighty in fancy clothes. They rub their own bellies: 'Today we served the Almighty in the best way possible: we prayed much, we studied much, we are completely quit of any debt to Him!' Woe upon this shame and disgrace! Woe upon this insult to prayer! Verily, this is nothing other than idolatry! It is bringing strange fire to the altar of the Lord! A man who is truly righteous, who serves God out of love, never feels satisfied with his worship of the Creator, blessed be He; he never can do enough for the Almighty. On the contrary, the more he prays and studies, the more surely he feels that he has not so much as begun to pray or to study.

"A Jew must always be moving on to the next rung on the ladder. This is what is meant by 'Come, let us go' —never to be standing still. But there is one condition: that this striving upward must never, God forbid, lead to boasting that one has gone 'from strength to strength.' A man must never measure his progress. For no sooner does a man say, as in the Psalm of Degrees, 'I will lift up mine eyes,' than the question immediately arises, 'From whence shall my help come?' Ai, ai, ai! For 'If I ascend up into heaven'—that is if I assure myself that I continue the distance, far away from me. But if 'I make my bed in the depth below'—that is, if with all my worship, I consider myself the lowest of the low, abject beyond measure, why then 'Thou art there!' Thus a Jew must always be on his way but without being conscious of it. For as soon as he realizes that he is on his way, he becomes at once the one meant by the verse 'And he went'—that is, his going causes the anger of God.

"This, in fact, is the meaning—ai, ai, ai—of the verse referring to David, 'When he changed his behavior before Abimelech, who drove him away and he departed.' Here David represents the sum total of Jewish souls, as every sensible person knows. So the Psalmist says that when a soul repeats its deeds, that is, when it makes itself out to be something before Abimelech—that is, before the Father of Kingship, blessed be He—it must make sure that 'he drove him away and he departed': that is, he must drive away the one who goes, in order not to consider himself a mover forward in the worship of the Creator, blessed be He. Thus, in the whole matter of worship and prayer, no man may consider his own self. We do not pray to the Almighty for ourselves, for our physical needs, for what we lack in this world, since, 'What is man, that Thou art mindful of him?' The only thing we must pray for is revealed in the verse, 'I am with Him in time of trouble'—for the Divine Presence, for the exiled Shechinah, so to speak, for the Shechinah in trouble. But as soon as a Jew begins to believe that by his study and prayer he is doing the Almighty a favor, to him you must apply the test of *aizehu hasid:* Who is pious? He who behaves with piety toward the Creator. Here the word *aizehu* is used in the sense of *I-Kavod* [Ichabod]: The glory is departed—which means that a person who believes he is doing God a favor is no pious man at all.

"So we see that the entire essence and substance of being Jewish is to strip oneself of materialism through total denial of one's own existence. But if, God forbid, one should stumble into pride through much prayer and study, then a man must immediately hasten to the righteous man of his own generation. For the wickedness of delay is the messenger of God's presence—that is, it is the advocate who uses his influence, who after receiving an appropriate gift can transform a fault into virtue, or the soiled into what is clean, softening austere judgments, as in the sacred verse, 'Though your sins be as scarlet, they shall be as white as snow.' "

Following his discourse the rebbe meditated for a quarter of an hour. Then he raised his head and whispered, "Wine!"—whereupon Mekhtzie climbed onto the table to carry out his assignment. "The wealthy and distinguished member of our congregation pays honor to our rabbi and the assembled guests," he began with a gesture to one dignitary, who signaled to him in turn that he was offering twice eighteen bottles of the finest wine. "Hirsh, the communal leader of Krokodilevka!" Mekhtzie went on, pointing to another guest, who announced that he was contributing three times eighteen bottles of the best wine and twice eighteen bottles of ordinary vintage. "The tax-farmer of Khabarevke!" Mekhtzie continued, and the response was a pledge of twice eighteen bottles of high-grade vintage. "The gabbai of the burial society of the holy congregation of Vetzeeoni!"—and the response was, "Eighteen bottles of the best wine and three bottles of ordinary vintage. "This," the official explained, "is in gratitude for a secular teacher who dropped dead this year. And if, God willing, a few more secular teachers should give up the ghost in the coming year, the contribution will double. Am I right, Reb Nochum? What do you say, rebbe?" To which the rabbi mumbled, "Easy, there."

After he had called on all the adult guests, Mekhtzie said, "Each of the young men here will contribute two bottles of first-grade wine. Whoever objects do so openly and give his name." Naturally, no one dared affront the rebbe even though he might find himself without money for the return trip. He made no mention, however, of the *hevra borsht* or the crew of ragamuffins in general. Then he turned to the rebbe's wine dealer—it was the rebbe's own oldest son who maintained a winery on the premises —with a cry of, "Mendel, bring up the wine!" Of the approximately twenty times eighteen bottles of high-grade wine and the twenty gallons of ordinary vintage that had been pledged, only a few bottles of the best vintage and a gallon of the ordinary borsht were placed on the table. And on Saturday evening the guests in attendance were ordered to pay at the rate of two rubles for a bottle of the best vintage and two rubles per gallon of the ordinary kind. The guests seated at the table were served the good wine in tea glasses, while the rest of the Hasidic crowd were handed small beakers of the ordinary stuff. Our rebbe handed the drink to each one in person, wishing him *l'hayyim*. You can imagine the commotion, the shoving and jostling among the Hasidim seated on benches away from the main table, since everyone was anxious to get close to the rabbi, or at any rate not to be left out altogether.

I did not escape my share of being pushed and pummeled and stepped on before the rabbi wished me *l'hayyim*. One was ready to go through fire and water—and even to submit to *kiddush ha-Shem,* the supreme sacrifice—for the sake of hearing the rebbe wish one good luck. Fortunately, no one was ignored; everyone had the privilege of going through this ritual with the rabbi and was contented as a clam at high tide. And the things I heard from the Hasidim about the rebbe's hands are past describing. For instance, if someone remarked, "It is almost as though Moses raised his hand," another might rejoin angrily, "Blockhead, can't you do better than that?"—to which the reply would be, "Fool, I'm telling you all Israel saw that great hand."

When the benediction was over, the rebbe withdrew to his private chamber and the Hasidim went their ways, some of them to the houses of their sons or sons-in-law, others to see the rebbe's youngest son, a child of eight.

Here, indeed, you came face to face with an angel! Have you ever observed a child engrossed in ripping the pages out of holy books and tearing off their covers? Nonetheless, may I have as many good years as there were old men there! Men of seventy or eighty addressed him as "rabbi" and knelt down so that he might bless them! Lessees consulted him concerning the squires they did business with; commissioners of the postal service spoke with him about their horses; tax-farmers sought his advice about cattle; merchants, about trade; and the Hasidic flock in general asked his help in dealing with wayward thoughts. . . . It didn't really matter how he responded: he was, after all, a celestial manifestation. Sometimes he answered as a child would, sometimes as a lunatic; occasionally his answer would be to pull an old man's beard or ritual sidelocks, or to snatch off someone's skullcap. I am ready to take an oath on the Bible about the rumors of hundreds of miracles said to have been performed by this angel, this eight-year-old last-born son of our rebbe, and I can swear as well that all the Jewish communities in Poland are calling on the Lord for just such children of their own. Meanwhile, he is well into his ninth year and yet actually deficient in elementary schooling. But why should I discuss this spoiled youngster? In fact, he has already surpassed me in ingenuity, in the liveliness of his imagination! If all the Yiddish authors in Poland together owned a part of the value of the gifts showered upon this brat, they would not have to plead with those same cultivated donors for a position that pays ten rubles a month, and listen to the unfailing response: "Excuse me, but what use would you be in business, since you are a writer?" Well, is it not better to be the son of a rabbi who tears up books than a father of children who writes them?

In short, the Sabbath day was no worse than the Sabbath evening. The rabbi's discourse in the afternoon, and especially during the third Sabbath meal, was inexpressibly beautiful, since it was beyond comprehension and was couched in the grand style of Avremel Hirik. And it goes without saying, where the meal to usher out the Sabbath Queen is concerned, that one swallow of the rabbi's borsht is worth anything else you could name. To put the whole thing in a nutshell: if paradise is as gratifying as a Sabbath at the rabbi's court, I pity the heretics who, alas, must be deprived of such bliss for eternity.

30

*Without virtues and without morals,
without the Torah and without prayers—
yet, swift was my rise to greatness*

Little by little, at the synagogue, I began to be in my
element. I was soon regarded by the *hevra borsht* as one
of their own; I was on good terms with the rabbi's male
and female servants, and within a year I had gotten into
the good graces of the wardens, the rebbe's gabbaim.
Already they had begun to employ me for some of their
missions, such as paying a visit to the Gosedar synagogue
for the purpose of vilifying its rabbi. That had been a
somewhat risky venture, but I succeeded, thank God!
Then I was commissioned to trail a non-Orthodox rebbe
in the public square at night, and cut off some of his hair.
I also had to hunt down the secular teacher late at night,
and give him a thorough workout under cover of darkness. There were still other tasks of the same sort, naturally.

Word got round of my successful missions, and this
brought me into the good graces of our rebbe's offspring. The rebbitzin would greet me, and even the
rebbe himself would deign to smile on me occasionally.
Once I had gotten on the right side of the rabbinical

family, I found myself being gradually taken into their confidence. Also, in Sirkov there was an old stodgy Hasidic rebbe named Reb Avremele, to whom strays from our congregation brought a *pidyon* from time to time, and now and then this seedy sage would come up with a feeble sort of miracle. And so I would relay gossip and slanders concerning Reb Avremele to our rabbi, who took a certain interest in such things. This service added to my prestige with our rebbe; also, I would occasionally bring him his slippers or summon the rebbitzin to him at night, or collect the *pidyon* notes that accompanied the money offerings and fasten them to a hook in the usual place—namely the rabbinical privy, which was always locked. And I did many other services of this nature.

Once luck has struck, it is certain to strike again. All of a sudden two women made their appearance, each of them noisily declaring Mekhtzie to be her husband and to have deserted her and their small children some fifteen years before. One of the women came from Hirevka and the other from Lazevka, and each produced depositions from rabbis and eyewitnesses; each raised a storm, demanding an immediate divorce and maintenance for themselves and their children.

To add to the polygamistic woes, his third and present wife began clutching at his beard and screaming at the top of her voice, "Let me have a divorce this minute, you old rogue, or I'll slit your throat! You dirty pimp, I won't look at your ugly face any more as long as I live! I want you to promise me a divorce this very minute, in front of the rabbi. You slimy rat, so you thought I didn't know about the thieving and the crime you were carrying on under the rebbe's very nose? May your parents, both of them, sink into the ground and be swallowed up! What happened to the string of pearls that belonged to the rebbitzin's maid, that you gave to your slut—and then took away from her again? You scrofulous son-of-a-bitch, if I really started saying what I know, you wouldn't care for it at all! I know it was you who took the silver crown!" (Several months before, the crown from the rebbe's Torah scroll had been stolen out of the synagogue.) "If you don't consent to a divorce this very minute, I'll advertise a few more of your virtues . . ."

So, to be brief, Mekhtzie had to grant his current wife a divorce, and left in disgrace along with the other two wives—whereupon it was I who replaced him as the rebbe's assistant warden. Putting my best foot forward in this new position, I came into still more favor with the rabbi and the rest of the household, carrying on my duties until the Almighty performed another one of His miracles: Shliomka, the chief gabbai, went to join his ancestors, having succumbed to a fright of some sort, and I was promoted to the status of chief gabbai.

May the name and the memory of the Berliners, those so-called enlightened ones, be wiped out for insisting that at the end of Yom Kippur, Baruch Talner caught Shliomka with his wife and beat him black and blue, and that the poor fellow died of his injuries. That is an outright lie! The actual events were quite different: Shliomka—may he rest in peace—was very anxious to persuade the daughter-in-law of Baruch Shaigetz, the infidel, and not his wife, to become a follower of our rabbi. Take my word for it, so delightful a creature—her beauty was ravishing—would sooner or later have been useful in extracting a favor from some official. He went to every length, naturally, using all his persuasive powers, until she agreed to attend the rebbitzin's house of worship on the eve of Yom Kippur to hear the solemn *Kol Nidre* (so it wasn't the end of Yom Kippur, as rumor had it). After the service he walked home with her, continuing his campaign until she was persuaded to become a devotee of our rebbe. As a result of his great fervor he went with her into the house—the rest of her household being still absorbed in prayer at the Talne synagogue. Indoors they both became so engrossed in pious conversation, and then so oblivious of all else, that their fervor overcame them and they strayed into a bedroom. It was their misfortune, however, to have her husband and father-in-law appear on the scene at just that fateful moment. Not unnaturally, their unexpected arrival curdled the chief gabbai's blood; he went into convulsions that lasted ten days, and he yielded up his kosher soul for the sanctification of the Divine Name, on Hoshana Rabbah, the seventh day of Tabernacles.

Now you can see how far the scoundrels will go in fabricating unheard-of charges, simply to humiliate a great rebbe. But death bore witness to the truth: our rebbe attended Shliomka's funeral, and during his discourse on Hoshana Rabbah he stretched the truth a bit, proclaimed the deceased to have been God-fearing all his life, and absolved him of all guilt. However that may have been, what did it matter now that I was the rabbi's chief gabbai?

Could anyone, I ask you, be more fortunate than I was? Still bad luck is likely to creep on good fortune. A thing befell me that I least expected and that almost toppled me from my high status. And what was the cause of it all? Only listen to the lengths those Berliners, so-called enlightened ones, will go to in order to blaspheme and humiliate our rabbi.

One Friday morning I was sitting alone in the rebbe's anteroom, writing a letter to the community of Hirevka to urge against undue delay, for God's sake, in secretly denouncing their secular teacher to the authorities, and in delivering the golden Hanukkah menorah they had promised our rabbi as a gift some time before.

But just as I was about to bring the rabbi the letter to be approved and signed there was a frantic pounding on the door. I knew no one ever visited the rabbi at this time except in emergency. Opening the door, I was confronted by a distraught-looking young woman, who tearfully begged admission to see the rabbi—and at once, since she had come from another town and was in a hurry to get back. Seeing me hesitate, she slipped a three-ruble note into my hand, and I proceeded to write a *kvittel,* a dictated memorandum of the petition she wished to submit to the rabbi. And what do you suppose that petition was? Let me quote it, word for word:

I, Bassia, the daughter of Esther, implore the rabbi to pray for me, so that the demon may cease haunting me every night, and also that I may be chaste for my husband's sake. And since I am pregnant, I implore that the Almighty grant my offspring perpetuity in the community of Israel.

That was her petition. I ushered her into the presence of the rebbe, who read through the note, sighed and rolled his eyes heavenward, talked with her for ten minutes or so, promised that her three wishes would be fulfilled, and gave her a blessing. I was delighted to see the interview go so smoothly, and I surmised that the tzaddik was in a favorable mood just then.

After the blessing, the rebbe asked where she came from. "From Hirevka," she replied.

"Then why didn't your husband come with you?" the rebbe pursued.

"My husband? But, but, but—whoever said I had a husband? That's precisely my misfortune—I am without a husband!"

A bit baffled, the rebbe now asked, "How long has it been so?"

"For about three years now I've been a widow," replied the petitioner.

"But you say in your note that you are pregnant!"

"That is another of my misfortunes!" she exclaimed through her tears, and prostrated herself.

At a sign from the rebbe, I pulled her up and led her out into the courtyard, to be rid of her—and at just that point she began to yell. As people came running, she suddenly began taking her clothes off—and as she removed her dress, it became evident that she was a man in disguise, with his beard shaved off. All of our gabbaim now pounced on him, ready to beat him within an inch of his life. But then he gave a shrill whistle, and in response a dozen policemen emerged from the rabbi's orchard. They let fly with their clubs, arresting a few of our men while they were at it. The scoundrel also told the police sergeant to recover from me the three rubles and from the rebbe the *pidyon* of eighteen rubles that we had accepted.

Now that I think of it, we had to deal with men who were not only wicked but idiotic besides. In such circumstances, one of our group would have demanded a sum at least three times—and more likely ten times—the amount he had turned over to us. And we would have paid gladly. Woe to the honesty of such stupid knaves! What's more, the rebbe would really have come to grief if the police sergeant had not been a gilgul of—guess who? None other than that libertine and debauchee, the secular teacher of Hirevka. But that teacher didn't put anything over on our rebbe—not for a minute! As a matter of fact, our rebbe later declared with his own sainted lips that the secular teacher was haunted by a reincarnated soul, a woman's soul, a gilgul of the wife of a misnaged of Vilna. . . .

But our rabbi was so very much provoked that, since

he held me responsible, I would have forfeited my position as a gabbai had I not hit upon a novel expedient. Maneuvering and subterfuge are nothing new among our Hasidim, but ideas as ingenious as mine occur only rarely. Fortunately, however, that idea dawned on me in the nick of time and saved me from ruin—a veritable miracle from heaven! Only listen to what happened.

31

Mekhtzie's bull neck and Shliomka's potbelly are no help—a quick mind is what matters.

Some three or four years before I settled in Sirkov, the lessee of the postal service had begun calling on the rebbe twice a year—at Rosh Hashanah and again at Purim. Each time he brought a cash offering, a *pidyon* of a hundred rubles, along with other gifts, and implored the rabbi to pray that his wife would give birth to a son. The rebbe, for his part, declared every time that the supplicant's wish was about to be granted; but the years went by without any result—which might of course, have been the fault of the lessee himself.

Nevertheless, he had continued making these visits and contributing sizable *pidyonot* to the rebbe; occasionally he even brought his wife along. As for the rebbe's Hasidic followers, they were not in the least surprised that so lukewarm a Jew as the lessee should continue his pilgrimages and his substantial donations to the rabbi. All this merely served, they said, to increase the rebbe's prestige, since he was able to attract even such half-hearted souls regardless of whether they derived the least benefit from him. The misnagedim and the Berliners, however, were astonished, and more than once they attempted to wean the lessee away from the rebbe; but in this instance he ignored them, remaining loyal to the rebbe while also staying on good terms with the skeptics. In the third year, moreover, he became a still more frequent visitor, giving without stint to the rebbe and even to his retainers, though the rabbi's promise that the lessee's wife would give birth to a male child had not been fulfilled. A mystery? A riddle? And, can you Berliners solve it? Yet we Hasidim cut this Gordian knot with no trouble at all. It's all so simple.

At the age of thirteen a niece of the rebbitzin—a plump and ravishingly lovely girl, may no evil befall her! —was sent to be brought up in the rabbi's family. Why do you stand there gaping, you Berliners? It was quite possible, was it not, for the lessee to have taken a liking to her? After all, he was handsome and robust, he had a leaning toward the Berliners, his wife appeared nearly old enough to be his mother and, to compound the lack of attraction, had failed to present him with a son. So one may give free rein to a lively imagination when it comes to such a creature as the niece of the rebbitzin, and one can never tell—life is stranger than fiction. . . . So, indeed, she did become infatuated with his manly appearance, with his generosity and with the longing gaze he cast on her. When she was sixteen they began to meet secretly, and by the time she was eighteen their love knew no bounds. I was fully aware of all this—the lessee could be generous with a bribe so as to keep such an affair secret. As you'll discover presently, I was myself laboring under a totally false assumption. In reality, the lessee had a genuine and blameless love for Rachel, and supposed her to be as chaste as an angel. And this fitted in with plans of my own. I must also mention one other thing: whenever the lessee's wife visited our rabbi, the rebbitzin was fascinated by a splendid brooch and earrings, valued at seven or eight thousand rubles, that were worn by the visitor. After a time these ornaments became an obsession with the rebbitzin, who would gladly have traded her soul to the devil himself for them. On the basis of these two secrets—neither of them known to anyone but me—I evolved the following scheme: the moment the lessee arrived at our rabbi's regal court, I took him aside and brought our conversation around to the subject of the rebbe's niece. And when I convinced myself that he was really enamored and eager to marry her, I casually asked, "And what is there to stand in your way?"

"What do you mean by that? Are you pretending to be simple? I am a married man, after all. Are you forgetting my wife?"

"Oh, no!" I answered nonchalantly. "That needn't be a hindrance—that is if you are really sincere about marrying the niece."

"Do you doubt my sincerity about Rachel?" exclaimed the lessee, stirred to the depths. "I tell you, my very life depends on her! And if a marriage could be brought about, I would gladly part with half of everything I own. But how can I get rid of my wife, Reb Itzikel? She would never let me divorce her, no matter what!"

"Excuse me, my dear Reb Kalman," I answered, pretending to emerge from deep thought. "You go on talking about your wife; but what concerns me is a thing of far greater importance. If that were the only drawback, there would be no problem at all. The crux of the matter is: are you really determined to divorce your wife?"

"For heaven's sake, Reb Itzikel! How else can I prove that I mean what I say?" pleaded the lessee. "By all means, if you know of any way to make my wife consent to a divorce, please let's hear about it. Then you'll see whether I don't follow your advice, no matter what I may have to do—just so long as I can marry Rachel!"

"Excuse me, my dear Reb Kalman, but this could be a statement made in the heat of the moment," I insisted with feigned anxiety. "I happen to know that you are a progressive Jew who likes to please everybody, including the Berliners. But if things did come to a head, you would not wish to wrong your wife. Am I right?"

"Far be it for me to wrong her," the lessee pleaded, still without grasping my intent. "As a matter of fact I would gladly sign over most of my possessions to her, there would still be more than enough for myself."

"That's not the problem at all, Reb Kalman; I know perfectly well that you have a heart of gold," I replied. "What I mean is this: on having to accept a divorce she would be very much humiliated—she would have to eat humble pie, as the saying goes. And that could possibly have a further adverse affect, since no one can predict how matters will turn out. At such a moment your ambition is likely to predominate—and thus disrupt everything. But let me repeat, Reb Kalman: there is still a greater drawback than your wife—"

"Pardon me, Reb Itzikel, but you fail to comprehend the innermost feelings of others," the lessee said obdurately. "I give you my word—and you know me to be a man of integrity—that nothing would deter me from being joined with Rachel in holy wedlock! Show me how that can be accomplished, and you'll be convinced of my true feelings. After all, for my wife this is not a matter of life and death. What if she is humiliated just a little? I don't mind that in the least. And so far as those belonging to the other camp are concerned—it means nothing. I only play along with them; they can go to the devil for all I care. Only show me what to do, Reb Itzikel, and we'll win the game, God willing. Oh, yes—you keep hinting at some other drawback. Is it the rebbe's consent to all this that you have in mind? Well, altogether I am not such a fool but that I can well imagine the expenditures involved. And if it turns out to cost me another five thousand rubles—what does that matter, as long as Rachel is to be mine?"

Whereupon he pledged on his word of honor to cooperate with me in whatever action I might take. And now that I found him ready to go to any length, I said slyly, "Reb Kalman, you are right about the rebbe; it may be a matter of perhaps another thousand rubles. That need be no concern; but there is a thing no bigger than a pin that could be the monkey wrench if it got into the works. And on that very pin hinges your divorce. To be more specific: that pin is the pivot that is going to move your wife so that she will be sure to sue for divorce, and that is tied up with her humiliation. And that humiliation, in turn, is going to reflect upon someone in the other camp—"

"Stop talking riddles, and say what you mean!" the lessee cried impatiently. "I've already given you my word of honor, so out with it, Reb Itzikel! What are you talking about?"

"Reb Kalman, that pin stands in your way like a wall of iron," I went on, continuing to play my role with the greatest seriousness, so as to be sure that he would do my bidding. "But I have a scheme that will not only enable you to achieve your goal, but also do it in such a way that your reputation and the high esteem in which you are held will not suffer in the least—and what is more, the rebbitzin herself will as much as entreat you to become almost the same as her son-in-law. But—" And here I paused for a moment to whet his interest.

"You say that my reputation will not suffer at all?" he asked in astonishment. "Look here: is there anything

I have done to warrant disrespect? Do you perhaps refer to the impropriety, the imprudence in a man of my age and position, of wishing to marry an innocent girl because I'm smitten with her? Well, I suppose that could be regarded as uncouth and undignified on my part. Is that what you mean, Reb Itzikel? Naturally, I would very much appreciate your sparing me the embarrassment of playing the part of an adolescent. Is that what you have in mind, Reb Itzikel?"

Observing his naiveté, I wondered whether he was really so simpleminded, or was trying to hoodwink me. So, shifting my ground, I said with a pretense of ignorance, "Well, it might perhaps be that, but—"

He took all this in and embraced me, exclaiming, "May the Lord smile on you for reassuring me! Only, Reb Itzikel, what did you mean by that 'but'?"

"I meant simply that you would have to present your wife's brooch and earrings to the rebbitzin—and do it cleverly, with finesse. If you follow my advice, everything will turn out splendidly. Listen carefully to my plan of action, Reb Kalman, and do as I ask. . . ."

32

The Jesuit maxim that the end justifies the means is fair and just

"This is the situation, Reb Kalman," I began. "Reb Mekhuntzie, our rabbi's elder son, is also head over heels in love with Rachel." (At these words the lessee trembled visibly.) "But since his wife demands twenty thousand rubles as a settlement in exchange for a divorce, he is about to go on a fund-raising tour that will make it possible to divorce his wife and marry Rachel. The rebbe still does not know about all this; but the rebbitzin does, and as the mother she is naturally unhappy about her son's losing his head over Rachel. On the other hand, she is both ashamed of the situation and distressed by the idea of a divorce for the daughter of Rabbi Hanina—an event that could become notorious throughout the Hasidic world. What's more, the rebbe himself is likely to frown on such a tour, quite aside from the threat it poses of undermining his own income from those same sources. As matters stand now, Reb Mekhuntzie is determined to begin the tour, and the rebbitzin doesn't know what to do. So now you can see that when I propose you as the new bridegroom for Rachel, the rebbitzin will be delighted because in this way the scandal of her son's divorce, his planned tour, and her husband's embarrassment will all be avoided. But to ease a mother's anxiety, I would advise you to present her with your wife's brooch and earrings, especially in view of your wife's last visit here.

"I will see to it that she personally urges you to marry her niece, and that the event takes place on the Sabbath Shirah, when the Song of the Red Sea is recited, so that her son will be caught off guard. Now have a safe journey, and God willing, everything will be attended to in the best way possible. After you receive a letter from me, you and your wife should visit the rebbe on Sabbath Shirah, bringing along her jewelry as well as a gift of some sort for the rabbi. Also, it is essential for the secular teacher to attend; that can easily be arranged: as soon as you get home, mention to him casually that in our rabbi's town there is a great demand for teachers of his category, and he ought to visit it. Then, since the poor soul will not have the fare to make such a trip, you could mention, again casually, that you expect to go there again soon, and he could climb aboard your cart and travel with you. All of this should be done in a most offhand way. When he gets here he will naturally have to be our guest for the Sabbath; and then all the pieces of the puzzle will fall together. Don't ask me any more, Reb Kalman, but a safe journey to you!" And after a few glasses of wine I was on my way.

Quite probably, within a few weeks the rebbitzin became aware that Rachel was pregnant, and concluded that her son was involved, since she had now and then seen him making advances to the girl—even though he was looked upon as a respectable person. It is easy to imagine the distress felt by the rebbitzin, especially after Rachel hinted to her who the culprit was. (This was after

I told the girl the good news that she was to be engaged to the lessee, of whom she was enamored.) And when the rebbitzin learned that her son Mekhuntzie was indeed implicated, she tore her hair and wept.

At this critical juncture I began insinuating myself into her good graces, with hints that I knew what was going on. And I went further, suggesting that a way out would be to marry Rachel off to someone else, with no damage to the honor of either the rebbe or his son. I went on to say that the whole affair could be hushed up without arousing the least suspicion. And in addition, as a result of this maneuver she would acquire a thing she had been eyeing for the past two years, and which she could not have obtained in any other way.

The rebbitzin was beside herself with joy. "Itzikel," she declared, "if you can really get me out of this predicament I'll be grateful to you forever! But what is it you mean when you say I will acquire a thing I've had my eye on?"

"Can't you guess, my dear lady?" I said. "I know you've been admiring a certain brooch and earrings belonging to the wife of the lessee for a long, long time. Well, this is your opportunity to own them!"

"Oi, Itzikel!" she exclaimed. "You put new zest into me. I don't know how you can go about getting those jewels for me—but it doesn't matter, so long as I'm able to wear them."

"What do you mean?" I asked, in a tone of righteousness. "Surely you don't expect me to steal? After all, I am not one of the former gabbaim. And what's more, how could you possibly put on stolen jewelry and wear it in public?"

"That would be no problem, Itzikel," the rebbitzin answered with a shameless smile. "Our goldsmith could restyle the jewelry and then I wouldn't have a worry in

the world! But, of course, you are right," she said, blush-
ing. "Naturally, you wouldn't steal. Except—how else
could it be managed?"

"With God's help," I told her, "it will be managed,
so that the lessee himself hands the jewelry over to you.
But you must listen to me. You must approve of the
lessee's marriage to Rachel. The lessee is smitten with
her, and he is also very eager to have a male child. If this
marriage is arranged, he will be in such rapture that he
will reward the rebbe handsomely—and hand over the
jewelry besides. And he is so madly infatuated with Rachel that he will not ask questions later on. Do you follow? You need only make sure that the rabbi gives his
consent."

"As for the rebbe's consent—that's all but certain,"
she beamed. "But how, Itzikel—"

"How about the lessee's wife?" I broke in, anticipat-
ing her question. "Don't let that worry you. Leave it to
Itzikel. The lessee and his wife, God willing, are scheduled to visit here on Sabbath Shirah. And that is when
our purpose will be achieved."

The rebbitzin shook my hand on this, and even proposed that the wedding should be on the fifteenth day of
Shevat, the holiday of the New Year of the Trees.

I promptly sent a letter to the lessee, bringing him
up to date on these developments, and another to the
leading elder of Tzeplik, urging him to come, at the
behest of our tzaddik, and bring along the tax-farmer. In
due course, sure enough, the lessee and the secular
teacher appeared, together with the leading elder and
the tax-farmer. And I went ahead with my scheme, never
failing to look out for my own interests.

I had known from the start that the leading elder
and the tax-farmer were at odds with the lessee's wife.
The cause went back to a time when two would-be *poima-*

niks, abductors, had pounced on the secular teacher of Tzeplik, with the intention of taking away and destroying his passport, and then handing him over to the czarist army—in which, as the custom of the time decreed, he would have had to serve for twenty-five years, and for which Jewish boys no more than ten years old, called "Cantonists," could also be abducted and conscripted for life. As it happened, the lessee's wife was passing by, and after managing to snatch the passport from the assailants, she went to the town bailiff, who in turn ordered the teacher released and slapped a jail sentence and a hundred-ruble fine on each of the two abductors. From then on, the pair were on the watch, biding their time for an opportunity to settle accounts with the lessee's wife. So you can see that I had only to say, "Here is your chance to even the score with the lessee's wife and the teacher. . . ."

What, you ask, did I plan to have them do? A mere trifle, really: at a signal from me they were to affirm before our rabbi that on several occasions they had seen the lessee's wife and the teacher go into the stable in the courtyard of the house, and that on one of those occasions, when they had hidden behind a gate, they had seen her emerge half an hour later, in a flush of excitement, while her companion staggered out disheveled and unbuttoned, like a tailor's apprentice. The witnesses would say that they had refrained from exposing her so as not to disgrace her husband and to avoid slandering a Jewish woman. In view of everything, however, they were now ready to take their oaths, in prayer shawls and white linen robes, that she was a mere shameless harlot.

When the lessee arrived, I suggested that the teacher take a separate room at the inn for the weekend; then, just before setting out at dusk for the rabbi's feast, he was to tell his wife in a casual way to invite the teacher to the evening meal, as an act of charity. The rebbe already knew how to deal with the lessee's wife when she and her husband made their call on him. And what do you suppose happened? It goes without saying that the minute the two guests appeared the rabbi greeted the lessee with an embrace, at the same time glaring at the lessee's wife, rolling his eyes heavenward and muttering, "The laws, the laws! It is terrible!"

After the evening services, the lessee stayed in the synagogue to await the rebbe; but when one of my men appeared and whispered to me that the teacher had joined the lessee's wife for the evening meal, I nudged the lessee and said, "Let's go to your room at the inn. As soon as you enter, you will take the brooch and earrings along with the ring and then hand them to me privately."

The lessee did not for a minute suppose that I would make off with the jewelry, for during the course of the day the rebbitzin and Rachel had both smiled at him encouragingly several times, thus promising a favorable outcome for his hopes.

Accompanied by a quorum of Hasidim whose help had been enlisted beforehand, the lessee and I entered his room with a cordial greeting for his wife—and then stood with eyes riveted in amazement on the teacher and the lessee's wife. What was going on here? What business could a Berliner, a secular teacher, have with our rebbe's devotee? And above all, what business had he to be alone with a married woman?

But the lessee ordered wine for the assembled guests, and as things grew lively, handed me his wife's jewelry. Still more quietly, I slid the ring into the breast pocket of the teacher's overcoat, which hung from a hook near the door. Before long we were poking such fun at the teacher that he showed signs of feeling ill at ease. And then, sure enough, he was putting on his coat and going off to his room.

Half an hour later, as had been prearranged, the lessee somehow recalled that he had brought along a precious little object as a present for the rabbi. We naturally implored him to show it to us. He pretended at first to be reluctant but finally, yielding, he said to his wife, "Would you please get out the little box with the gift I brought for the rabbi?"

On opening the box, she turned pale. "Kalman," she screamed, "the jewelry is gone!"

"What do you mean?" asked the lessee with a show of astonishment. "It was there when I went off to the rabbi's to welcome in the Sabbath. Where could it have gotten to? Perhaps, you put it somewhere else, and then forgot. Look again; don't be excited."

We all helped her look for the jewelry, but to no avail.

"Reb Kalman," I declared, "you should search all of us at once. As the Gemara says, *kabdehu v'hashdehu*—respect him, but suspect him just the same."

At first he wouldn't hear of such a thing; but finally he gave in and searched us all. The innkeeper and the servant were summoned and they declared their innocence and submitted to a personal search.

Finally, the servant exclaimed, "The Berliner! He was here a while ago. . . . I beg a hundred pardons, since I don't know the man, but perhaps . . . he, too, ought to be searched. Woe is me! If I were to be accused of stealing I would lose my livelihood—no one would hire me!"

"The teacher? God forbid!" the lessee broke in, with a great show of indignation. "Why, the teacher is a reputable man—we've known him for years. How could I humiliate a decent person?"

But the innkeeper and the servant were determined there should be a further search to avoid being suspected themselves. So the lessee and his wife and all the rest of us went to call on the teacher. And, of course, that search led straight to the ring in the breast pocket of his over-coat. The lessee made a show of pleading not to expose the teacher and stir up scandal, but the innkeeper and the servant lost no time in sending for the police, and the accused teacher was taken into custody. Meanwhile, we began jeering at the lessee's wife, hinting none too subtly about her being in league with the culprit. Eventually we all returned to the synagogue.

Now, my dear sirs, it should not be difficult for you to imagine the end of this charade. By the next day the news had spread like a house afire, and the Hasidim all maintained that the lessee's bitch of a wife must herself have handed over the jewelry, or at the very least, by her own dissolute ways, encouraged her paramour to steal it. On the Sabbath eve the rebbe summoned the lessee and his wife to his private chamber, where he proceeded to roll his eyes and mutter about a terrible accusation against the lessee's wife that he saw written across the heavens. Then, to top everything off, in came the leading elder and the tax-farmer with their testimony about having seen her carrying on with the teacher. Whereupon, the lessee's wife toppled over in a faint. Finally, she was brought to and led back to the inn.

I needn't describe what passed between the lessee and his wife, except that they were divorced on Sunday morning in the rebbe's private chamber, and the cast-off wife went home heartbroken and in disgrace. On Monday evening the lessee and Rachel were betrothed. The rebbe was richer by five hundred rubles, the rebbitzin had the cast-off wife's jewelry, and I also came in for a little something. On Wednesday, the fifteenth day of Shevat, Rachel and the lessee were married.

Now you can understand how it was that my prestige with the rebbe had suddenly risen.

33

A rebbe's bidding must be scrupulously carried out—even though it be contrary to law and justice

If you will pardon me, my dear readers, how is it that not one of you has shown the least interest in what may have become of my wife? To place you among the sort of saints that Boaz was—the Gemara is amazed that he should even inquire about a woman—would be going too far. Even a genuine tzaddik such as our rebbe will occasionally ask a wealthy devotee, "How is your good wife?" And to say that you are ashamed to intrude on the life of a married couple would be a downright falsehood. What other nation in the world does more poking of noses into other people's private affairs than the Jews? Then again, perhaps you have failed to inquire about the fate of my wife because you object to my having totally ignored her. On this point I can assure you that I most certainly did not ignore her: and the proof of this is that she has thus far presented me with five children. For at least every year, sometimes for as long as two days, I go to visit her—on which occasion I also hand over a few rubles. Well, and what else would you have expected of me?

On the other hand, if you have failed to inquire about my wife because of having become deeply engrossed in my narrative, that would be most surprising and I can scarcely understand you! When it comes to that, do you find anything new in these stories of mine? It would seem to me that all of you must be better acquainted with them than I. Where, after all, does this entire affair and all these yarns originate, if not with you? And if it had not been for you, I would have had nothing to write about, there would have been no grist for my mill. Of course, I realize that if my spouse had been a beautiful woman, you would certainly have been interested in learning for yourselves how she was faring. If this is so, then out of pure spite I will tell you just how she fares now, and how I have treated her of late, and then you will realize that a Hasid is more of a gentleman and more gracious toward his wife and children than all of your Berliners and yeshiva students.

Some six months after the affair of the lessee, the daughter of our rebbe's sister, a young widow, a creature with rosy cheeks and glowing dark eyes, came to visit. I fell in love with her instantly, and both the rebbe and the rebbetzin dropped hints that I might marry her. It appeared that I was not to her liking, although she had no say in the matter. But what would I do, since I was already saddled with a wife and family? You can imagine my anguish, with fortune and felicity so close at hand and yet totally beyond my grasp. Only think of it—why, it was the next thing to becoming a son-in-law of the rebbe! And to have so luscious a playmate was not to be disdained, either! It amounted to paradise on earth! And to think of the wretch, the monstrous eyesore, whose face would stop a clock, who barred my way to that paradise! As if all this weren't enough, she kept sending me word, through various Krokodilevka Hasidim, that since she and our children were freezing and on the point of starvation, it behooved me to send her at least a tenth of my earnings. Well, and how would you answer such a shrew? First of all, you must know that I bank all my earnings with the rebbe, so that I could not touch any of those funds whatever happened. Second, why couldn't the baboon knead and bake, or go into some business, to feed herself and the brats? I couldn't abide the sight of her from the very day of our marriage—and once I had met the rebbe's niece. . . . Also, she raised objections to being divorced without a maintenance settlement—can you imagine such a thing? But after you have learned, as you soon shall, of my kindheartedness, of my plans to divorce her according to the Law of Moses and Israel, you will also realize that her impudent arrogance toward me was such that an angel could not have endured it! Only listen to what happened.

On a Sabbath eve, just before the ceremonial blessing, the *Kiddush,* the rabbi summoned his niece and me, along with his wife, to his private chamber, and brought up the question of my marrying his niece. "Itzikel," he said, "I want you to know that I am under constant direction from above, from heaven itself—in my dreams I am forever hearing the names of Isaac and Rebecca." (The young widow, you see, was named Rebecca.) "Therefore," he went on, "the rebbitzin and I have decided that you must go to the holy congregation of Krokodilevka and divorce your wife. As for the obligations spelled out by the marriage contract, you will be unable to meet them, for it would amount to a sin to use up your savings in my possession, which will enable you to begin a new life with my niece, on an equal footing with our most notable citizens. Therefore I say you ought to get an arbitrary divorce, involving only nominal expenses—for transporting yourself and your two witnesses to Krokodilevka, and such small change you probably now have in your pocket. There will be a delay of a couple of weeks until Sabbath Hanukkah, when that abominable half-wit of a Hasid, your father-in-law, takes to the road along with your mother-in-law, for a Sabbath visit to the rebbe of Zodkowetz. Then at twilight, when Sabbath Hanukkah is over, you must hire two thoroughbred horses. With them, you and my two assistant gabbaim should be able to cover the two and a half miles to Krokodilevka and be back here in plenty of time for the meal that ends the Sabbath. Meanwhile, in the name of the Holy One, blessed be He, I declare you and Rebecca betrothed. And, God willing, within a fortnight after you return from Krokodilevka divorced, the two of you will be united in holy wedlock." With these words he pulled out his silk handkerchief and had me and my wife-to-be grasp it as a token of our future bonds, and then his holy lips pronounced his blessing. There were actually tears in the young woman's eyes, but she could hardly expect to go against the rebbe's wishes. You can well imagine how elated I was—and how impatient for the two-week interval to end.

I survived somehow until Sabbath Hanukkah. Also I had word from Krokodilevka that my two dear brothers-in-law were away from home. So, as soon as the twilight prayers were over, the two gabbaim and I climbed into the cart that I had ordered on Friday, and we were off for Krokodilevka. The rebbe had pronounced a brief vale-diction: "Farewell! May God be with you on your way—and let no dog whet his teeth on you!" And although the rebbe—may his life be long!—had urged me not to grant a judicial bill of divorcement, wishing to be considerate, I had brought along my last hundred rubles, so as to fulfill the Law of Moses and Israel. Now, you Berliners, you can see whom you have to deal with: I was willing to violate my rebbe's behest in order to act justly. And it was probably this very disobedience that proved my undoing—disregard of a rabbi's order is no trifling matter! Be that as it may, I also had in my pocket a compulsory bill of divorcement that the rebbe's scribe had drawn up for me on Friday. And so we were bound for the holy congregation of Krokodilevka.

We arrived at our destination around eight in the evening, got out of the cart at some distance from my wife's house, and edged up to the windows to eavesdrop. There was not a soul in sight; not even a dog barked, although ordinarily a cart passing through Krokodilevka would set every last one in town to yelping, until the canine chorus echoed throughout the community. The silence appeared to confirm the rabbi's prophecy, and convinced us that the entire venture would go off smoothly, without any untoward result. It never occurred to us that our cart had halted near the house of a Berliner who had very recently been made tax collector for Krokodilevka. While we were chatting merrily some distance away, this curious official caught sight of our cart and went out to question the driver, a boy of fifteen or so. This boy informed the official that the three of us were the gabbaim of the rebbe of Sirkov—and gave our names, while he was at it. No doubt, if this adolescent moron had known of the purpose of our coming, he would have told all about that too. Obviously, if the heretical Berliner knew that Itzikel, the rabbi's chief gabbai and the talmudic wonder's son-in-law, was in Krokodilevka, he would have been quick as a cat to find out what was going on at my wife's fireside, and would have nabbed us then and there.

At any rate, it was clear that my intention to adhere to the notion of justice that prevailed among Berliners but ran contrary to my rabbi's wishes had caused me to take leave of my senses, so that I had failed to warn the youngster in time to keep his confounded trap shut. Daredevil though I was, able to accomplish such a feat as the lessee's divorce and remarriage, I had not had the wit to forestall a slip like that. . . . Well, it is all water over the dam now. And you may as well hear out the story of my compulsory divorce, down to the end.

34

A most curious event, enough to drive one mad—however, the rabbi's reputation takes precedence over all

I hesitate to tell you of the sorry plight in which I and my two fellow gabbaim found my wife, since you thin-skinned sensitive souls are so prone to weeping on the least provocation—especially when the matter concerns a *Frauenzimmer,* as you like to put it. But for the honor of the Hasidic sect, I am duty bound to fill in for you at least a tenth of the details, so that the world may learn from us Hasidim how a man schooled in the Torah is forced by circumstances to act the barbarian when his dignity is at stake! As our holy Gemara propounds, "A scholar who cannot be as vindictive as a snake is no scholar." Not only a wife, but even one's own parents, when they fail to render the honor due to a man learned in the Torah, must be dealt with even as serpents are. So let me give you a bird's-eye view of what I saw as I peered into the room inhabited by my wife.

A candle flickered in the corner of the room, where the cold came in through cracks in the walls and the broken panes in the single small window. My spouse sat crouching on the floor, on a cushion of musty straw,

suckling an infant at her breast. A girl of three lay next
to her, and a boy of two napped at her feet. At a little
distance, two boys, aged five and seven, only half-clad
and with scurfy heads, sprawled on the bare floor, trembling with the cold and periodically coughing. Snatches
of an embittered, barely audible complaint reached our
ears: "Lord of the Universe, relieve me of this wretched
misery, and let me die!" (At this point a child shrieks.)
"What am I to do, my darling baby, when there is no milk
in my breast? Go on, then, suck out the marrow from my
bones." (A wheezing cough from one of the others.) "I
worry until I'm sick about that cough of yours. Woe to
the mother who has seen you these three years, and can
do nothing to help you!" (An outburst of hiccoughs from
another child.) "Woe is me, to have to hear you go on
coughing these two years! You'd think that death by slow
starvation would be punishment enough—but no, you
are doomed to still other troubles. Woe, woe that I must
watch your misery! Dear God in heaven, have pity on my
living orphans, who suffer for the sins of their parents!"
(One youngster whimpers again with the cold.) "Oi, I
must be out of my mind! Woe, woe! My poor children,
take my last rags and cover yourselves. I am not cold—
I am covered with troubles. My broken heart keeps me
warm; I go on smoldering with rage, there's no end to
it. Almighty God, what have I done to deserve this punishment? And even if I am a sinner, why must innocent
little souls suffer so? What does that scoundrel, my husband, want with my life? When I still lived with my parents, poor as we were, I found some enjoyment in life.
When there was bread in the house, nothing else mattered; and when there wasn't any, I could get it from a
neighbor, and be free as a bird again. But from the miserable day of my marriage I've known nothing but trouble,
day after day, and the Lord alone knows for how long I'm

doomed to this wretched existence. There are all kinds of misfortune; my mother didn't fare so well, either, but there's no comparison between those hardships and my endless wretchedness. And who is to blame for it all? Why, none other than that rat, that villain, who deserted me and his five ailing little ones for the sake of his Hasidic sect, and who left us at the mercy of the four winds. Oh, that miserable Hasidic sect has been the ruin of many a Jewish young woman! Because of their saintly sages and their synagogue wardens and all the other parasites and hangers-on, we are condemned to an existence of grief and sorrow. What cannot be kept secret from God will be kept secret from men; and so I will proclaim to the whole world that my husband's rabbi is the cause of my ruin. Because of some Hasidic dance at their *melaveh malkeh* festivals, I and my five ragged, ailing children must squat here on the bare floor, enduring cold and starvation. Perhaps it is a sin for me to say these words, but I am doomed no matter what. Oh God, take me away from here—take us all away from this wretched living grave, away from this miserable world we live in. Dear God, let me die. . . . There, there, poor little thing, suck on my empty breast! May your father know the taste of my bitterness, even though I pay with my life for that satisfaction!"

After listening to this brazen disparagement of myself and above all of the rabbi's reputation, I resolved not to give her a single kopeck. At a signal from me, one of my companions knocked at the door. When my beauty asked in dismay, "Who is there?" he replied, "Don't be afraid, Tseitele. Be so kind as to open the door—I have a letter and a few rubles for you from your husband."

As soon as she opened the door, I thrust the bill of divorcement into her hand in the presence of two witnesses. In another minute the three of us were back at the cart and hurrying home despite the wails of woe that issued from the dilapidated house. And we were actually back in Sirkov in time for the celebration of the *melaveh malkeh* at the court of the rabbi. There all was joy and jubilation, and the rebbitzin lost no time in setting the wedding for the eighth day of Hanukkah. The male servants bustled about; the cook and the maidservants were busy stewing, boiling and baking, since the holiday began in only two days. The wine merchant went to work decanting various wines and spirits into bottles; well-to-do merchants flocked from all directions with gifts for the rabbi and for the bride and bridegroom. The eighth day of Hanukkah arrived at last, and the assembled guests were ready to proceed to the synagogue for the ceremony. The bride never stopped crying—but after all, is not that the custom? In the evening the rabbi's synagogue was lighted with innumerable candles, both Havdalah and the ordinary kind; all the guests were in their most festive clothes. Finally the rebbe and his entire family appeared, his sons and sons-in-law wearing long gabardines and round fur-trimmed hats, the rebbitzin resplendent in the noted brooch and earrings, along with the rest of her jewels, and the daughters and daughters-in-law arrayed as though for the Rejoicing of the Law.

Then the bride and I were ushered into the synagogue and stood under the canopy. I was attired in white linen and a fur-trimmed hat, the bride in the traditional gown and veil. The eldest of the rabbi's sons and sons-in-law served as groomsmen, and the rabbi himself performed the marriage ceremony. But when the moment came to put the *kedushin*-ring on the bride's finger and pronounce the benediction, who should burst in but the commissar of rural police for Krokodilevka, with two gendarmes and the Berliner tax-farmer, followed by my wife! They rushed at me like a lot of tigers assaulting their prey. Everyone was astounded, and I stood there unable to move. The commissar told my wife to calm herself and in a whisper asked the tax-farmer to hand him some document or other. After glancing at it, the officer intoned aloud: "Itzko Yoskowitch Tzepliner! Mordko Mordkowitch Trogharb! Shmulke Shmaienwitch Fishchelke!"

Well, since there was no wriggling out of our predicament, the two gabbaim and I acknowledged our respective identities. The officer then began reading the document to us in Russian. But since we gave no sign of understanding (Mordecai, as a matter of fact, was well versed in Russian, but feigned ignorance), the uncircumcised flunky called on the tax-farmer to act as interpreter and we learned that the officers were well acquainted with the details of the arbitrary divorce. Since we had supposed that no living soul was privy to our secret, we tried at first to disclaim any wrongdoing. The tax-farmer whispered something to the commissar, who in turn ordered a gendarme to bring in the lad who had been our driver—as soon as he entered we knew who had betrayed us. Accordingly, we had to admit our journey to Krokodilevka, though we still went on denying the accusation of the arbitrary divorce.

It was then that the commissar sat down at a table, opened a leather portfolio that held various documents along with the bill of divorcement, and began interrogating the accused—eventually bringing in the scribe, the bride, the driver and as if that weren't enough, the rabbi himself. The entire assembly stood as though petrified. As the initial shock subsided they were in suspense over how the drama would turn out; and the rabbi's entourage still hoped for the storm to blow over, so that the merrymaking could proceed. For in the past, our rabbi's court had again and again been the scene of protests by

the Jewish women of Krokodilevka against arbitrary di-
vorces—but thanks to the rabbi's overwhelming merit all
those mix-ups had always been ironed out. And here was
the proof of that merit: as soon as the commissar ventured to impugn the rabbi, the assembly was thrown into
a dither and the tax-farmer of Krokodilevka, who was
one of the guests, edged over to the official, ostensibly
to examine the bill of divorcement but in fact to whisper
something into that official's ear. From then on, the commissar backed off, gradually changed his tune, closed his
portfolio, and wound up mumbling to himself, "Well, it's
rather late now; we'll postpone the case until tomorrow." Finally, eyeing the three of us, he added, "I hope
you won't have disappeared by then."

And he headed for the door, with a disconsolate
entourage, including the tax-farmer, trailing behind him.

The assembled guests were about to resume the
festivity, but at the moment the commissar opened the
door he was thunderstruck, and so were all the mer-
rymakers. Oh, I am too excited to tell you just yet what
happened! Let me take a deep breath first.

35

*Quench one false charge and another
springs up in its place—there is no respite
for the tzaddikim*

Before I give an account of what took place in our synagogue following the incident with the commissar of rural
police, allow me to revert momentarily to past events.
For six months the cause célèbre involving the postal
lessee seemed to have been forgotten completely. During the six months that followed, only the merest ripple
ruffled the placid surface of events, such as a casual visit
by the local police sergeant to the synagogue, or a trifling
affidavit submitted by the town bailiff of Tzeplik, or an
interrogation by a police inspector that lasted no more
than ten or fifteen minutes. The rebbe himself had been
cross-examined once or twice about some seemingly
trivial matter, and then the awkwardness seems to have
been disposed of once and for all.

Throughout the two months between Sukkoth and
Hanukkah, not a word was said about the lessee's divorce, and things seemed to have settled down. The only
possible reason for concern was that the lessee passed
through Sirkov just once during that entire year, on
which occasion he paid a perfunctory call to the rebbe,

bringing him no *pidyon* or gift of any kind, and leaving quite abruptly. Nor did he convey any regards from Rachel to the rebbitzin. That was the lessee's only visit to the rabbi after the events at the synagogue.

The lessee did drop a hint in passing, however, that something was brewing at the county seat, although he did not say what. Well, and what of that? Some people will let their imaginations run wild. And anyhow, the rebbe's agent at the county seat had given no inkling of any trouble or subterranean rumblings there. On the contrary, in a letter to us written early in the month of Kislev, he hinted that the secular teacher was likely to be kept locked up for some time. And so there appeared to be no grounds for concern. Indeed, the entire incident might have been forgotten if our own beloved brethren could just have refrained from poking their noses into it! Why, after all, should there be trouble over a mere secular teacher? Even if he had been locked up for eighteen years, would anyone in his own camp have bothered to extend a helping hand? A plague on all the Berliners; they don't give a tinker's damn for one of their own who finds himself in hot water! They will merely offer a sanctimonious remark—"An outrage!" or, "Think of it, such a noble soul having to suffer so unjustly!" or, "Alas, that culture should be the victim of fanaticism!" One such phrase is as meaningless as another, but nobody who mouths them is likely to offer assistance to the victim— which is not surprising, since there is so little rapport among them. And the liberal school of thought is based entirely on the most prosaic version of righteousness, just as the philosophy of the misnagedim is based on an austere, cold-blooded interpretation of the Torah. Both are merely golems without a soul, each striving to exert its own will and intent—one through speculation and Haskalah, the other by way of the Talmud and the commentators who came after it.

Both movements are based on a mere passion that is like any physical urge; any passion calls for personal gratification, but if several devotees can indulge in it jointly, so much the better. Also, although those devotees all yearn to indulge their appetites jointly, nevertheless each one is concerned primarily with himself. Therefore, when one of the company is missing, the rest are undisturbed, since each can still indulge himself to his heart's content. Of course, they felt sorry for the captured brother, since one more devotee adds to the fun and zest of the occasion—but they can do without him.

When it came to our crew, however, you were looking at a horse of another color altogether. The ideology of our sect called for rapture and ecstasy. And these require numbers: the more there are, the more the performance is accelerated and intensified. That is why each one of us did all he could to bring others into the collective undertaking. And if one of the members found himself in trouble, the rest were distressed over it, and were prepared to sacrifice themselves for the victim's sake, because each of us was concerned entirely with the collective welfare rather than with himself alone. Which is why, no matter how much one might have transgressed against the Torah and against righteousness for the sake of some member (to say nothing of having a concern for the entire association), his error was regarded as a mitzvah, a good deed done for altruistic reasons. For the transgressor was not seeking his own aggrandizement but the furtherance of the association. So why should there be any concern over some action or other on the part of those who were merely bodies without souls, cold-blooded philosophers without a trace of Hasidic fervor.

The trouble was that one of our own had become entangled in this affair, and when one did that, others were sure to follow. They knew quite well how to manage the affair gradually and surreptitiously, one step at a time, through a series of small intrigues such as we Hasidim were capable of—until the final outcome erupted like a tornado on a lovely summer day. As soon as one of our members turned traitor and got into this affair, the men from the other camps joined in, bringing in money along with their heretical practices.

Here is how the new scandal evolved. The divorced wife of the postal service lessee had received more than twenty thousand rubles as a settlement of her claims. She was not stupid, after all; having retained some of the spirit of our sect, she had seen through our stratagem from beginning to end. But she also knew perfectly well that she could not expect much out of merely getting the cooperation of our Hasidim, or even with the help of other sects. So, biding her time, she did her best to find a suitable new husband within our ranks. Within six months she was married to an entrepreneur, a widower from Hitrovka (Silly Village), who was sociable and a good mixer, had close ties to officialdom, and was an ardent devotee of the rebbe of Antel—and I don't have to tell you how the followers of one rebbe denounce and persecute the followers of all the others. But let me tell you about the hatred and rivalry prevailing among the rabbis themselves and in particular between the sage of Sirkov and the sage of Antel.

You will probably wonder, my dear sirs, why our Hasidim of Sirkov could have failed to grasp the situation —or if we, as ordinary mortals, had some inkling of it, how it was that our farsighted spiritual leader had himself foreseen nothing and taken no precautionary measures. Let me assure you that we were indeed aware of what was afoot—and that on the Sabbath after the lessee's onetime wife was married, our rabbi had fulminated in his sermon, even quoting the passage, "I will embroil one kingdom with another, and every man shall war against his brother, and against his friend. . . ." But we had supposed first of all that a Hasid, no matter what rabbinical dynasty he adhered to, still detested the Berliners every bit as much as he did the pork of gentiles, and that even when it came to taking revenge against other Hasidim, he would not stoop to certain measures without a proper motive; it was also rumored that the woman was perfectly content, and led a happier life with her new husband than she had with the lessee of the postal service. Who, then, could have dreamed that this wicked shrew was dissembling, all the while harboring dreams of revenge as despicable as those of an erstwhile talmudic scholar. In the second place, we did in fact counsel our agent at the county seat to be on the alert, and he did in fact keep his eyes and ears open. In a war, one side is bound to win while the other loses, and this time it was evidently the false prophet of Antel who was destined to triumph. Our rabbi did receive an advance tip from heaven about it, but he viewed the impending trouble with charity, as a sufferer for a sinful generation.

At any rate, the shrew had stirred up her new husband, who in turn stirred up the Hasidim of Antel, with whom the Berliners eventually made common cause. There was no lack of funds: the woman herself contributed half of the capital she had acquired through the divorce proceedings (having promised no more than ten thousand rubles to her new spouse, who had been badly in need of that), and one must not forget the savings she had set aside while she was married to her first husband —another ten thousand, in all likelihood. The rich Berliners and the well-to-do Hasidim of Antel also contributed, and two prominent lawyers were engaged to handle the case. And the whole proceeding was launched with the utmost secrecy. (The stupid oafs supposed they had foiled our rebbe, too.) And so the indictment of our rebbe along with all the rest who were involved in the affair—except for the women—came on the very eve of Hanukkah festival. Leave it to the Berliners!

So on the eve of the eighth day of Hanukkah the secular teacher was set free; in Tzeplik the lessee of the postal service, the sheriff, and the tax-farmer were arrested and thrown into jail before they had time to communicate with the rebbe. And at the very moment the rebbe's niece was stepping under the bridal canopy, the sheriff opened the door, and at least eighteen police officers sailed into the synagogue like a cloud of hungry locusts. The party included the chief of police, the prosecutor, the police inspector and other officials—plus a score of uniformed officials and plainclothesmen who cordoned off the synagogue and swung into action when some of us tried to escape. The teacher, the two attorneys and Rachel herself—as a witness of it all—were likewise on the scene.

I soon realized the full import of the situation, and became resigned to whatever might ensue. From a glimpse of the teacher and Rachel, it was all too plain that they were not indifferent toward each other. I shall spare you the details of our interrogation by the officers. Let me merely sketch the situation and mention the decisions that were reached several hours after midnight, after the rebbe's house had been ransacked and all its contents sealed, and there had been a confrontation between Rachel and Mekhuntzie, the rabbi's son, followed by an interrogation of the teacher, the rabbi and myself.

You will finally realize what it is that people were making such a hue and cry over. But no matter how hard one may try to explain to a goy the meaning of Hasidic jests and cavils and pranks and double entendres, the goy will still view things in his own strange, goyish fashion. Let me give word for word the list of infractions and felonies set forth in the indictment.

36

The indictment based on trumped-up charges by goyish judges

The Charges against the Rebbe Were as Follows:

The tzaddik of Sirkov was accused, in general terms, of deceiving the world at large by hoodwinking it into believing that he was God's intermediary on earth, and of making his rounds in that alleged capacity; and in his name his agents and Hasidic followers were said to have committed offenses of every sort, causing distress among the citizens, such as were most detrimental to the state. In particular, according to the testimony of the lessee of the postal service at Tzeplik, the local sheriff and tax-farmer; according to what transpired during the confrontation of these three with the former lessee's divorced wife and the secular teacher of Tzeplik; and according, finally, to the investigation of the local authorities at the synagogue of the tzaddik of Sirkov, in connection with legal proceedings begun at Krokodilevka, the tzaddik had been placed under indictment on the following counts:

1. That through deception and fraud over a period

of five years he had extorted from the lessee of the postal service at Tzeplik more than three thousand rubles in cash, in addition to gifts and entertainment amounting to more than a thousand rubles, for the false promise of interceding with the Almighty in answer to his wife's prayers for a male child.

2. That in order to cover up a scandalous liaison between Mekhuntzie, his oldest son, and his wife's niece, as well as for a monetary consideration, the rebbe of Sirkov—contrary to the Mosaic Law, which requires that all religious disputes, and in particular those involving eyewitness accounts, be adjudicated by a rebbe or by a dayyan—had listened to testimony which he knew to be false against the wife of the lessee of the postal service, thus causing a rupture between a happily married adult couple, and slandering a devoted and upright wife and matron.

3. That he had defrauded the lessee of the postal service at Tzeplik by inducing him to marry the rabbi's wife's niece under the incorrect assumption that she was a virgin, although the rebbe was well aware that his son had made his wife's niece pregnant; and that, moreover, said rabbi had relieved said postal lessee of five thousand rubles, as well as a brooch and a pair of diamond earrings valued at from seven to eight thousand rubles.

4. That in a ruse to marry off a niece who was a divorcee without a dowry to one of the conspirators in his swindling operation, he had urged said conspirator to impose an arbitrary divorce on said conspirator's wife, and had also persuaded his clerk, with two other Hasidim, to draft and sign a bill of divorcement, and had also forced two of his gabbaim to act as witnesses during the fraudulent divorce.

5. That he had compelled this same niece to be married against her will to this same despicable conspira-

tor, the chief of his gabbaim; and that said rabbi had purported her to be an authentic widow, whereas he was perfectly aware that she was a divorcee, whom he had personally coerced, eight years before, into divorcing her beloved husband on the grounds that he was a maskil, an opponent of the Hasidim.

Mekhuntzie, the Oldest Son of the Tzaddik of Sirkov, Was Accused as Follows:

1. Of having raped his cousin Rachel one night in his father's private study.

2. Of having induced her to swallow certain preparations with the aim of inducing a miscarriage.

The Chief Synagogue Warden Was Accused as Follows:

1. Of having, as part of the conspiracy, and for considerations of monetary gain, instigated the lessee of the postal service at Tzeplik to divorce his wife and to marry Rachel, the rebbitzin's niece, although said chief warden was aware of the latter's pregnancy.

2. Of having, through fraud and flattery, extorted from said lessee of Tzeplik a diamond brooch, a pair of diamond earrings, and a diamond ring, the property of said lessee's wife, which had then, with the exception of the ring, been presented to the wife of said rebbe of Sirkov through sleight of hand, the chief warden having planted them in the pocket of a coat belonging to said secular teacher of Tzeplik, thus branding an innocent man with the theft of all the jewelry.

3. The record of the proceedings also indicted the rebbe's scribe, along with the two witnesses of the compulsory divorce, for drafting and signing the bill of divorcement, the two leading wardens for bearing witness during the proceedings of that divorce, the tax-farmer of

Krokodilevka for bribery, and the recipient for accepting such bribe.

The prosecutor further ordered the rebbitzin, since she had not been incriminated, to pay out of the funds due me from the rebbe twenty rubles a month to my divorced wife and our children in Krokodilevka until such time as the trial should be concluded.

And what, my dear sirs, is your opinion of these developments? Frankly, it is difficult to believe that there should still be such numbskulls as would fail to grasp things even a backwoods Polish Hasid has no trouble understanding. Just for the exercise, suppose we examine one by one the charges listed in their indictment; and let us further consider how persons who ostensibly possess each of the five senses exactly as we do could misconstrue the difference between a genuine and unequivocal transgression and mere play or joking or carrying off a prank. To go on making mountains out of molehills, take, for example, their solemn question: How could it be that the rebbe took money under false pretenses? Now, if they were only to recall their own goyish aphorism, "The fool giveth and the wise man taketh away," they would laugh at such obtuseness. But if you delve into the question more seriously, you will find it merely absurd—not to mention the fact that for us Hasidim a rebbe's promises are practically the same as the Mosaic Law, or a truth itself, and a rabbi is therefore deemed omniscient. But such a phenomenon is one that those imbeciles will never be able to fathom. Even the maskilim and the misnagedim, the enlightened ones, who after all are schooled in the Gemara, are ignoramuses and have not the foggiest notion about this either.

But let it be granted for the sake of argument that obtaining money under false pretenses is wrong. Nu?

And what of it? Does the rebbe entrap them, saying, "Here, I can give children, and subsistence, and forged receipts"—and so on and so on? Rather, people themselves beat a path to his door, importuning and clamoring, "Give us children, give us rain and snow and wars! Give us rebbes and ritual slaughterers, and scribes and teachers! Exorcise our demons and dybbuks, banish our wayward thoughts! Confound and befuddle the squire for us; order the Angel of Death into action! Seize Satan!" Suppose we agree that the tzaddik will be unable to fulfill all the petitions cited here. Nu? And what of it? But Hasidic Jews have such abounding faith that they won't give him a minute's rest!

In any event, he is entitled to compensation for his effort, for the endless annoyances and the backbreaking labor, with never a pause for breath. Nu? After all, his fellow Jews are bound to go looking for miracles and signs and wonders—for the reason that a Jew's whole life and breath consists of pure miracles, of things that transcend the natural order. So it becomes necessary for someone to carry the burden of their enthusiasm, their rapture and exaltation to the realm of heavenly things. And if one won't, then another must supply their demand. Necessity is the mother of gefilte fish. So he happens to be the one who responds to necessity. Shouldn't he be given the wherewithal, as befits so high and noble a station?

Or take, for example, the allegation that our tzaddik listened to testimony—and false testimony at that—without the participation of a rabbi, thus leading to the separation of a married couple. Why, such nonsense is enough to die laughing at! Just try to explain that the tzaddik is himself a scroll of the Torah—or as the holy *Zohar* declares, "The Torah, the Lord, and Israel are one!" Now in this instance, "Israel" symbolizes the tzaddik, who after the manner of the patriarch Jacob is to be the victor over the Shechinah, the Divine Presence, in that the Lord, blessed be He, issues the decree and the tzaddik annuls it. It follows that the tzaddik and all the leading rabbis and judges are insignificant as compared to him. How could any sensible person question the right of the rabbi to hear testimony? As for the contention that it was false testimony—there, again, you are dealing with the intelligence of morons! According to their slow minds, unless the culprit has been caught in the act, all testimony concerning him is to be regarded as false. What is at issue here, however, is not the transgression but the procedure.

Just try to clear up so abstruse a point as that one accursed cannot be attached to one who is blessed. Should a Hasid—or, God forbid, a Hasidic woman—make an overture to a misnaged or to a Berliner with a remark, or exchange a glance with someone, or even grant a loan without interest, that will already be seen as a calamity. Nu—after all, suppose the wife of the lessee was gracious toward the teacher; does that testify to their intimacy? Doesn't it mean simply that she can no longer abide her husband? What is so hard to understand about that?

The same may be said of the rebbe's declaring Rachel to be a virgin. What was he to do—shout from the housetops that his son had seduced Rachel and made her pregnant? Why, only a lunatic would behave that way! The same applies to their so-called offenses of my compulsory divorce and of forcing his niece to marry me. The rebbe's motives for these actions came as a decree from heaven. He had, after all, heard in a vision the names of Isaac and Rebecca. Was he also supposed to peer down the throat of a stupid woman? Furthermore, how was one to interpret the passage, "One can do a good deed for another without that other's being present?" And likewise the passage, "You bring pressure to bear until he says, 'I am willing.'" Measured against such lofty matters, the divorce of some lowborn woman from Krokodilevka, whether legal or compulsory, fades into insignificance.

So how is one to communicate with numbskulls who fail to grasp any subtlety on the part of an ordinary Jew? And if this can be said of an ordinary Jew, how much more is it true of a tzaddik—especially if the matter is beyond human comprehension? The same may be said of Mekhuntzie's transgressions. Imagine the son of a tzaddik who is thus himself a tzaddik, who has grown stout with the joy of living in the reflection of the Divine Presence—may no evil fall upon him!—who always receives inspiration from below rather than from above: can any ordinary man fathom such strange phenomena, can he grasp how such fervent exaltation begets passion —as it is written, "Through your blood you should live"? Such ardor must undoubtedly find some means or other of overcoming Satan. If there is any temptation to transform the Law of Violence into idolatry, however, the tzaddik must use restraint. But how can these abstruse matters be discussed with slow-minded men?

As for my own alleged transgressions—why, the charges are preposterous. I am accused of "inciting" the lessee of the postal service. You would think I had misled some poor innocent—or, for that matter, that I had swindled him out of his jewelry for the benefit of the rebbitzin. Wouldn't the poor fool have parted with his very last gabardine to win his inamorata? And why should he not consider what a privilege and honor it is for such a lout to become a son-in-law of the rebbitzin! Magnates and officials, as well as other saintly sages, are all eager to marry into our rabbi's family—the more since the rebbitzin, as the granddaughter of Reb Shmitzi, was already a patrician in her own right. Alas, if it hadn't been for Rachel's mishap, that potbelly of a lessee wouldn't have had the privilege of shining her shoes. And those morons frown on me for having induced him to marry a dishonored girl! Did they really imagine that I could have proposed a match for the lessee of Tzeplik—a costly bargain!—if she had truly been a virgin? Indeed, the rest of my offenses were no less trivial. Where was the tragedy if that heretic, that scoundrel of a teacher from Tzeplik, did go to prison? Or if my wife did receive a compulsory divorce? Only take a look at those Berliners: those creatures are the scum of the earth! Was it necessary to make trouble for the scribe, and the tax-farmer, and the witnesses, and even the sheriff, over such a trifling matter? How can there be any communication with such scatterbrains? Not to mention their granting my wife alimony of twenty rubles a month. Imagine it—even the rebbe, who is the incarnation of lenience and generosity, exhorted me not to grant her anything, even a legal divorce. So, you can see that this whole imbroglio was the work of Satan. The Berliners and the other villains had let their imaginations run wild—and, alas, the rabbi and Mekhuntzie were doomed to suffer unjustly, while I and the other victims were turned into scapegoats for no reason at all.

And so, after the decision was announced, the prosecuting attorney ordered that the rebbe and his son be taken to the county jail. The scribe, the witnesses of my divorce, and the tax-farmer of Krokodilevka were to be sent to prison at Sirkov. The sheriff was released with a reprimand. And since I and the two other wardens were natives of Vetzeeoni—the district that included Krokodilevka—we were sent to prison in our native place. Two fur-lined overcoats, two fur caps, and two pairs of felt boots were brought to the synagogue for the rabbi and Mekhuntzie. And while they dressed for their journey, in full view of the congregation, its members broke into loud wailing and sobbing, reminiscent of the destruction of the Temple at Jerusalem. Woe to us, that we should see the tablets of the covenant come crashing down! Woe to us, that our crown of crowns had toppled!

At a signal from the sergeant, the uniformed police entered the synagogue and surrounded us. As we were about to file out, the secular teacher whispered to the prosecuting attorney, who appeared to concur. Evidently the teacher had asked permission to address the gathering—to reprove the prisoners, condemn them, extol the imperial authorities, and praise the common people. Blasphemy triumphant! The police sergeant having granted permission, the secular teacher strode to the lectern and began to speak.

Here Is the Secular Teacher's Address to the Rebbe:

"To begin with you, rebbe—I have you to thank that I have pined away in prison for a whole year, for the sake of your false honor and your gold! I have you and all the rest of the Hasidic rabbis to thank for the great honor and laurels you have bestowed on all Jews by your miracles and your benevolence. I am obliged to all of you rabbis for embezzling the funds intended for Eretz Yisroel, whenever and wherever you have officiated. I must also thank the overturned Bear, who after working nobly for the Hasidic cause, has indeed become a procurer of harlots and a public consumer of treyfe.

"My thanks, also, to the tzaddik of Boyan for the glory he brought upon himself over certain jewels appraised at a thousand rubles, which he contracted to pass to a woman, whereupon he put his two wardens on her trail, with instructions to rob her of those same jewels.

"My thanks, as well, to the heaven-blessed sage of Boyan, who after the formal settlement of a dispute with his brother, to whom he conceded the exclusive rights to rabbinical activity in the Gosedar region in return for forty thousand rubles, accepted the stipulation that he himself would never again encroach upon that territory; as soon as he received the amount agreed on, he proceeded to establish himself in a town only a mile and a half from Gosedar and close to the Russian frontier, so that he was in a position to intercept en route all Hasidim coming from Russia to visit his brother, and was thus able to do a thriving business under the banner of the Hasidic cause.

"And by the way, rebbe, I suppose you approve the practice of one religious swindler in selling and mortgaging thousands of his fellow Jews to another for the purpose of exploiting them just as the serfs are exploited by the goyim on the great estates. And so one swindler is hoodwinked by another.

"My thanks, further, for the benevolent visits paid by you Hasidic rabbis—for surely they could not be merely for the sake of a ruble—to informers, stoolpigeons, thieves, tavernkeepers, procurers and the like.

"My thanks, also, to the rebbe of Komodova for the lovely and tantalizing story of how, simply to humor his wife, he caused Monpauk to waste fifteen years of his life in prison.

"My thanks, also, to the sage of Nachmestrivka for coming to blows with his sons in the courtyard one night over the sharing of an inheritance. What an edifying spectacle it is when the entire community, Jew and non-Jew alike, come running to stare while a venerable saint, his sons, his daughters, and his sons-in-law, all in their nightclothes, carry on the dispute with oven-rakes and spades, all swearing at one another like troopers. But on the very next day, supplicants were arriving with their *pidyonot*, offering sizable contributions while the brawler of the night before once again rolled his eyes to heaven, heaving sighs and making the same outlandish promises!

"My thanks, also, to the two martyrs of Savilat for their statesmanship—that is, before they were flogged; and my thanks, as well, for the response to all the requests brought in with cash offerings by thousands of Jews who come to Vetzeeoni; all those requests that were found spiked on convenient nails in various hallowed latrines.

"My thanks, also, to the saint of Sraketchka, who made his people pay through the nose on the authority of his father's last will and testament, which read: 'Yekel Asher, my son, you must continue to bring grist to the mill, to welcome and accumulate as much as you can, since no matter how much you accumulate, the donors will still be getting a bargain. . . .' And this mandate Yekel Asher executed faithfully, along with Naritzkin the heretic, by levying exorbitant excise taxes on his fellow Jews. The two three-story buildings he owned at Atzimir—acquired through the expenditure of Jewish blood and sweat—he lost by mortgaging them to Naritzkin, who publicly related to him the familiar passage concerning the soldier and the melamed's prayer shawl and phylacteries. Yet he went on consorting with the shaven Naritzkin. And tenderhearted fellow Jews reimbursed many times over the losses suffered by the Jewish collector of excise taxes.

"My thanks, also, to the twelve-year-old tzaddik, Reb Hunem-Berikel, for the great pride and honor he brought to Jewry while he toured Poland with his mother, by berating and humiliating elderly talmudic scholars, lowering the status of rebbes and dayyanim and ritual slaughterers, depriving hundreds of families of their means of livelihood, all as a result of his pronouncements on every visit. No sooner had he crossed the threshold than he would exclaim, 'Fie, for shame! An abomination! The devil and his evil spirits at work!' And sure enough, a page from Isaiah with a forbidden exegesis, which would have been planted there by one of his adjutants, was sure to be found in the house. A decade later, he was begging me to steal a rare folio from his father and deliver it to him as soon as possible. May I be spared the benevolence of such saintly sages!

"And as for you, rabbi—let me thank you in the name of all Polish Jewry for your thimblerigging, your confidence games, your brass fobbed off as gold, your fabricated miracles and wonders, for which all of Polish Jewry pays with its prestige, its wealth, its honor, and its very blood. And I wish, further, to thank your adorable sons, who indulge their whims and sow their wild oats, who abuse the poor, who snatch shtreimels from gray heads, who pluck gray beards and ritual locks. The more they squander in riotous living, the more arrogant and insolent they become, the more they are revered by your Hasidic vassals. But I would ask you to answer one final question of mine. Descend for a moment, I pray you, from your celestial sphere, and give heed to a rude mortal like myself. Forget for a moment the aureole the Hasidim have bestowed on you, cease to think of your house of worship as a sanctuary, of yourself as the high priest, and your children as heirs of that station, your dining table as a sacrificial altar, and the *pidyonot* as the sacrifice; cease to regard your pipe as a censer and your tobacco as incense, or to suppose that when the smoke goes straight upward, it is to be taken as a sign that in that moment you are conferring blessings and success and prosperity on the world but that if, God forbid, the smoke fails to rise evenly, it is conferring a severe condemnation of all Jewry, whereas if it rises in swirling spirals, the Archangel Michael and Satan have joined battle, and if it makes surging billows, some future father and mother are in harmony, and that a rabbi along with the angels in heaven will be ushers at their wedding. Forget all this pious claptrap for a moment and be truthful, rabbi—that should not be beneath your dignity, since I am without doubt no less a descendant of the saintly sages than you are, if the word 'saintly' can be used here. Is it not an error for me ever to excuse you in my heart? I often reflect that in a way, after all, you rabbis are cultivated persons, the issue of respectable parents, and that surely you must harbor some shred of conscience and noble feeling, some relic of an uncorrupted mind!

"Nu, does it never occur to you to ask, 'How does it happen that some thirty thousand Jews have beaten a path to my door, that they follow me like locusts, shower me with gold, and are ready to sacrifice themselves for me at my slightest bidding? Why do their hopes and aspirations, their faith, their very lives, so depend on me? And how, then, do I reciprocate? How do I reimburse them? All the luxuries and worldly pleasures and miracles in their behalf are, after all, no more than a hoax. Thus, for the sake of appearance, while receiving a *pidyon,* I roll my eyes and heave a sigh to the Almighty. After all, it would be foolish if even the king's own minister were to go on importuning the king for five or six hours at a time with endless petitions and requests. However, I forget each supplicant as though he had been a bad dream as soon as he is gone. This is because, first of all, no one could remember an accumulation of appeals by the hundreds every day. In the second place, the scene is repeated all over again with each succeeding day, so that one's head is in a whirl. In the third place, I am quite aware that when my rabbinical duties are over I am the same mortal, made of the same flesh and blood as the rest of mankind: I eat and drink and sleep and enjoy my family and go for walks, and occasionally I glance at a talmudic tractate.

" 'Alas, with all the hurry and scurry, with all the petitioners besieging me from dawn to dusk, I have hardly the leisure to breathe. As for the belief of my devotees that during my leisure time I inhabit the celestial sphere, that I barely touch food and scarcely sleep a wink, and that my taking a stroll and other such relaxations are but the serene worship of God and a *tikkun neshomah,* a source of spiritual improvement—well, I know that these notions are all erroneous, that all this sort of thing is not incumbent even on a genuine tzaddik. As to their marveling at my wonders and miracles, well, certainly I am aware that they amount to humbug and mumbo jumbo. Indeed, I am familiar with all the deceitful and perfidious practices to which my Hasidim resort, consciously or unconsciously. Yet who, not excepting even Moses himself, ever did or could have manifested as many divine miracles as my followers attribute to me, whether sincerely or with calculated intent—whether ingenuously or disingenuously.

" 'They derive courage from their staunch faith in me, they have the illusion that all their pleas are being granted. For this service I deserve no more than a word of thanks and possibly a meal, a cotton kaftan, a pair of slippers, maybe even a roof over my head—but not lavish riches and worldly pleasures. Rabbis of other sects, as well as all sorts of religious officials who undoubtedly render service to their fellow Jews, are paid far less generously. And our venerable leaders, in antiquity—the judges, the prophets, the tannaim, the amoraim, the gaonim, the commentators, and those tzaddikim who truly exerted themselves in behalf of their fellow Jews, whom they instilled with faith and courage—did they, God forbid, exploit their people for their own purposes? Those who came from prosperous families had no need of financial reward, whereas the less fortunate lived in privation and humility, shunning extravagant donations. Alas, not a few of our most distinguished tannaim were struggling artisans and workers. Rabbi Hillel was an ordinary day laborer, Rabbi Yehoshua a coal miner, Rabbi Yohanan a cobbler, Rabbi Isaac a blacksmith; Rabbi Kahana a common knacker. There were hundreds more —for instance, Rashi, the renowned commentator, was a goldsmith; and so on and on.

" 'Now, even to subsist on funds from one's poor followers—what, that is tantamount to robbery! . . . And now, since I contribute very little to their well-being, and since my whims and my Hasidic activities only serve to arouse the displeasure of the other nations against the Jews—can I still pursue such a sinful life and such a deceitful role, can I maintain such royal luxury, even steering my indolent and laggard children in the same direction, all of this at the expense of my twenty thousand blind and hungry sheep? . . . Does it even occur to me to try to extricate myself from such a way of life, which would be abhorred by any righteous person?'

"Yes, rebbe, this is how I think of you, and while I deliberate thus, the Almighty knows I truly sympathize with you, my heart bleeds for you . . . Surely I cannot be mistaken: it is probable that you do engage in spiritual stock-taking from time to time—it simply must be so. But why, then, do you not finally abandon your false and harmful way of life? Of course, we can always discover extenuating circumstances. That is how I rationalize things: the rabbi is undoubtedly aware of his intolerable situation and would certainly like to escape it. But since he is only a mortal, he is reluctant, he finds it difficult to give up such a lucrative enterprise and go from a luxurious way of life to one that is drab and meager, in accordance with his reduced earnings. And even if the rebbe were himself to become reconciled to an impoverished but honorable existence, in keeping with his reduced income, he would be deterred from such a move by his wife and children, who have become accustomed to a life of comfort and luxury. They would not relinquish such good fortune, but would insist on their perquisites even though he were conscience-stricken. Didn't Reb Berennu Levit plead with his wife for many years to disavow the contemptible way of life led by the Hasidic rebbes, and return to the simple and modest ways of other upright Jews? No matter how hard he tried, he could not persuade her, since she was unwilling to give up a life of affluence, until he himself became corrupted. . . .

"The pressure upon the tzaddik increases from day to day; he is beset by supplicants arriving in a steady stream from every direction. Some are in trouble over forged documents; others are desperate for snow and rain; lessees are haunted by installments, incoming and outgoing; adorable creatures are in distress over a spouse or a marriage; divorcees over the prospect of a husband; barren women come in hope of offspring; public figures come in search of rebbes and ritual slaughterers and vice versa; business partners come in quest of arbitration, and Hasidim for a tikkun and renewed enthusiasm; merchants come hoping for credit; not to speak of the halt, the lame, and the blind, or of dybbukim and gilgulim and sleep-demons, of the insane, and so on and on. Indeed, every one of them is clamoring for an amulet, a cure-all, a good-luck charm. Some even come proposing to buy some of the rabbi's personal effects, or to acquire a coin from the rabbi as a souvenir and a luck piece.

"All the while, he has no respite for even a moment; his head is swimming. But still, he must give some attention to every petitioner after he has accepted a *pidyon* from that petitioner. Moreover, the rabbi would be unable to make the rounds of all the local communities, even if he had a thousand heads, and so he is forced to delegate authority to his wardens and his deputies, and his secret agents—all of whom must be privy to his secrets and his plans, and who go to extremes in their turn for their own personal aggrandizement, and so he falls under their influence and becomes quite powerless to extricate himself from their snares. Even before they are out of the nursery, the rebbe's children assume that their father is a man of wealth and that the Hasidim and their belief are at his service—and so they are prodigal in indulging their appetites. They are being crowned as Hasidic rebbes and celestial beings. While they are still young they suppose that angels consort with them, and in their old age, when they grasp the true state of affairs, just as their father did, it is already too late—and so Judaism sinks still lower. This is what all of you young rebbes think, and it distresses you, and yet you simply cannot help yourselves.

"But it must all come to an end someday! Someday, alas, this necromancy is certain to evaporate into thin air, and then your pampered and worthless children will become indigents obliged to take up begging. Therefore, rabbi, pluck up your courage, do away with all this foul intrigue; begin to live according to the voice of your conscience—and give a respite to your fellow Jews. You will most certainly be set free: your devotees will scrape up their last savings for your acquittal! Let this be the final atonement for someone else's sins, and your conclusion of so ignominious a life . . . By now you have ruined the lives of not a few of your fellow Jews; if, God forbid, you were to pursue your nefarious way, many more would be doomed to the same bleak fate as mine. Rabbi, I am not referring to my year's imprisonment— that is a trivial matter compared with the injury done me by you and your agents. You have shattered the lives of two unfortunate souls whom God had joined—and for whom separation was the next thing to death. For eight years now, those two souls have been tormented with longing for each other, and because of you they are doomed to an existence of agony. Rebbe, at this fateful moment let this be your first step toward redemption— give happiness to two innocent souls by certifying their reunion, and I, rabbi, will be the first to thank you. Then, having performed this first act of contrition, you will be certain to continue thus until you have earned the gratitude and esteem of all our brethren. Utter one good word, rabbi, and confer true happiness on those two souls!"

Now, my dear sirs, what do you think of this reprobate, this impudent son of a fiddler's bitch? And to think of how the rebbe, his children and all the rest of those assembled there, who were obliged to listen to this drivel and keep quiet!

Unable to endure the blasphemy any longer, the rebbe cried out, "Heretic! Scoundrel! Woe to the exiled Divine Presence!" Whereupon he lowered his head in grief and the entire assembly burst into tears, some wailing loudly as though in mourning for one dead. In the next moment Rebecca, the rabbi's own niece, ran over to the teacher, exclaiming, "My dear Solomon!" The teacher burst out, "My darling Rebecca!" and the two embraced. Then the police sergeant ordered us all to leave the synagogue, except for the teacher and Rebecca. Only now did it dawn on me who it was she had been in love with all along; and only now did I become aware that the fifth count against the rabbi had been expunged from the record of the proceedings.

Three days later, I was committed to the Vetzeeoni prison.

37

*Woe, when Berliners turn maggidim and
moralize to sages and Hasidim*

The teacher addressed the general gathering as follows:
"My unfortunate and misguided brethren! I am able to
perceive that although you know my righteousness
before God and man, and are aware of the frightful injus-
tice, the untold misery and anguish that for no reason
whatever have been inflicted on me and other innocent
persons, you nevertheless look on me with hatred and
contempt, and the accused with tolerance and compassion, even regarding them as martyrs.

"The truth is on my side, and therefore I am in need
of no one's favor. Thus it is not my own misfortune that
concerns me, but rather yours—the honor and welfare of
my poor fellow Jews. Only look about you, brothers—at
the miserable situation in which we find ourselves among
other nations as a result of our evil deeds and our corrupt manners and behavior, and because of our isolation
from cultivation and decorum—from all worldly things.
Take stock of yourselves. How do you propose to im-
prove your wretched standing among the nations, so that
our brothers may be regarded as upright and useful citi-

zens of the country they happen to live in. Let us not forget that it is we, the Jews, who were singled out by God for the title of the Chosen People, and who ought to serve as a model for all the nations of the earth, rather than as a burden and a disgrace.

"A living body exists only because all of its limbs and organs work together in harmony, each according to its function, to keep the mechanism in operation. But when a limb or organ is weakened or paralyzed, it obstructs the operation of the body's mechanism, and so may have to be amputated. Now, you are aware of this. You also know from the Kabbalah that the whole world is like a single body and each person is a small world within it, so that the individual is a branch of mankind, the human organism; and in order for that organism to live and endure, each part must contribute its share to the functioning of the whole. But when an individual— not to speak of an entire people—grows indolent and useless, he becomes a burden to the entire body; and quite aside from his own sloth, he interferes with the functioning of all the other limbs, since they must sustain the flagging member.

"Still, such a limb can be tolerated: it is prodded to perform its task, and if that fails it is ignored and denied any benefits from the collective enterprise. But what of a limb or organ that becomes detrimental to the entire body—as, for instance, when a foot develops gangrene, which not only causes excruciating pain but is also likely to spread and infect the entire body? Alas, my brethren, if you were merely an ill-fated member of the world organism, a whole nation becoming a burden and a mortification to mankind, that would be distressing and deplorable enough. That would still not be the worst of it —it could still be tolerated. But what if mankind began to complain of you, not simply as an unfortunate member indulging in all sorts of fantasies but as a diseased part that might undermine the whole body? Not content, even with a God and a Torah all your own, and synagogues and houses of study and rabbis and dayyanim and ritual slaughterers and related functionaries, as well as charity boxes and other such spiritual expedients to inspire your souls—you also crave zealots and intermediaries and angelic advocates in heaven.

"And then, still unsatisfied, you make things worse by giving rise to bickering, altercations, rivalries, intrigues and outrages that injure mankind in general and Judaism in particular. And the State, which is your guardian and which has you laggards on its hands, must waste endless time, effort and resources keeping an eye on your cruel and dangerous schemes. I shall forbear to mention the countless individuals and families—yes, even entire communities, all of them as guiltless as myself—to whom you have brought immeasurable hurt and misery.

"As if it weren't enough for you to lavish on the intermediaries between heaven and yourselves funds that might in every city and borough have supported schools, hospitals, orphanages and homes for the aged, have given assistance to all the destitute, the sick, the handicapped and the widowed, helping to feed, clothe and shelter the unfortunate, while those intermediaries squander your hard-earned money on pearls and diamonds, and sumptuous tableware, on fine carvings and expensive furs, even then you are not content. No, you must still fritter away the funds that remain on lawsuits and bribes to politicians to win your senseless victories and carry on your disgraceful conspiracies, simply in order to see your rabbi exalted ever higher as a miracle-worker and celestial being. And for the sake of so worthless and stupid and insane a triumph, you don't care in the least how many innocent people are ruined in one reprehensible way or another. Look about you, brothers, and see how you yourselves, together with the rest of Jewry, are held in contempt and ridicule by the other natives and by the authorities because of your wrangling and intrigues; and see, too, the suffering, both physical and spiritual, of the rest of Jewry.

"How much you spend in money and effort and time, how much trouble you give yourselves, so as to attribute your rabbi's shortcomings as a miracle-worker and outright wrongdoings to supernatural forces; to inflate his troubles with the sheriff into a thing of earth-shaking importance, meanwhile glossing over his bowing and scraping before the goyim, his avarice, the shortening of his sentence, and treating all his errors of judgment and his discourses on mundane matters as sacred utterances and esoteric allusions, which would prove totally useless to you or anyone else in the world. If you were to contribute the money thus wasted to charity, to the welfare of the community, or if you were to concern yourselves with your own households, your wives and children, you would be helping the entire country and all of Jewry as well as yourselves.

"You would be able to carry on a tranquil family life; you would rear your children in a manner pleasing to God and man and in keeping with the demands of our times; your women would become physically and spiritually more attractive; and you would have leisure to attend the morning and evening services and to dip into the Mishnah and the Gemara, devoting the rest of the day to earning a living honestly, instead of following the crude and graceless Hasidic way of life—squalid, shabby, threadbare and down at the heels, starving and irresponsible. Your homes are full of gloom and echo with curses; your wives are sullen, slatternly and in despair; your children are tattered, ill-fed, untutored waifs—and all because your efforts and aspirations are dissipated in the synagogue and the ritual baths, and in spreading fairy tales about your saintly sages. On holidays and festive occasions you desert your firesides and rush off to visit the saintly sage in the next town—and come back with accounts of brand-new miracles and wonders, primed with fresh intrigues and squabbles, and ready for new feuds.

"I myself come of Orthodox stock, and up to the age of twenty I was no different from any other Hasid—that is, an idler and a drone. But the Almighty took pity on me and opened my eyes, making me realize what a morass I was in. So I know only too well what goes on in your Hasidic world, about the cost in money and sweat to the community of the rabbi's smallest pseudo-miracle. It is only the simple and indigent folk who can be duped into believing that there is a fair going on in heaven. But you can't deceive me! I am well-informed about the so-called miracles of the rebbes. We need not waste any words on a rabbi's prediction: he is tipped off beforehand by his secret agents and hangers-on, of whom he has enough and to spare, from the highest official to the lowest peeping Tom—not to mention the way every Hasid serves as an undercover man for his rebbe. And when some supplicant comes to the rabbi with the standard written request accompanying the *pidyon,* the rabbi has been tipped off beforehand about that petitioner's problem, and is thus regarded as a prophet and an angel from heaven. The rebbe's miracles are disgraceful and ludicrous. Take, for example, the miracle of the present trial: the rabbi predicted that the Tzeplik teacher, that heretic, would not weather the storm—but he did weather it. The lessee's wife, that bitch who stood up for the teacher, was publicly humiliated by the rabbi, and was abruptly divorced by the husband. The lessee suddenly presented the brooch and the earrings to the rebbitzin—even pleading with her to accept them. As for the rest of the miracles in the current trial, I am ashamed even to speak of them. As for the comparatively few miracles and wonders of the saintly sages that are brought about through bribery, calumny, forgery, conspiracy, larceny, false imprisonment, and occasionally even murder, they are sheer juggling and manipulation of rumors. The squire, a dotard of ninety with one foot in the grave, has been paralyzed and unable to speak for the last three years. But on the eve of his death, his youthful wife happens to demand payment due the squire from the Jewish lessee —and so the lessee hastens to present his last eighteen rubles as a *pidyon* to the rebbe, who rolls his eyes heavenward, sighs and (being well aware of the squire's moribund condition) says, 'Go in peace. The squire will soon give up the ghost.' And so it turns out. What if, after the squire's death, his widow orders a dozen or so of her huskiest farmhands to beat up the lessee? Somehow no outsiders get wind of this, but the squire's decease and the prophecy concerning it are spread far and wide.

"Or, from a secret dispatch by his agent at the county seat, the rabbi learns the contents of a royal manifesto that has already been promulgated in the national capital and in a few days will be broadcast throughout the Russian empire. Meanwhile, a desperate Jewish woman visits the rebbe with a *pidyon*, wringing her hands and moaning that her husband has been in prison for three years, and that she and her children are desperate. Again the rebbe rolls his eyes, heaves a sigh and then says, 'Go in peace—within a week your husband will be set free.' And so it turns out. The manifesto becomes a side issue, a mere incident, but the rebbe's marvel of a nonprophecy is the day's sensation. Or the gabbai arranges with an itinerant huckster to proceed to a certain town on a Friday to carry out certain instructions at the ritual baths: another bather will address him in such a way, and in his turn he is to reply thus and thus—and eventually he will marry the daughter of the other bather . . .

"Then, another Jew visits the rebbe with a *pidyon*, imploring the spiritual leader to pray for a bridegroom for his daughter, who has a pockmarked face and no dowry. Once more the rolling of the eyes, the sigh, and the bidding, 'Go in peace—you will find your daughter's predestined bridegroom at the ritual baths on Friday. Your shibboleth shall be such and such, and he will answer thus and thus.' And so it shall come to pass that another mystic turns up as a bridegroom for an unsightly bride. There is a miracle for you: a saintly being able to see from one end of the world to the other!

"And what about peculiar miracles the rebbe manages by the use of an equivocal word or a vague gesture? For example, on being presented with a *pidyon* in behalf of a woman in childbirth, the rebbe will say something that is an equivocation but that could in any event be construed as an oracular miracle—'One dies, one lives,' for example. If the woman should survive but give birth to a dead child, his statement would apply to the latter, whereas if she should give birth to a live child but die herself in doing so, the statement would apply to her; or if both mother and child should die, it would apply only to the mother, the saintly sage discounting the stillborn as having never been a living creature. Should both mother and child survive, it would be construed that the rabbi had actually saved the infant from death. . . . And there are vast numbers of such hoaxes which the common man does not fathom, and which are bruited about as miracles.

"Rid yourselves, my brothers, of these heavenly intercessors who indulge their appetites here on earth, who live on the fat of the land and burn the candle at both ends, all at your expense! They don't give a tinker's damn about you on your occasions of rejoicing, let alone in times of adversity—a thing you are well aware of, since you see it happen every day, as it is happening at this very moment. Does the rebbe show the least concern for the lessee of the postal service, now that he has bled him white and betrayed him? And, of course, he hardly pays any attention to the rest of the accused.

"The greed and avarice of these sages have no bounds. They exploit and fleece and extort from everything you own, yet almost never hold out a helping hand. Don't be deluded by the way some moguls and professional do-gooders and worldly politicians, including even some of the maskilim and the so-called heretics, even the unbearded and the debauchees visit these sages and occasionally contribute a *pidyon* to them. That is simply because, given the general corruption of our time, they are afraid of losing their possessions, of being disgraced or actually imprisoned. Some find this sort of intrigue to their advantage; others make use of it as a goad to scourge and threaten whomever they please. As for you yokels, you merely look on the surface of things and are delighted to offer up Judaism, your wives and children as a sacrifice in return for the privilege of touching your rabbi's shtreimel, I give you my word of honor that I made no effort whatever to bring about my own release, knowing that this would only lead to the imprisonment of the rebbe for his various misdeeds—and that in turn would only impel the Jewish community to make further sacrifices to get him out. This I was anxious to avoid, whatever happened. But, through no fault of mine, despite my innocence, honest persons also contributed to my having to suffer without any reason.

"Stop this sacrificing of yourselves to the golden calf! You have endured more than your share of destitution and misery and indignity, of pangs of conscience and wretched worldly pleasure, not to speak of the seven circles of hell in the world to come. Alas, it is high time for the rest of Jewry to cease having to atone for your transgressions! . . ."

38

The rebbe was saved by Jewish money—but who knows whether his prayers could save me?

After about a week my father was permitted to visit me in prison. And although much distressed by my misfortune, nonetheless he consoled himself and me with the declaration that I was atoning for the saintly sage—might he have a long life—and that because of my being so devout a Jew the Almighty would set me free. And he told me of reports from Sirkov that the moguls of Kiev had furnished bail amounting to three thousand rubles for the rabbi and Mekhuntzie, providing the bondsmen were repaid within six months. So the rabbi and Mekhuntzie were out on bail. Two weeks later my father came again, along with a spiritual leader and two wealthy local dignitaries. I was urged, on rabbinical authority, not to implicate the rebbe and Mekhuntzie in the forthcoming trial—or, God forbid, I should pay dearly for it. In return for this forbearance, the rabbi would pray for me continually, keeping at it until I had been set free.

My father exhorted me, "Itzikel, it is incumbent on you to carry out the rabbi's behest; moreover, it will be to your benefit as well. I am already old and infirm, and evidently not long for this world. So you can hope that the rebbe will once again engage you as a gabbai; and even if that doesn't happen, you will still be able to keep the wolf from the door by collecting funds in the neighborhood for the rabbi's maintenance. You already have authorization to do so from the local Hasidim and dignitaries, and if you now do as the rebbe bids you, in due time you may, God willing, inherit my position and thus be able to make ends meet, however humbly, so long as you are not a mere supplicant."

At first I found life in prison very difficult and upsetting, since I had been accustomed to a life of ease and self-indulgence. Gradually, however, I became reconciled to the hardships, especially after the Jewish prisoners were granted permission to have a little bit of schnapps for *Kiddush* on the Sabbath. The "little" bit was later expanded to a quart for the three of us, which would last us until Wednesday. This privilege helped to brighten our lives when the going was rough, and after the first year of our imprisonment we seemed to have accepted our fate. For days at a time we would entertain ourselves with stories about the rebbe and the lives of all the tzaddikim, going back to the saintly Baal Shem, and we would recite all the miracles and wonders of that rebbe, the Master of the Good Name, as well as his parables and pithy passages. In short, it was like the worm finding comfort in horseradish. Each one of our trio kept his innermost feelings about the Hasidim and the saintly sages to himself. But for the sake of appearances each of us did his best to make a show of belief. And on the weekly occasions when we were permitted to leave our cells along with the other Jewish prisoners, the three of us would stand up for the saintly sages before the rest of the prisoners, refusing to tolerate the least criticism of them, since practically all of the Jewish prisoners were

Hasidic adherents, most of them having been locked up for offenses similar to our own.

Not a few Polish Jews openly commit far more serious offenses, with not a whisper or protest; in fact, they play the role of leaders and dignitaries. They are highly respected in the community and arrange the best marriages for their children, and they live surrounded by reverence, pride, and indulgence. But they need only become involved in some grave but spurious charge and they are sentenced to long prison terms, or occasionally even transported to the bleakest part of Siberia. Consider, for example, the two Hasidim who were jailed for forgery, tampering with wills in a case involving the estates of two deceased squires. Trifling matters, certainly —mere rubbish, don't you agree? Why, such cases occur every day in Poland; they're scarcely worth mentioning. After all, the profligate heirs of those gentry would be inheriting some two million rubles from their fathers, in addition to the estates—so how are they hurt by such relatively trivial matters? Let us say that instead of losing ten thousand rubles in a single night's gambling at cards, or the cost of one night's carousing in a brothel, they lose only 9,950 rubles; whereas that same ten thousand rubles will enable the two Jews to marry their children well, contribute handsomely for being called up to the Scroll of the Law in the synagogue during a Sabbath morning service, present their rebbe with a substantial *pidyon* twice a year, and so on and on. Thus the money is put to better use than it would have been by the precious sons of the gentry. Don't you agree? But no; some Berliner or misnaged, or even some follower of a rival Hasidic rabbi, because of some trivial dispute or slight, will turn them over to the authorities for what amounts to hardly more than a practical joke, a prank—and imprisonment is the result.

Or take the case of the tavernkeeper who was jailed for receiving stolen goods—if you consider that a crime. Let us say that a peasant owes him several rubles for vodka consumed at the tavern. The peasant offers a few stolen turkeys or a copper frying pan, dirt cheap, to the tavernkeeper, who accepts the loot in his turn and proceeds to extend further credit to his patron for vodka. Is there anything illegal about such a transaction? After all, if *he* doesn't engage in it, someone else will, since it provides mutual satisfaction. But before he knows it, some scalawag will denounce him—once again as a mere practical joke—and a trifling offense will be blown up so totally out of all proportion that the innkeeper is ruined for life.

Another prisoner was serving time for having used the mails to defraud, still another for a fraudulent petition of bankruptcy; two had committed assault and battery in a synagogue; one had been in the business of selling moonshine and unauthorized marriage licenses, and other crimes equally horrendous—all in fact quite negligible. What a misfortune, indeed, that the imperial treasury should lose a few kopecks in postage! (Bear in mind that several poor Jewish corpses will be provided with shrouds costing several kopecks less!) So the Jew is deprived of the loot and all but beaten to death. You would think that he had already been sufficiently punished for such a trivial offense. But no, on top of this he must be kept locked up, too. Will the tax-farmer be so gravely damaged if he is to net a little less this year? Why, he spends on a bouquet for the actress enough for the Jew and his family to live on for some time, and set aside a little money for the rebbe as well.

Such loudly advertised transgressions as these are a commonplace in Poland—especially among Hasidim, respectable Jews who marry young. These young men,

supported by their parents or in-laws, cluster meekly in
the synagogue and at the ritual baths. An allowance set
aside for the dowry, which is usually small and is held in
trust by a third party, enables the bridegroom once a
year to make a trip to some saintly sage for the High Holy
Days. The wives of these young men give birth regularly
in accordance with Hasidic tradition. And when the in-
laws' support comes to an end and the trustee goes bankrupt—as is likewise the tradition—or embezzles the entire two hundred rubles of the dowry and squanders it
during the first year of the marriage; or he himself opens
a store and leaves to his wife, the mother of five children,
the business of running it—since for him there are
spiritual matters to look after—and the venture, alas,
goes on the rocks, then what is he to do? There can, of
course, be no thought of resorting to a craft of some sort
—even you, my dear sirs, would not go so far. He is unfit
for business—that is also the tradition; so he hasn't a red
cent, he can't be a melamed because he has a weak heart
—as befits a well-bred young Hasid—and he is too ignorant to be a rabbi. So he turns to a vocation that can be
pursued without capital, without intelligence, without
knowledge of the Torah or a robust constitution. And so
if he is a congenital liar, he becomes a matchmaker; if he
is long-winded, he becomes a badchan, an entertainer at
weddings; one who had grown up in his father's winery
will become the keeper of a tavern where the gentry
spend their leisure; one with a smattering of Polish will
become a middleman. If he is gifted with fine penman-
ship and mastered Russian grammar in his youth—or
even without having done so—he becomes an expert in
forging documents, contracts, passports and so on—
which, after all, is also an art of sorts. If he happens to
live near the frontier, he will take up smuggling. There
is no shortage of vocations, to be sure. And one does the

best he can with whatever little the good Lord provides him.

However, since such a well-bred young man, the protégé of some rabbi and the heir of saintly sages, is nevertheless not equipped to pursue any dignified vocation, he will have to content himself with a menial job which may be as far beneath his dignity as it is beyond his strength. It might reasonably seem that such a one had already received his chastisement. But reality is not acquainted with reason: on top of everything, he must be sent to prison.

To be brief: I had already served nearly five years before any substantial news reached me from the outside. Then I learned of various disputes and feuds and conspiracies as well as of the new miracles and wonders of the Hasidic world. I even found out that that heretic long since married Rebecca again, and that for the past two years he had been the government-appointed rabbi in Vetzeeoni, where he had been doing very well. I learned further that the rabbi and Mekhuntzie had been acquitted, and that after the first year the rebbe had ceased to give even a cent to my wife. Well, it may be that in this he was justified: he had, after all, spent a small fortune on his own defense in court, and so why should he pay old debts—particularly to me?

Meanwhile, my father had come once to visit me, for the last time before his death, bringing with him my eldest son, whom he was having assist him in collecting funds for the rabbi's maintenance. My father was already failing and would indeed be gathered to his ancestors that same year—with "May His Soul Be Bound Up in the Bond of Life" duly carved on his tombstone. I was delighted with my boy, though I could not understand why he had been enlisted. Among other things, he told me that had it not been for the Krokodilevka excise-tax collector, his mother and the rest of the children would have had to kill themselves.

As for the trumped-up charge against me and the others, it was a thing we were still at a loss to understand. It was clear, however, that I had been made the scapegoat for all the crimes, though there could be no doubt that the rebbe must be stirring up the celestial realms in my behalf. Well, time would bring everything to light.

39

A moot point emerges

Another year had passed, and my father was dead. There were now rumors that my young son had become a habitué at the rebbe's court; but everything there was shrouded in mystery, though he was known to be making the rounds to collect funds for the rabbi's maintenance. Meanwhile, I had languished six whole years in jail, still with no inkling of when I would be released. And no doubt the rabbi was still beseeching the Lord in my behalf. Shmuelek, one of the two gabbaim who were in jail with me, finally began to be heard making critical remarks about the rebbe's apparent lack of concern for us and to sound somewhat skeptical about the Hasidic cause. But the other, Mordecai ben Mordecai Tronhorb, was more than ever ready to endure fire and brimstone for the sake of the rebbe and Hasidism, accepting every tribulation like a true Hasid, with fervor and devotion. As for me, I usually held my peace and acted as intermediary between the two of them.

One day gripping news reached us from outside: Ferilhein of Drobitchev, renowned as a Hasidic millionaire, was on the verge of bankruptcy and headed for the poorhouse. Moreover, the disaster was rumored to have been brought about by none other than Hanarz, a Berliner. Soon afterward there was further news: Itzchak Ber Levenson, the notorious Jewish heretic had turned up his toes. My response to the two reports was merely to nod my head and make a wry face. Shmuelek was much excited over the second report, and had no interest in the first. Mordecai, on the other hand, was happy over the second and distressed to the point of tears over the first.

The morning after the two reports had come in, Mordecai looked gloomy, and I asked him what was the matter. "Bah! It's hardly worth talking about," he answered, "I had a strange sort of dream last night. It was really sickening."

"Nu—tell us what the dream was about," I urged him.

"I've told you, Itzikel, that it's not worth discussing —it's so dreadful," Mordecai answered.

"That may be, but since you are obviously so distressed over it," Shmuelek said, "wouldn't it be better for you to try to explain the dream?"

"Well, you may be right," he responded halfheartedly.

The three of us sat down near the barred window and Mordecai began this way: "It was really a ridiculous dream. In my sleep I seemed to see a moonlit night, more beautiful than any I had ever seen before. I seemed to be in the cemetery at Kremenitz. Then suddenly I heard the most awful noises, and all around me were hundreds of corpses, wearing prayer shawls and white linen shrouds, gathering in a circle. In the midst of that circle I could see a gilded bier covered by a splendid marriage canopy that had an angel holding each of its four corners. Just in front of it was a dazzling pillar, which in my dream I supposed might be the Divine Presence itself. Suddenly a mellifluous voice, with the words, 'Justice must go before a man as he travels that way,' issued out of the pillar. As I lay there trembling, a corpse dressed in a soiled prayer shawl and a white robe rushed over and prodded me, calling out angrily, 'Villain, why are you dawdling there? Get up and accompany Reb Itzchak Ber Levenson of blessed memory, the great tzaddik and zealot of Israel, on his way to Jerusalem!'

"I was shaken to the very depths, for I recognized the voice as that of the old maggid, whom I had heard more than once in my youth. I shrieked, 'Is that any way to talk about such a heretic? Anyway, how did you get here from Atanovka?"

" 'Silence, you Hasidic fool!' was the corpse's apprehensive reply. 'Now that you've recognized me, keep it to yourself! My name is anathema here. Only in your world of illusion was I considered a celebrity or a man of distinction. Here, in the world of the hereafter, my name is in disrepute. As soon as the funeral procession has passed by I will give you a brief account of my end, so that you may communicate it at once to your rabbi and to my sons in the world of illusion.'

"The funeral went on for what seemed to be about half an hour, and then all the corpses reassembled. 'Villain, you must go no farther!' cried a horrifying voice. 'This is the boundary of Eretz Yisroel. No such money-grubber may set foot on holy ground!'

"I was not sure where this voice came from, or to whom it was addressed. But the elderly maggid prodded me again, saying, 'Come. That is the voice of the Angel of Destruction, who follows me about in my world of chaos, and who gives me the order to turn back.'

"As he retreated, this is what he told me: 'You know

something of the role I played in the world of illusion, since you recall seeing me on a Sabbath day in Vetzeeoni. And the rest you must have heard about. In my youth I could not explain how I had become renowned as a tzaddik, a prophet, a miracle-worker, and a celestial being. Now and then I would laugh to myself at seeing such deeply devout and wise people revering an empty vessel and a scatterbrain such as I am. But over the years, as I saw an anxious world beat a path to my door and people going to extremes to gratify every whim of mine, and how the more injustices and acts of folly I committed the more I was honored and glorified, to say nothing of the thousands of rubles that were showered on me, I began to be deluded into thinking that I was truly a master of learning. And I no longer scoffed at the deeply devout and wise. By the time I reached old age, and came to be known as the "Old Maggid," I was oblivious of my own identity. I had come to regard myself as a celestial being; I lived in the grand style of royalty, and reared my children in the same fashion. And I felt confident that in the hereafter I would be no worse off than during my life on this earth.

" 'And so when, shortly after my demise, an angel opened my sepulcher and asked who I was, I replied with anger and disdain, "Don't you know that I am the Old Maggid?" On hearing this the angel plucked out my intestines, flung them into my face, and shouted, "So you are the person who bled your brothers white by fraud and deception, who persecuted all the maskilim and the movement of the Haskalah from the eighteenth down into the nineteenth century, and above all that illustrious Jew Reb Itzchak Ber Levenson?" And with that he caught me by the nose with his flame-tipped spear and flung me through a huge door into a vast auditorium, blazing with light, where a session of the heavenly tribunal was in progress. There was the Archangel Michael on one side of the table and Satan on the other, and stacked between them were the gigantic chronicles, inscribed in blood on pages of fire that record all the transgressions of mankind. The tribunal then opened a book of the chronicle, in which Satan pointed out all my recorded sins and transgressions. And let me inform you, you Hasidic fool, that every sin and wrongdoing—from the most insignificant folly to the most heinous crime—that I had committed, in word or deed, was recorded in that book, in my own hand. Even such minute errors as adjusting a woman's marriage wig, not to mention approaching the lessee with the alms box for a donation of silver in the midst of the Eighteen Benedictions, were likewise registered. And although this may sound incredible to you, there was even a record of the trick resorted to at the table in Vetzeeoni on a Friday night, when I pretended to fall into a momentary trance so that the shtreimel fell off my head, and then screamed, "Bring on the grapes for dessert! Grapes for dessert!" And as soon as this delicacy was placed on the table, I would toy with a cluster for a quarter of an hour, grimacing all the while. Then, selecting a single grape, I would cut it into tiny pieces, and after swallowing one piece, according to the gabbai, I would fall into a deep sleep, wheezing like an ox with its throat slit, while the guests sat spellbound, believing I was in communion with the celestial realm and standing on the very threshold of the throne room of the Almighty. And there was the Archangel Michael, all in a sweat as he tried to find one good deed in my record—all to no avail. And then, as though for spite, Satan gave a laugh and pointed to a passage conveying my deathbed admonition to my second son: "My dead Yekel Asher, you should accept all the contributions you can, in cash or in kind, and go on accepting them—for no matter how much you take in, my followers can never repay me fully!"

" 'According to the verdict of the celestial tribunal, the three principal transgressions were: (1) a terrible greed for money; (2) having victimized supplicants through deceptive promises and predictions in the name of the Almighty; and (3) the persecution and vilification of contemporaries. For these three transgressions the penalty was to spend in the realm of chaos as many years as the transgressor continued to defraud in his role as sage; and throughout this period he was to continue his role as a false and avaricious sage, even as he had done during his existence on earth. Accordingly, Satan was to carry out this sentence upon him: to be cast into Gehenna in a sepulcher of imaginary virgin silver, where his greed for gold would flare up at every moment, compelling him to snatch at a handful of the glowing gold pieces that floated through the air—only to have each coin disintegrate into dust and ashes, as it trickled through his fingers. And each time he snatched at the illusory gold, one or another of his deceased Hasidim was to appear and mock him. He was to roam night after night through the cemeteries of the nether world, posing as a saintly sage among the dead—who, while appearing to be still alive, would come to him as supplicants and have the false saint promise them offspring, long life, health and prosperity. And after each false prediction, those same supplicants were to confront him as no more than corpses, mocking and pointing the finger of scorn. And he was to go on and on in this deathly charade of receiving petitioners. In addition, at the close of the Sabbath, he was to be led, wearing his holiday attire, into the celestial auditorium, where he was to be made a laughingstock before the great true sages of Israel.

" 'This verdict was executed forthwith, and now for thirty years I have been made to suffer because of my wretched thirst for imaginary gold. Night after night, I enact once again the contemptible role of a spurious saintly sage among the corpses, and at the close of each Sabbath I am put to public ridicule before the great sages of Israel. Whom, you ask, do I see among those sages? Woe is me! Along with such venerable masters as Maimonides, Ibn Ezra, Ramban, Judah Halevi, and Abravanel, are Moses Mendelssohn, Baruch Spinoza, Naphtali Hertz Weisel, Mendel Stern, and ever so many others, all of them wearing crowns of gold, with ministering angels dancing attendance on them. Last night, as I was being held up to the laughter of these great sages of Israel, there was a commotion, and all the assembled sages were on their feet as the Archangel Michael ushered in the soul of Itzchak Ber Levenson of blessed memory, glistening like the full moon. The sages welcomed the soul of Reb Itzchak with awe and reverence, and a host of seraphim appeared to greet him. One seraph brought out the ledger labeled "Utter Indigence" and placed it on the table, and an oracular voice issued from the heavenly throne: "Because Itzchak Ber Levenson has suffered distress, privation and indignity at the hands of such hypocrites and flatterers as the maggid and his retinue, but continually sacrificed himself for the honor and welfare of his people, his tortured and sanctified body is to be taken to the holy city of Jerusalem and interred there with royal honors."

" 'I beg of you to hasten and convey what I have told you to all my sons, as well as to your rabbi, so that they may take stock of the lives they lead. And let them do penance and give up playing their sham role as saintly sages. Such a step might atone for some of their sins, and thus perhaps my bitter lot would also be alleviated.

Hurry along, and warn them to break loose from eternal ignominy, disgrace and misfortune.'

"At these words I awoke in fright at so ominous a dream."

40

It is hard to say whether the sects of the Hasidim, the misnagedim, and the Haskalah are a blessing or a curse

Mordecai recounted his dream with contempt and annoyance, and Shmuel listened to the whole strange tale with aversion. When it ended, both spat in disgust, with the pious exclamation, "Heaven preserve us!" Now, I had known Shmuel, from his earliest childhood up to his present age of thirty-five, to be a misnaged and a talmudic scholar who was in fact eligible to be ordained to the rabbinate. And I knew Mordecai to be a leading maskil, who had embraced the cause of the Haskalah and was versed in four or five languages, and who had already published a Hebrew translation of a work by a certain well-known German named Goethe—a book acclaimed by all the followers of the Haskalah. In addition, almost up to the age of forty-five he had been a heretic, had transgressed nearly all the biblical commandments, and had, moreover, feathered his nest to the tune of ten thousand rubles. But about five years ago both completely disavowed their former mode of life and in their fervor as Hasidim surpassed even our rabbi's devotees.

They were, in short, Hasidim ready to immolate

themselves for the sake of the very slippers the rebbe wore. Thus, more than once I had heard Shmuel declare, "The Talmud and all the posttalmudic commentaries are not to be compared with our rabbi's everyday remarks!" And Mordecai had said he would swear on the Bible that Mendelssohn was not worthy to mention the name of the Baal Shem Tov, of blessed memory. Yet both Shmuel and Mordecai had witnessed the entire affair at the synagogue just as I had. What is more, they were privy to some other secrets and now they had languished in prison for six years just as I had, all because of their rabbi. And even though they were less culpable than I, nevertheless they showed such zeal for the rebbe and for Hasidism that it amounted to self-immolation. So I ask you, my friends: What, after due consideration, was I to think of the whole Hasidic cult?

Naturally, I wished to be sure whether they were really sincere or were merely hypocrites putting on an act because they were suspicious of each other—and especially of me. They knew me, after all, to have been a devout Hasid all my life; and they were all the more wary of me because of my taciturnity while I was in prison with them. They could very well have supposed my uncommunicativeness to be a ruse I was using to test them. It thus occurred to me, since I had had more influence in Hasidic circles than my fellow prisoners, to engage them in a halfway candid discussion of Hasidism, and thus to learn their true colors. They were not likely to hoodwink me completely, I thought; and so I began by observing to Mordecai, more than half-seriously, "According to the Gemara, one's dreams are a reflection of what he thinks while he is awake."

"I'm really surprised to hear such foolishness from you, Itzikel!" returned Mordecai, sounding ruffled. "Why, we heard about the heretic's death only yesterday.

And if I did give it any thought, it was to recall only vividly that fellow who had posed as a pillar of society. So what could it have to do with such a loathsome and idiotic dream about such a despicable scoundrel, and what relation could there be to the Old Maggid, of blessed memory?"

"How could I know?" I answered with a shrug. "Shmuel, what do you make of it?"

"It's very simple," said Shmuel. "Since Mordecai knew the heretic, it is not surprising that he thought of the matter—and in that fleeting thought the past was recalled to his mind, with the way of life and the sinful notions of that period. So when his mind was turned loose in sleep, he dreamed of all these things. But to say that Mordecai harbored such strange thoughts last night, you must be out of your mind! Suppose, for instance, that I were to learn today that Reb Hayyim Volozhiner had died. Having known him personally, I might have been reminiscing about the old days when I conversed with him and was associated with the Vilna Gaon. If I dreamed of all that at night, would that fact be proof that I still clung to my heretical views at the time, God forbid? So, Itzikel, what is there to be so puzzled about in all this?"

"I know I shall never have such a dream as long as I live," I declared.

"Is that so, Itzikel? And do you expect, perhaps, to dream like a fool of paradise?" Shmuel slyly inquired. "You hardly knew anybody of that persuasion; and even if you did, you had little in common with any of them. And so why should disturbing ideas come to you in your dreams?"

"The Lord be praised that I didn't know such people, or have any wish to know them," I said with some deliberation.

"True enough—and for a Hasid born and bred, it is best that way," Mordecai replied. "But don't forget, Itzikel, what the Gemara says: 'A true tzaddik cannot attain such lofty heights as a repentant sinner.' Shmuel and I have at least already experienced the need to resist temptation; but as for you, all you did was to advance from a minor synagogue to the rabbi's house of worship. A brave fellow, indeed!"

By now, I could rejoice at the thought that they both regarded me as a zealous and even fanatical Hasid. And I could exploit this as leverage toward an open discussion of the entire question. So I plunged ahead.

"I don't quite see what temptation you had to resist," I said. "What is so extraordinary about misnagedim and the entire Haskalah movement that it should be necessary to resist temptation in renouncing them?"

I had intended to provoke them—and I had succeeded.

"Listen to me, Itzikel," Shmuel broke in angrily. "Of course nobody can discuss music with a deaf-mute. But is the deaf-mute therefore entitled to look down on those endowed with an acute sense of hearing, or to boast that he has never heard a woman's voice, as normal people have? If you had been endowed as we were with proper hearing ability, and if you had been privileged to listen for many years to the melodious voice of a famous woman singer, then you would not doubt the temptation that must be overcome in the voluntary repudiation of certain beliefs. Of course, it is easy to be a pious Jew without having tasted the fruit of the Tree of Knowledge. But afterward, Itzikel, it's a different story altogether."

"As a matter of fact, what you have said supports my argument. So you regard your behavior at that time as equivalent to the Tree of Knowledge, as an important event?" I inquired. "Well, then, good!"

The question was not, my two fellow prisoners answered at once, how they regarded that bygone chapter at present, but that it had been a matter of great importance at the time.

"If that is the case, let's go a little deeper into the question," I said, smiling in the true Hasidic fashion. "We don't have to sound our own trumpets like the Gypsies. It is common knowledge that the three of us are ardent Hasidim, and not likely to be corrupted by such a discussion. So, my friends, give me some idea of your former opinions, and in what ways you now find them running counter to Hasidism. To be more specific: Have you come to regard those former views of yours as absurd—or perhaps even as belonging to the devil's territory? Or did you renounce them because you found the cause of Hasidism superior to the other school of thought—although both have some merit of their own?"

I shall not drive you mad by giving a detailed account of our discussion, which went on for at least three hours. Rather, I shall summarize for you the views of my fellow prisoners on this matter.

They argued that both Misnagedism and Haskalah had merit: one could adhere to the first school of thought and still remain a pious Jew and a good person, or one could adhere to the second and still remain a good person and a pious Jew. . . . Both schools of thought, however, appealed only to *cold-blooded* persons (Mordecai used the word "conservative"), namely, those who follow the beaten path and give attention only to the *outward* aspect of things, without heed to the *internal* aspect (naturally, each individual according to his own perception). For instance, the doctrine of Misnagedism stipulated that prayer and the study of the Torah, the observance of the six hundred thirteen commandments of the Pentateuch, and so on, are to be carried out, without exception, at a specific time and in a specific place and a specific way. Haskalah, on the other hand, disavowed all the official commandments concerning good works, and urged its followers to act entirely according to their consciences. Even so, it advocated only outward observance with certain reservations; and as for inner observance, certain commandments were to be complied with, whereas others were to be ignored. In general, the followers of both schools of thought called for adherence to the prayer book, in an obedient and disciplined manner but with total respect.

A person endowed with enthusiasm and rapture, however—one with a heightened spirituality—could not conform to these schools of thought since such a person could not submit to specific rules and regulations and was averse to discipline. They are like roosters: when rubbed under the wings, they must crow. Moreover, they must associate with others in order to share and give vent to their own fervor. Therefore my two fellow inmates found Hasidism to be the best course, since Hasidism was essentially a living spark. They were not troubled by its being a self-seeking course; indeed, they maintained that Hasidism in itself was only a chimera, insignificant as compared to the other two schools of thought. What mattered to them was that this was a course that allowed complete freedom in Judaism, which was why its devotees were always exhilarated—a mood that brought accord and rapport among its followers. This accounted for the self-sacrificing mutual aid among Hasidim— something my two fellow prisoners regarded as a rare virtue, while this rare virtue was also assessed according to law and justice, the two inmates are unemotional angels and obedient lackeys and dutiful soldiers, devoid of any spark of fire, or of a moiety of enthusiasm. (Mordecai admitted that Haskalah did seem to entail a bit of enthusiasm—that of reading a good book for instance, or of composing a poem—but that enthusiasm, too, must be brief and restrained, a thing felt only within oneself.) And so each one could get along by himself, without companionship. Neither a misnaged nor a maskil would offer you a meal, let alone put you up for the night, or grant you a loan without interest, or join in your festivities, or come to your aid when you were most in need. The Hasidim, on the other hand, would put themselves out for one another; when one of them was in trouble the entire sect would stand by him to a man. Thus, my two fellow jailbirds considered both the other schools of thought, with all their merits and virtues, as *dead*, whereas Hasidism with all of its flaws and deceptions, they saw to be very much alive. And however that may be, if one was capable of exuberance and ecstasy, that was all that mattered. But since I favored neither of the other schools of thought, was I not justified in following Hasidism and idolizing its saintly sage?

Yet I felt trapped and suffocated: somehow I could not reconcile myself to all the machinations I had witnessed at the rabbinical court and among the Hasidim. But, then again, perhaps all of that had been right and proper; perhaps our rabbi was indeed a celestial being, and it was my fault that I had not fathomed the actual aim and the inner secret of Hasidism. In short, I found myself at an impasse, groping blindly for a new position—supposing that I were to be released from prison at all. The two schools of thought were not the question, since I was familiar with neither one. The question was simply whether I would go on clinging to the traditions of my old way of life, regardless of its flaws and shortcomings, or repudiate it, bracing myself for a life of humility and deprivation, simply in order to ease my conscience. In the midst of these bewildering thoughts, I dozed off on my prison cot and had a double-barreled dream.

41

My first dream: the gluttonous spider is dead, and the trapped fly takes heart

In my dream I was at death's door. All of a sudden, the Angel of Death stood there glaring at me out of a thousand eyes, clutching in one hand a vial of poison and in the other a slaughterer's knife, and ordered me to confess before I died. My mind was all in turmoil; I seemed unable to get hold of myself, and could not decide what to confess. Ought I to confess all the mischief and outrage I had perpetrated during my Hasidic life for the sake of a saintly sage, and the Hasidic cause? Or ought I to confess that of late I had begun to harbor doubts about the cause of Hasidism, and even to suspect our saintly sage himself? In my utter confusion, I began to wonder whether the whole idea of the creation was delusive, no more real than the tricks of a prestidigitator.

After all, I had seen a multitude of Jews giving our rebbe more veneration than Moses, and treating the most casual remark of their idol as superior to the Torah. These Jewish followers maintained that the tzaddik partook of the nature of the Holy One Himself, blessed be He—and that the tzaddik's every utterance was tantamount to the Mosaic Law. But in the course of many years I had witnessed this same rebbe and his children behaving contrary to the dictates of the Torah and the commandments of the Lord of the Universe. So now I was faced with two alternatives: that the Holy One, blessed be He, and the Torah were opposed to all the misdeeds of the rebbe and his Hasidim in this world; or else, God forbid, that everything was in a state of anarchy, without any law and without any judge.

In the midst of this mental agony the Angel of Death slit my throat, and immediately my soul left my body to soar above the clouds, above the stars, through the celestial spheres and each of the seven heavens, until finally it came to a vast hall where it cowered out of sight in a corner. Before long, the heavenly tribunal could be seen sitting down at a table and the presiding judge could be heard calling out, "Bring in Ferilhein of Drobitchev, that old villain, the enemy of Haskalah, defrauder of widows and orphans, and let him give an account of himself!"

My spirit was dumbfounded to hear the name of the venerable Hasidic millionaire who was thus summoned to trial. Alas, here was a plutocrat, rumored to have been on the verge of bankruptcy and about to topple from eminence to a hand-to-mouth existence—and what, I wondered, could he be accused of by the celestial tribunal?

At that moment a handsome young man in splendid attire appeared on the scene, and the sexton at the table called out, "Welcome, Reb Simcha Kotzi." Next, in came angels with stacks of ledgers and promissory notes and other negotiable instruments by the armload; and one of them deposited the rich man's ledger on the table. In a little while the accused Ferilhein was escorted in, along with a lewdly decked out female in velvet and cloth of gold, blazing with precious stones. Behind them trailed a beautiful young woman, blue-eyed and golden-haired, who appeared tearful and downcast in her shabbily respectable clothes—evidently a servant to the bejeweled woman who preceded her. Still farther behind, a tall elderly woman, in the dress of a housekeeper, looked beseechingly toward her mistress.

The young man began turning the pages of the ledgers and exhibiting the promissory notes, as proof to the celestial tribunal that Ferilhein was both a swindler and an embezzler, who had perpetrated a sham bankruptcy proceeding. The young prosecutor's accusations were examined and confirmed, and Ferilhein confessed to all the charges. Then the presiding judge announced, "Ferilhein has perpetrated a sham bankruptcy, and under our Code of Laws he is condemned for life to the prison at Drobitchev. As for his grave transgressions against justice and against the Torah, and his robbing of widows and orphans, as well as his peculation of communal funds; as for his persecution of the Haskalah movement and its followers, his giving homage to the Hasidic cause and its leaders—in order to bolster his financial credit and sweep away all impediments in his drive for gain, yet all the while posing as a devout and righteous Jew in the community; and as for yet other grave sins and misdeeds which he himself has recorded with his own hand—for all of these he will be tried as soon as he is dead, according to the Code of Laws."

The ruthless and hardhearted Ferilhein stood there stricken, with bowed head, while the bejeweled woman shrieked hysterically and then fainted. The comely young woman and the tall elderly one smiled faintly and sighed as though relieved of a heavy burden. The young prosecutor then approached the young woman, and in cadenced phrases offered his congratulations:

Welcome, dear lady Haskalah!
Now I shall proceed to clean up this Jewish clutter;
Your persecutor has met with defeat—
For now I shall take you under my wing.
Look about you—brazen Hasidism, your erstwhile mistress,
Lies prostrate, with her patron.
For you this augurs a great future;
Soon, Jews will kneel before you likewise—

"One moment!" called out the presiding judge. "Standing there is someone much older than the youthful Haskalah, who, although she suffered less than the younger one, also had to bow her gray head before that impertinent Hasidism, and to put her shoulder to her wheel in abject humility. Here we are confronted with ancient Rabbinism, to which the brazen woman now refers as Misnagedism. And we were silent! We held our tongues because Rabbinism had failed until now to protest publicly in her behalf against Hasidism, as the more energetic Haskalah had done. And that was because, alas, Rabbinism has no spokesman in the nether world. (The Torah, alas, has been thrust into the background.) Ever since its solitary defender, the Vilna Gaon, was gathered to his fathers, the Torah has been, alas, like a flock without a shepherd; it must submit to the leadership of Hasidic rabbis, who instead of acting as spiritual leaders, or ritual slaughterers, or related functionaries, follow their own deceitful interpretation. It is precisely because ancient Rabbinism bowed down before Hasidism, and made no attempt to free itself, though fully aware of the good example of the Haskalah, that the fulfillment of redemption must still be postponed for a while. The day will come when the celestial tribunal will sit in judgment over the tenets and creeds of these three schools of thought according to the interpretations of their three exponents—Mendelssohn, the Vilna Gaon, and the Baal Shem Tov. Then the masses will learn which school has stayed nearest to the truth and which has gone astray.

"For the time being, we wish to inform the masses that as of this moment we condemn the despotic arrogance of Hasidism, because it has gone out of bounds. But the verdict on the continuation and the authority of these three schools of thought must wait until another time. We have at least silenced the brazen woman and deprived her of her dangerous patron Ferilhein. That in itself is the beginning of salvation."

These words were followed by a solemn chant from the angels:

The Lord of the Universe has condemned
The arrogance of Hasidism,
The curse which haunts our land
With its shams and despotism.

With Hasidism finally exposed and overthrown,
Other schools can claim their right
To truths which Hasidism can no longer own—
Let us go forth and conquer in our fight!

And let us not disdain the good in Hasidism—
Its creed should not be wholly despised.
It could still be a source of idealism
Through which the ancient Jewish hopes are realized.

Apparently, as I watched this scene and listened to the chanting, I became totally delirious. But after some time in a dead sleep, I went on dreaming. And now I found myself in a totally different scene.

42

My second dream: all the trouble and adversity in the world are rooted in the Jews' having no sense of proportion

In my dream, I was now in the company of my two synagogue wardens. We were somewhere in a desert, at the foot of a high mountain, on whose summit we could discern a pillar bearing a tablet inscribed in letters of fire: "I have set before you life and death—therefore choose life."

The three of us stared at one another in surprise and confusion. Then, after I had described my first dream to them, we all shrugged and grimaced as though we were ashamed of ourselves. And in the midst of my dream, it seems, I was thinking that they had now revealed themselves to me: they were having their doubts about the entire question, and were hesitating to commit themselves, just as I was. And while we stood there lost in thought, a gorge opened up before us and we were now in a dreadful, dark abyss, which in my dream I supposed must be the infernal region of Sheol itself. While we stood there in mortal fear, all around us a multitude of voices broke into a howl of mocking laughter. Turning around, we found ourselves confronted by throngs of

destroying angels, demons and evil spirits, who pointed
at us, shouting, "Here they are, the three of them—two
who traded one rag for another, and a third who died as
a result of his doubts, without a confession of faith, almost the same as a heretic!"

For a moment it appeared that our death warrants
had been signed. But then the commotion of wings subsided and a whisper ran through the throng. "Oh, oh, the
Archangel Michael is coming to defend them, to plead
the cause of the two malefactors!"

At that moment the entire scene became as bright as
though lit by eighteen blazing suns, while the Archangel
Michael with his six fiery wings descended. He hovered
above us as gently as a white dove over a dovecote, and
in a melodious voice, whose sound was like a cooling
fountain in a garden full of flowers, said, "Peace! Cease
your noise and laughter! These persons are still among
the living and have their own free will, and so we have
as yet no right to judge them. You can see for yourselves,
alas, that they are in a sorry plight. It is hard to say how
they will fare in their declining years. Though we are
angels, even we do not know what is in store for them
tomorrow. We know that for the time being they are
groping for the right path; but as long as they can choose
their own course we have no right to direct them. And
if they had acted of their own free will since childhood,
they might long ago have found the path of righteousness. The trouble is that the Jews of Poland, once their
childhood is over, do not act of their own free will until
they themselves become fathers, and when they are able
to act of their own free will it has already been so weakened that it is practically gone. Then the anxiety of earning a livelihood, and bodies weakened by the struggle
and tribulations of life, cause them to resign themselves
to a life of remorse and despair, of suffering and anger.

So how can they be accused in their present predicament? Neither are their fathers to blame for having reared them as children in the same way as they had themselves been reared—all of them following the well-trodden path, the time-honored pattern bequeathed by their ancestors.

"And if the first generations had understood the principles envisaged by our forefathers when they founded their schools of thought, and on which they base their philosophies, then later generations, and especially the present ones, would not have found themselves in the sad plight of the three before us, and of thousands of others in the nether world. For undoubtedly every founder of a new school of thought had good intentions, and designed his plan for the welfare of his people—I refer to honest folk and ardent Jewish patriots, not, God forbid, to hucksters and swindlers. And if the successors to those men had really heeded their principles and intentions and had developed and carried them out, then each sect would have flourished materially and spiritually; and the diversified schools of thought would have merged into a general and perfect doctrine for all Jews, in accordance with the Law of Moses and Israel.

"Let us evaluate the three doctrines, Misnagedism, the Haskalah, and Hasidism. Now, the Vilna Gaon, Moses Mendelssohn, and the Baal Shem Tov, their respective founders, were unquestionably righteous persons and true Jewish patriots; and each one built his own particular creed on sound and commendable principles for the welfare of people at large through generations to come.

"The Baal Shem Tov was not, God forbid, a swindler, as some people maintain. His Hasidism was an indispensable and salutary reform in the religious life of his epoch—as compared to the cold austerity of Orthodox Rabbinism, which reduced the divine service with all of the commandments of the Torah to the status of rules mechanically obeyed, so that the Jewish worshiper no longer felt any ardor or ecstasy in prayer, but performed the ritual like an automaton, as an order carried out by a soldier. With his Hasidism, the Baal Shem Tov naturally achieved his final objective: the fulfillment of a task spontaneously, by one's own volition, experiencing the glorious meaning of a commandment together with its true benefit—that is, of being a *voluntary* soldier in the service of divinity. Had the three founders united in their efforts to reform the religious and spiritual life of the Jews, each according to his point of view and his principles, they would no doubt have established a complete and unified doctrine for generations to come, and there would have been no need for sects in Jewish life. Moreover, if the respective schools of thought had been adhered to according to their original intent, the condition of contemporary Jewry would have been happier. Unfortunately those who came after the three founders gradually fell away from the original concepts—some of them out of ignorance, and others for their own aggrandizement and profit.

"In the course of time, the three doctrines so diverged from their original outlook that hardly any resemblance to their original form remains. If the three founders were to see their corrupt and distorted doctrines now, they would find them unrecognizable. So how can they be arraigned? Indeed, they played fair with the tens of thousands of Polish Jews who are now sunk in perpetual squalor. These precursors at least strove against their corrupt upbringing. The oldest of the three, having sinned at will under a fallacious doctrine that became obsolete in his own time, retaining not a vestige of the Haskalah, became conscious of his errors and began looking for spiritual nourishment; since such a one would not wish to fly into the airless cage of Rabbinism or the dilapidated prison of Haskalah, he entered the spacious cell of the Hasidic sect.

"The second of the three, who has suffered greatly through his own illusory doctrine, submitting automatically and under rigid constraint to the six hundred thirteen commandments of the Pentateuch and numerous other restrictions and decrees, likewise had his eyes opened and began, as a free individual, to search for a concept to nourish his eager soul. Since such a bird was not likely to fly into a cage with its door wide open—the delusive Haskalah—and since he did not intend to renounce the mandate of the Torah and its commandments, therefore he, too, strayed into the Hasidic cult, a cage which by that time was half shut.

"The youngest of the three, floundering about from his youth in the fallacious Hasidic sect, and discovering what went on in a cage of that sort, became conscience-stricken and yearned to find something better. But from the start he was less fortunate than his associates: they were equipped to fly to a new abode. The first was versed in languages and science, and was well-bred. The second was learned in the Talmud and the rabbinic writings, with a modicum of scholarship as well; and having a minimum of piety and good manners, he was something more than a wild animal. So where did he fit in? Moreover, his comrades had already informed him that the other two doctrines were worthless. So, finding himself in such a miserable situation, with a mediocre education, and humiliated, poverty-stricken, he was bound to despair and lose faith in everything.

"The older two could still somehow extricate themselves from the delusive Hasidic sect and work out an acceptable composite of the three doctrines, because they were equipped with some learning; and if they failed to discover the path of righteousness during their lifetime, they might perhaps be taken to task at their death —with their poor upbringing as an extenuating circumstance. The youngest of the three, however, could be accused of nothing, not even after his death, because his freedom of will had long ago been extinguished. I foresee that he, along with thousands of other Jewish lads in Poland, will be kept with his nose to the grindstone for the rest of his miserable life. Upon their death I will plead the cause of each to the best of my ability, in order to obtain for each of them a nook in paradise. Yes, their wretched and fanatical upbringing must atone for their foolish behavior, just as their privations and humiliations and illnesses and all their suffering and misfortune must atone for their wicked and wasted lives. There is one thing for which I myself would condemn such a one in the hereafter—and that would be for bringing up his own children according to the same sophistry. Were he to insist that he knew no other way to do it, I would urge him to seek the advice of reputable men, to let his children find their own way in life—so long as he steers clear of the wretched manner of educating Jewish lads in Poland!"

At that moment I awoke, drenched in a cold sweat, and found myself and my two fellow prisoners face to face with the prison warden. He held a document of some sort, and he told us that we were being let out of jail: amnesty was being given to thousands of prisoners by a royal decree. All the same, Mordecai was ready to attribute this deliverance to our miracle-working rabbi, and Shmuel was ready to agree. As for me—I simply shrugged.

43

Out of the loom comes the fabric; out of the upbringing, the life

When I came out into the bright, free world after six years behind bars, I found myself so dazzled that I could not collect my thoughts—especially during the first few days, when the Vetzeeoni Hasidim of Sirkov had so golden an opportunity to offer a toast to their rabbi's miracle, and to give old friends a chance to meet after so long an absence. In fact, there was so much drinking and singing and dancing that I was all in a whirl. It was not until the third day, when the excitement had died down, that I could bring my thoughts together and examine my situation for the first time in my life. Consider my plight: past thirty, haggard and ailing, without a nook to rest my aching bones in, and without hope of even a bare subsistence, except by soliciting contributions for the rebbe—a task I would now rather die than perform. Somewhere or other, my wife and children were also in a bad way—a thought that sharpened my pangs of conscience as I recalled my Hasidic buffoonery, the rebbe's conniving, Mordecai's dream, Ferilhein's downfall, the chanting of the angels, and Archangel Michael's prophecy concerning my future. And to top it all off, I was destitute. "Oi, oi, oi!" I gasped, and began weeping. "What is to become of me? I am at the mercy of the winds, I am an abject failure in both body and soul!"

I sat there for hours, moaning over my lot until finally I cried out in despair, "What the Archangel Michael said is true! I am doomed forever; I have no strength to struggle against the current. My freedom of choice expired from the moment I was born, and I must go on in the same way I was brought up by my father— the way the traditional Jewish education has formed us all!"

So I now decided to hold on to the Hasidic sect for as long as possible, since it would give some sort of sustenance, a little something to drink, and a group of companions to talk with endlessly. Otherwise I was alone, an outcast: the misnagedim regarded me as an ignoramus, the maskilim as a savage, the dignitaries as a loafer, and the rabble as an ex-convict. Since under such circumstances there was no alternative but suicide, I had to stay close to the old trodden path. There was no escape—where else could I go unless I joined my ancestors? So I would join the Hasidim, but I would not observe the Hasidic doctrine, nor would I be a real Hasid. My only protection now would be to hold my tongue.

To solicit funds for the rebbe's maintenance, one had, of course, to get his approval. So on the following day I went along with my two gabbaim to spend the Sabbath with the rebbe. (I even had visions of the rabbi handing over to me at least some part of the three thousand rubles I had deposited with him.) But all three of us, and I especially, got a cool reception from the rebbe. I can assure you that this didn't surprise me at all: often enough in my life I had seen him estranged from people who had given him their meager savings, their blood money, and whom, when they were totally destitute, he would scarcely recognize, sometimes even cutting them dead—a thing that was actually regarded by the Hasidim as a miracle. So it is no wonder that he ignored my two comrades now that they were no longer of use to him— and all the more in my case—a pauper and an ex-convict, to whom, moreover, he was indebted. But who would have acted any better? Another in his place would probably have refused to see us altogether. What earthly use were we three lame ducks to him after all—especially since we were involved in the same affair with him? To slam the door in our faces, however, would have shown him in a bad light in the community. But imagine his sanctimonious air when I ventured to ask meekly for a little bit on account of the money he owed me! He first flew into a rage and was ready to jump down my throat. But in another moment he had calmed himself, rolling his eyes heavenward and answering with a smile. "The money I owe you? Ah, well . . . a mortal owes the Lord of the Universe his soul every moment of his life. So how can one speak of *debts?* Moreover, for a whole year I supported your wife—something you owed her under the law. And then there is the money I spent in financing your marriage to my niece—may her name be blotted out! And how much, after all, did I spend on *your* case —on getting it postponed until I could deliver you from the hands of the goyim? And yet you have the audacity to ask still further repayment?"

There he was—all innocence, his conscience clear as crystal. . . . My wife was entitled under the law to what had been allowed her, and she had been victimized by a compulsory divorce, and he had spent money on *my* case, and he had gotten me released from the goyish jail. And, of course, the expenditure for the wedding was no small matter, either. (He seemed not to remember that the lessees and other followers of his had given generously toward the legal expenses.) And still I had the gall to ask further repayment from such a tzaddik! Assessing my precarious situation, I decided to salvage whatever I could as a move toward getting him to allow me to solicit funds for his maintenance. To forestall a possible refusal, I quietly produced a deposition from the leading local Hasidim, and then asked for his sanction. At first he hesitated, but finally his great compassion for his fellow-man won out over my having been disrespectful to him, and he said with a sneer, "Very good. I am sure you'll carry out your task properly—and wherever necessary you'll resort to a little self-sacrifice. . . . But as you are aware, Itzikel, *your* case has bankrupted me, and because of your numerous sins, my income is greatly diminished —oi, oi, oi! And your late father, in the good old days, used to get ten gulden a week from me. Moreover, you have no family. So I will pay you just seven gulden a week." (Now he was no longer concerned even with be-ing "within the law.") "Have a good trip. May God be with you on your way." Then, turning to the gabbai, he said, "Write out a statement authorizing him to solicit funds in my behalf, in the place of his late father."

I picked up my credentials and hurried away. For you could never tell: at any moment he might very well perceive my aversion for the entire Hasidic sect, himself included—after all, he was said to be capable of seeing from one end of the world to the other!—and in that event I would lose the seven gulden a week and soon turn into a sack of skin and bones . . .

Back at my lodgings, there was another toast to my anticipated earnings as the rebbe's solicitor of funds. I rented a cubbyhole for myself and my young son at twenty gulden a year. All during the next month, I tried to discover what progress he had made in acquaintance with Judaism, and found he knew nothing of the various schools of thought in the realm of Hasidism, nor had he any wish to inquire into them. He aspired to be no more than an ordinary God-fearing Jew and a respectable member of the community. From the non-Orthodox rabbi he had gotten a smattering of the Pentateuch and an elementary knowledge of the Russian language. His teacher had not stressed any particular religious ideology. I remembered the Archangel Michael saying, "Let them go their own ways rather than receive the wretched education now given to Jewish children in Poland." I did not take issue with any of the boy's statements. He had passed his Bar Mitzvah a few months ago, and his teacher had bought him the phylacteries. I can only tell you that I became very much attached to my son, and then a feeling of commiseration for my wife and our other children gradually welled up within me. I reasoned with myself this way: "How can a shiftless ne'er-do-well in this world like you still consider yourself superior to your wife? How could you dare think of marriage to some attractive woman? How could you dare—a fellow from Poland, a broken reed adrift at sea, and prematurely aged, hope for a mate of any but your own kind? Is your wife not doomed to the same fate as you simply because she is Jewish and living in Poland? Then how can you aspire to anything better?"

Immediately I took ten gulden out of the funds I had collected for the rabbi, in addition to my earnings, and gave them to my young son, telling him to go to Krokodilevka and bring his mother and the rest of the children to Vetzeeoni. My unfortunate and ill-favored spouse came and joined me. I rented a larger attic and a kitchen at forty gulden a year; on Saturday evening we went through a new marriage ceremony and I was committed to provide for a wife and five children on an income of

seven gulden a week, plus an occasional nip in the synagogue.

You can, of course, readily imagine the pleasure and
contentment of such domesticity. Our only furniture was
a rickety table and a battered bench that had been lent
by the landlord as a mitzvah. And you can imagine the
luxury possible on seven gulden a week. To add insult to
injury, I was confronted day and night by a prematurely
aged and ailing spouse. On the other hand, did Polish
Jews generally fare better than I? The Lord of the Universe be praised, nevertheless, for the consolation I
derived from my eldest son. Other Jews fared less well
because they had not been privileged to heed the Archangel Michael's sermon and had reared their children
themselves. You may well wonder how seven ailing persons can keep body and soul together, pay rent and taxes
and tuition fees, buy any sort of clothes, and once a
month put on a freshly laundered shirt—all on seven
gulden per week. And what about those who, out of
similar earnings, must still manage a visit to the rabbi in
the city, taking along a *pidyon,* plus a donation toward the
purchase of a silver bowl as a gift to the rebbe? Now, I'll
let you in on a little secret: except by pilfering some of
the money I collected for the rabbi, I could not have
provided my family even with bread and onions. But how
long is it possible to go on cheating and stealing, especially under the eagle eye of the rebbe? Through devious
ways, I kept up the hanky-panky for about three years,
until the rabbi discovered he was short a hundred
gulden. It was no trivial matter to be caught stealing
money from a saintly sage: that was really going too far.
So naturally I was sent packing, and my family left destitute just before Rosh Hashanah. But then, on the very
eve of the holiday, my older son brought home two Sabbath loaves of bread, a plate of fish, two pounds of raw

meat, a bottle of wine and five gulden. I surmised that these items had been contributed by the non-Orthodox rabbi. During the services in the synagogue, I ignored the way the Hasidim looked at me askance for fleecing the rebbe. At the end of the High Holy Days, my son told me in a pitiful voice that the non-Orthodox rabbi and his wife wanted to see me.

Now, you may argue—and with justice—that I am a ne'er-do-well, a nobody and a scoundrel. But I must confess that all the same, as soon as I saw this rabbi's wife, the comely Rebecca, I became so enamored of her that I was all but swept off my feet. Was it through any fault of mine that my poor heart, heedless of its lowly origin, should aspire to one so well-bred and genteel?

At any rate, the rabbi and his wife welcomed me cordially, and spoke to me with all due respect. They appeared to know all about my plight, my straitened circumstances, and even my pangs of conscience. The rabbi offered me a position as a sexton, to attend to all his errands for a weekly wage of ten gulden. (In addition, I would be able to earn ten gulden a month for doing other chores.) "So, Reb Itzikel," the rabbi said to me in parting, "you will always be welcome here. Our merciful God will not forsake you."

The Lord is my witness that if I alone had been concerned, I would have endured cold, starvation, and every other tribulation rather than accept charity from anyone. But things being as they were, I concluded that such was the will of God.

So I went to work as a sexton for the non-Orthodox rabbi. But I still did not disavow the Hasidic world altogether: I behaved like all other Hasidim, prayed with them in the same synagogue, occasionally helping myself to a nip there, and conducting myself like an ordinary God-fearing jew—even to all intents and purposes, like an authentic Hasid but without the idiosyncrasies of Hasidism. I am not, God forbid, a hypocrite; I hear and see things, but say nothing. My young son comports himself in a like manner. As a sexton I have bettered my condition to the extent that our diet changed from bread and onions to bread and soup. Our home was as poverty-ridden as before, with the same bickering and the same atmosphere of gloom as before—but, praised be the Lord, we have our piece of bread.

I served this rabbi for about three years. During that time my oldest son married into a decent family, and began earning his livelihood as an elementary melamed. Next, the non-Orthodox rabbi helped get two of my sons enrolled in a trade school. Then my wife turned up her toes. So with my two younger children (one child had died two years before), I would have gotten through my miserable life somehow, except that the Hasidic clique still held a grudge against me and were waiting for a change to settle accounts with me. Though I was aware of their enmity toward me, I did not expect them to go to extremes.

But one day or, to be more precise, on the midnight of Shushan Purim—while I was celebrating in the Hasidic rebbe's court, his followers got me drunk and then proceeded to beat me senseless, leaving me half dead. At dawn my son found me and brought me home, where for a month I hovered between life and death; in addition to my other ailments, I was now tubercular. During my illness the non-Orthodox rabbi and his wife did all they could to ease my condition. I now lie here in pain and misery, day by day, expecting the Angel of Deliverance to sever my miserable soul from my declining body.

My dear sirs, I have no strength left to speak, much less to write. Perhaps, after I am dead, my son will tell you the rest of the story. Farewell, my friends and may